VERIFY

JOELLE CHARBONNEAU

An Imprint of HarperCollinsPublishers

HarperTeen is an imprint of HarperCollins Publishers.

Verify

Library of Congress Cataloging-in-Publication Data

Names: Charbonneau, Joelle, author.
Title: Verify/Joelle Charbonneau
Description: New York, NY : HarperTeen, [2019] | Summary: Chicago teen Meri
   Beckley's pride of living in a land of peace, prosperity, and truth crumbles when
   questions following her mother's death reveal buried facts, especially that words
   can have great power.
Identifiers: LCCN 2019009520 | ISBN 9780062803627 (hardback)
Subjects: | CYAC: Grief—Fiction. | Honesty—Fiction. | Government, Resistance
   to—Fiction.
Classification: LCC PZ7.C37354 Ver 2019 | DDC [Fic]—dc23 LC record available at
https://lccn.loc.gov/2019009520

Typography by Jenna Stempel-Lobell
19 20 21 22 23 PC/LSCH 10 9 8 7 6 5 4 3 2 1
❖

First Edition

For Rachel Maddow, who points to the past when searching for answers to the present and future.

And for all journalists who refuse to stop asking questions.

VERIFY

ONE

My stool creaks in the slate-gray silence. I stretch, then turn once again to stare at the partially finished canvas.

A single desk lamp bathes the picture in a soft light. Shadows dance outside of the light's glow as I attempt to imagine what my mother was creating when she placed the geometric lines on the canvas over an ash-black background. Some of them, around the edge of the canvas, are thick and strong. Others move at a diagonal and seem to fade into the empty white area in the center of the work, as if disappearing into some mysterious place that only an artist could understand. Some lines at the edge are silver. The ones in the center are a burnished gold. Small red stars in the corners of the image make me believe there would have been more color had Mom had more time.

Now it is up to me to take the next step.

Looking down at the screen in my hand, I pick up my stylus and begin to draw on the copy I made of my mother's work, just as I have done every single day of the last eleven weeks and six days. I extend the lines—add detail. Match the color of red she used with one from my palette and begin once again to draw.

Sunlight creeps through the windows of my mother's studio, telling me that the time to get ready for school is approaching. But I don't move. Not yet. I stay seated on the rickety stool my mother had set up for me years ago when I begged to be allowed to watch her wield her brushes against canvas—a medium no longer used by artists but one my mother refused to completely abandon for electronic screens and the high-tech accessories that could do everything the tools on her desk did.

They can't do everything, I remember her telling me as she frowned into my eyes. *The things on the screen aren't real. What we can touch—that's real.*

Maybe I should have asked what she meant. Or maybe she should have just told me why she was spending so many late nights in this room using tools the rest of the country had discarded to create images that are impossible to understand. If she had been clearer, maybe I wouldn't be here right now trying to finish this painting for her.

I push a strand of hair that has escaped my ponytail out of my eyes and return to my sketch, working from the edges inward. I add a door in the empty space my mother left in the center of the work. The door is partially opened, as if waiting for someone to push it and walk through.

Over half my attempts have this door. Although until now the entryway has been closed. This time, without thinking, I painted it open. Does that mean something?

Streams of golden sunlight through Mom's studio window chase the rest of the shadows away. I layer color and shading until finally, I cock my head to the side and study my efforts.

The image is . . . interesting. If I brought it to my art class today, Mrs. Rudoren would certainly praise my talent, something my mother rarely did. In the middle of the other geometric lines, the entryway seems almost otherworldly with the slight arch I have added at the top and the light coming from somewhere inside. The picture is the most compelling of the dozens upon dozens I have created thus far, with the red patch on the side acting almost like a warning to keep someone from walking through my door.

And still, I know it's wrong.

I punch the erase feature on the screen. My part of the image disappears in a blink. As if it never existed. But my mother's work remains. She's gone, but that is what is left of her, and that's all that's left to me.

I rub my eyes, pick up my stylus, and touch it to the center of the screen to begin again. Wait. . . .

Damn it.

A persistent beeping sound echoes from above me. I slide off the stool and hurry through the door of my mother's studio, into the hall, and toward the stairs. I've been so busy working on the puzzle of Mom's painting that I lost track of the time.

The beeping gets louder with each step. The fact that it doesn't stop before I reach the landing tells me exactly what I will find as I step across the threshold of my parents' room.

My nose wrinkles.

The wailing of the alarm continues.

I step on a crumpled shirt and kick aside a pair of wadded-up gray trousers as I pad across the light blue carpet toward the nightstand.

A push of a button and the room goes blissfully silent, but a look at the clock's display tells me I have spent far more time in my mother's studio than I'd intended. My father isn't the only one who is going to be late at this rate.

"Dad," I say, turning toward the bed to where my father still sleeps. His breathing is raspy. His dark, normally wavy hair is plastered against his head. The mouth that once so quickly curled into smiles is mashed against a dark blue spot on the pillow, and a large, empty go cup rests next to one of his hands.

"Dad! Get up!" I snap.

He doesn't move.

"You slept through your alarm," I say louder. "If you don't get up now you're going to be late for work." And it wouldn't be the first time.

I stalk across the room and tug open a window to let the fresh, almost-summer air chase the heat and stale smell out of the room.

"Dad!" I yell.

When he snorts and rolls over, I head into his bathroom and turn the shower on. Then I grab a slightly stiff washcloth, run it under ice-cold water from the sink, and stomp back to drop it on his face.

The cold washcloth does the trick. Dad yelps, sits up, and snatches the wet washcloth from his forehead with one hand while knocking the go cup off the bed with the other. The cup rolls under the bed. Dad blinks his puffy red eyes several times before shifting them to look at me.

"The shower is already running. You can't be late," I say as I wait for him to swing his legs over the edge of the bed and plant his feet on the floor. If I leave now there is a good chance he'll just lie back down. It's happened before.

"I'm sorry, sweetheart," he says, running a hand through his hair before pushing to his feet. I wait for him to sway, but he's steady, and despite the swollen redness, his eyes are mostly alert. It's an improvement over last week. Maybe I should find hope in that. But I'm not ready for hope.

"Be downstairs in fifteen minutes," I say, heading for my room so I can get myself ready for another day. It takes me half that time to yank on the pair of navy-blue pants and pale yellow shirt that make up my school uniform. I used to hate it, but now I'm grateful for the required sameness. Figuring out what clothes to wear is one less decision I have to make.

I brush my hair, start to pull it neatly back into a ponytail as is my typical style, but one look at my eyes in the mirror has me leaving it loose. Hopefully, the fatigue won't be as obvious that way.

The smell of coffee hits me as I hurry downstairs and walk into the cozy yellow-and-white kitchen. My father gives me what I'm sure he thinks is a cheerful smile, but it comes across as more than a little desperate. His hair is still wet from the shower. His face is shaved and he's dressed in a blue shirt and gray jacket that I picked up from the cleaner yesterday after school. His eyes still look a little tired, but they are way clearer than they have been in the past few weeks. If I didn't know better, I would think that he was back to the dad I used to know.

He holds out a green apple—my usual choice for breakfast. A peace offering. I shake my head and grab a banana, even though it has brown patches on the skin.

My father sighs, turns back to the counter, and pours himself a steaming mug of coffee. In an upbeat voice he says, "Only one day left of class and two days of finals before summer break. Has the City Art Program made their decision yet?"

"I don't know," I say, taking a seat at the butcher-block table. "I didn't apply." I frown at the banana, knowing that picking the thing up means I'll have to eat it.

"Wait a minute." Dad sets his mug down on the counter. "Why didn't you apply? You worked so hard on your portfolio pieces. What happened?"

"You know what happened."

Mom died and my dad started to drink.

We did what we had to do in order to get from day to day. Those things did not include essay writing and portfolio development.

Before he can try to initiate some kind of father-daughter-heart-to-heart thing, I shove back my chair, spring to my feet, and cross to the garbage. "It's okay." I drop the overly ripe banana into the can with a thump and shrug as if it couldn't possibly matter. "There's another project I'm working on. I'll have plenty to keep me occupied this summer without being a part of City Art. And I can always apply next year if someone drops out. So it's fine," I lie. "Look, I've gotta go."

"I can give you a ride to school," Dad offers.

No. He can't. Not without being late for work. It's an empty offer and I can see from the slump of his shoulders that I'm not the only one who knows it. More than anything I want to call him out. But I bite back the angry words and instead say, "Rose said she might wait to walk with me. She'll never forgive me if I don't show up." I shift the bag on my shoulder and make a beeline for the back door.

My hand is on the knob when my father says, "Meri, I'm sorry. I should have asked before about City Art. I know your future is on the line and I—I'm screwing it up. I'm trying to do better, it's just . . ."

I glance over my shoulder. My father looks down at the coffee in his hand so I won't see the tears. But I see them anyway, and even if I couldn't I can hear the sorrow thickening his voice when he quietly admits, "I miss her."

Everything inside me freezes. The red-hot anger I stoke like a life-giving fire suddenly extinguishes, leaving me cold and weak and raw.

I can't breathe.

I can't speak.

It's like the moment I relive every night when I try to fall asleep—the one where the police officers come to the door with their serious, rosy-cold faces and stiff words, telling us about the vehicle that slid on a patch of black ice and couldn't stop in time.

They were sorry. Everyone was sorry. My friends. My teachers. Our neighbors. The guy behind the counter at the market two streets over. Everyone told me first with their words and now months later with a shake of the head how *sorry* they were that the person who drove the vehicle too fast during a spring snow was alive and well and my mother, who had simply been standing on the sidewalk in front of a potential new design project, was dead.

We're all sorry. So what? It doesn't change a damn thing.

"I'll see you tonight." I yank the door open and head outside, clinging to the anger that once again sparks inside me. I hate the pain my father is in. I hate that I understand why he drinks, and I hate knowing that if I didn't force him out of bed every morning he would drink himself into oblivion to forget what we have lost.

His work gave him two weeks off after the accident, and people looked the other way for the month after as Dad showed up late or in the same clothes he'd worn the day before. Finally, Dad's boss came to the house with a warning that he had to do better or he would lose his job.

The drinking continued, but little by little, day by day, Dad seemed to be doing better. Surrounded by more grays and dark blues than shrouded in empty black. He didn't have to reach for something to add to his morning coffee in order to face a world without my mother's lopsided smile and observant gaze.

I hurry down the steps and around the house, toward the street.

A gray squirrel darts across the sidewalk in front of me and bolts under the moving van parked in front of the house two doors down. I used to watch every new person moving into a house on the block for signs of kids my age, especially in the last few years when so many older folks moved away for work or retirement—or just because they wanted something new. Now I was glad not to see any signs of teenagers in the back of the van.

Robins chirp in the branches of the fairly young trees lining the street. The city's gardeners planted them only two years ago. Between the golden sunshine, this being the final week of school, and my dad's less glassy eyes, I should be feeling positive about the day. Maybe if Dad hadn't brought up the City Art Program I would find it easier to be happy about the little things, but thoughts of all the work I had done—the time wasted—what I had wanted so badly until my mother's death—made it hard to find the good in anything.

I'd worked for months on my portfolio so that I could be one of the four sixteen-year-olds chosen to intern alongside the city's design and beautification team for the next two years. Being chosen isn't just an honor. Being chosen gives a student the chance to work with the very best imaginations in the city and maybe even assist in designing one or more of the city's ongoing projects. It's one of the sure ways to gain a coveted slot as a visual arts major. Without a visual-arts degree it's impossible to secure a job as a working artist here in Chicago's City Pride Department or in similar departments in other cities across the country.

Of all the government jobs, the City Pride Department's were among the most important and prestigious. Years ago, a pilot program spearheaded by the best artists in the country was launched here in Chicago under the theory that people who lived in beautiful surroundings felt better about themselves and their futures, thereby causing them to make positive choices that would benefit not only themselves but the community they were so proud of. It was a radical idea, but the new City Pride Department was determined to make every part of the city beautiful—especially those most touched by neglect and crime, because the people living on those streets needed to see that they were worthy of beauty.

And it was working. Bit by bit. Block by block. The citizens here blossomed under the inspiration of the city's new beauty. But the project is never ending, because the city is large and always changing. So often my mother worked long into the night to create the perfect mural for the side of a neighborhood market or select the ideal color palette for a sign intended to draw the community into embracing a new park. She had even received a silver plaque last year to celebrate the work she had done. She was one of the top designers. The work she uploaded into the National Elevation through Arts database was some of the most often downloaded for use around the country.

Was it any wonder that I wanted to capture beauty in an image the way she did?

Everyone assumes my mother wanted me to submit to the summer program. That she encouraged me to walk in her talented footsteps. I've let them think it because it's easier than talking about the way, in the months before she died, she pursed her lips whenever I asked her opinion about my work.

Are you sure that's the color palette you want to use, Meri?

Is that really what you want to work on or just what you think you should be working on?

Then finally the one I'll never forget. When she fastened her hair at the nape of her neck with a long-handled, tapered paintbrush and turned to me, eyes shimmering with disappointment.

Maybe you should think about doing an internship at Gloss instead. Designing layouts requires a sharp eye and there's a lot less competition for those positions than there is for government jobs.

Those words made it clear to me that she thought I wasn't good enough. Maybe if I hadn't shut myself off from her from that moment on, maybe I would have found out why. Maybe—

"Hey, I almost gave up on you."

I look up and spot my best friend, Rose, standing in the shade of an old elm tree.

"Isaac decided you weren't coming and went on ahead. He's going through a self-important phase because Dad got him a summer job with city security. I'm not sure what is so amazing about filling in for security officers who are spending the day at the beach, but what do I know?" Rose rolls her eyes, which tells me everything I need to know about her opinion of her older brother's plans. Then she frowns. "Actually, it's good Isaac left, because you look terrible."

I shrug. I could take offense, but she's just telling the truth.

"Well, you look perfect," I respond. "So we balance each other out." The thing is, I'm not kidding about the perfect part. With her thick black hair twisted into a French braid, her glowing brown skin made even more flawless by makeup applied with a skilled and light hand, Rose looks more like one of the models in the fashion e-zine her mother edits than a sixteen-year-old high school student on her way to class.

"I'm not kidding, Meri." Rose steps toward me. Her intense brown eyes narrow as she studies my face. "You didn't sleep again."

"I slept." Sort of. When Rose purses her lips and gives me her don't-mess-with-me frown, I add, "Okay, so I woke up extra early and couldn't get back to sleep. It's no big deal."

Rose sighs and slides the straps of her yellow backpack off her shoulder. She unzips the front pocket and pulls out her purple-and-white-swirled makeup kit. "You keep saying that it's no big deal, but when was the last time you slept for an entire night?"

I wish I could answer that, but it's been too long for me to remember.

"I've had some bad dreams," I say.

Pity swims in her eyes, then vanishes almost as quickly as it appeared. She gives a no-nonsense shake of her head as she flips open the lid of one of her dozens of makeup compacts. "Lucky for you I have just the thing to fix you up."

There's no fixing me. Even if I slept for a week, I would never look like Rose. Boring dishwater-blond hair, pale hazel eyes, and average height are not model material. "You don't need to go to the trouble."

Rose grabs my arm as I try to sidestep her. "If you don't want your teachers calling your father out of concern for your well-being or, worse yet, sending you down to the counselor, you'll stand still and let me work."

"We're going to be late."

"Not if you keep still and follow my instructions," Rose says. "And if we don't get to class in time for the second bell, a call from either one of my parents will get us out of trouble. Deal?"

I sigh, knowing there really isn't much of a choice. When Rose has her mind set on something, there is little chance of changing it. Besides, I don't have the energy or the time to put up a fight. "Deal."

"Good. This won't take long. Hold this." She hands me the makeup kit, and I can tell from the colors that half of what she has with her has been brought specifically for me. Knowing that Rose has been worried enough to go out of her way to get these things ties my throat into a knot. Tears prick the backs of my eyes. The world blurs and I blink to chase it all away.

"Stop moving," Rose chastises. She dabs a sponge under my eyes and on several other spots on my face. I stare at a light green leaf on a tree in the distance and try to clear my mind and my heart the way I can with my tablet. Rose attacks my eyes with a pencil and eye shadow and actually growls at me when I try to move away before she puts the finishing touches on her design. Finally, she gives a satisfied smile and holds a mirror up to my face. "There is no denying that I'm a genius. My mother and *Gloss* editorials have taught me well."

She isn't lying. My skin is no longer blotchy. The peach shadow she used on my lids is almost translucent, but somehow makes them appear less sleep deprived. I seem almost normal—as long as no one looks too hard. The anger and fatigue and distrust in my eyes cannot be smoothed away with powder and lip gloss. Those are beyond even my best friend's ministrations.

But when I look away from my image and see Rose's grin, I can't help but smile back. After so many years, all the changes in our lives, and the bitterness and hurt I have waded through, the thing I am most grateful for is Rose's friendship. "Thanks," I say, lifting my eyes to hers. "I owe you."

"Real friends don't keep score." Rose shoves the makeup case back into her bag. Once it's stowed, she shrugs the bag onto her shoulder and we start walking. "So what happened this morning?" she asks.

"What do you mean?" I wait for a red sports car to pass and cross the street with Rose beside me.

"Meri, I yelled your name three times before you noticed me. That's not like you."

I take a deep breath and say, "Dad asked about my submission to the City Art Program this morning. It's the first time he's brought it up since . . . before." I walk faster, as if I can escape the ache that comes with the reminder of my mother's death. "He was disappointed when I told him I didn't finish my submission. I guess I thought in some way he would be relieved."

"Why would you think that?"

"He never goes in Mom's studio. He took her award off the shelf in the living room. He can't bring himself to look at her art or talk to anyone she used to work with. And whenever I start sketching or even talk about one of my assignments for art class he goes into another room."

The things that keep me going drive him to search for a way to forget. The award lives on the shelf next to my bedroom window. I draw for hours every day. A nicer daughter would give those things up to help him. Clearly, I'm not that nice.

"Your father's hurting," Rose says quietly. "But he knows how important your art is. He's not like my dad—determined to make everyone just like him. Your dad would never want you to give up something that makes you happy. Speaking of the City Art Program, I know you said your portfolio wasn't finished, but—"

"The submission deadline was two weeks ago." I walk even faster as our school and the dozens of cars and buses navigating the street in front of the redbrick building come into sight. "It's over, Rose."

Maybe I'd still get into one of the college art programs, but my chances of becoming a City Art Program designer now were low. And I had only myself to blame.

"Nothing is ever over until you admit defeat. I talked to—"

"Can you just drop it?" I ask. "Please? I haven't had a chance to ask you about whether you convinced your dad to let you work at *Gloss* instead of at City Hall this summer."

"Did you see the new issue? Mom said she sent one to your account. She wanted to know if you have ideas for the logo redesign. She wants something more youthful and striking and thinks a younger designer's point of view will help." Rose shakes the smile off her face and settles back into a frown. "But no fair changing the subject. We can talk about me and my summer job later. After you—"

The first bell rings, which cuts off whatever Rose was going to say because in order to make it to our class before the second bell sounds, we have to run. Side by side, we race across the street and down the sidewalk, dodging the other stragglers and the large outdoor screens that flank the front door entry like sentries. The one to the right is dedicated to a running display of times and dates for school- and student-appropriate city events. The other is set to local news, as are the two screens in the cafeteria. As Principal Velshi has said in every assembly, the only way we can be sure what we want to do when we go out into the world is to first understand what is happening in it.

The truth, however, is that no one really cares what the chirpy anchor with the plastic-looking hair is saying about the stepped-up recycling effort as students shove their way to the front entrance. Assistant Principal Schmidt is near the door, shouting over the din for everyone to hurry up.

Breathing hard, Rose pushes her way forward. I'm about to follow when a bus pulls away from the curb. Out of the corner of my eye I catch the flash of red lights. I turn, thinking the light must be from one of the announcement screens, but it's not. The flashing is coming from atop a police car in the distance. I stop walking as men in charcoal-gray suits shove a struggling person with magenta-and-black-streaked hair toward an open police car door. One of the suits backhands the man he's escorting across the cheek. I flinch and hold my breath as I keep watching. The suit yells and points toward the street. He's too far away from me to make out what he said, but several navy-blue-uniformed officers nod and race toward some bushes near the edge of the street.

"Meri, come on!" Rose tugs on my arm, and I start moving again toward the front entrance. I glance back in time to see the suited men shove the cuffed, shouting perpetrator into the police car and slam the door. Just before I step into the school, a uniformed officer pulls something out of a bush.

As I race down the hall trying to beat the next bell, I picture the scene from across the street and the item the officer waved in triumph at the suits.

It wasn't something anyone used anymore.

Obsolete, but not illegal.

So why, I wonder as the bell rings just as I am sliding into my seat, did the police arrest someone over a piece of paper?

TWO

My father once told me that when I was little I would stare at an object for hours. My head cocked to one side. My hazel eyes wide and focused. Never moving or saying a word. He said it was the way that I studied the world that made him realize I was going to be a visual artist, just like my mother. It was as if I was compelled to learn everything about the color and shape of a thing in order to understand it and myself.

I am staring out the window of my math class now at the scraggly bush far in the distance where hours ago the policeman found that paper. There is no sign of the flashing lights or men in suits. Just a sparrow sitting on a rusty-brown branch and sunlight shining on the forest-green leaves.

But still I focus out the window, looking for—I'm not sure what. No matter how I try to think about something else, I can't erase the image of the man with magenta-streaked hair being struck by the officer before being shoved into the police car from my thoughts.

Had that white page the officer dug out of the tree truly been the cause of the violence and the arrest?

It didn't seem possible. Few people can afford the environmental tax that is charged to anyone who purchases anything made with paper. And even if they can pay the price, most would never bother. There was no reason to. Tablets are just as easy to write on and writing on paper is not only extravagant and unnecessary, it's selfish. It means you don't care about fresh air and the environment. My dad was proud that his parents were some of the first to recycle all paper in their house. Mom's insistence on using canvases was always a sore spot between them, even though the canvases were made of linen, not pulp. He thought it would reflect badly on our entire family if anyone learned we created that kind of waste.

"Five minutes," Mr. Greene announces. "Some of you might want to think about paying attention to the review in front of you instead of what you intend to do with your summer vacation. These are just like the questions you are going to have on tomorrow's final exam."

I look at Mr. Greene, who meets my eyes with a nod. He mouths, "You can do it," and points down at the tablet sitting on my desk. I clutch my stylus tight, and I force my eyes to focus on the problems displayed in black and white on the screen.

If I expect my father to pull himself together and focus at work, I should be able to do it, too.

My teachers for the most part have been understanding of my situation, but I am not the greatest student on my best day. Unlike Rose, I have to really study if I want to get good grades. As it stands now, I have to do well on my finals or, concealer or not, people will start wondering if something is wrong.

I scribble numbers. I list whatever information I can come up with on the proofs that I am not sure how to solve, while wishing that I had taken Rose up on her offer to study with me last night. She is seated near the door, and by the way she is toying with her stylus I can tell she has already completed the work. Not a surprise. Ever since first grade, Rose has caught on to assignments faster than me, probably because she just does the work and doesn't insist on understanding what practical use the information has. I'm annoying that way.

Somehow, I manage to come up with answers for all the questions by the time Mr. Greene says, "Time is up. Now let's go over the questions one by one. If we do this right, you should be ready to ace your final exam."

A bunch of guys behind me groan, and Mr. Greene laughs.

"Think of it this way," he says, pushing up his green-wire-rimmed glasses. "The sooner tomorrow's test is over the sooner your summer can begin."

There are several high fives and calls to cancel the final exam as Mr. Greene quickly talks through the review test. He is going through the last problem for the third time as the bell rings. Everyone grabs their stuff and scrambles for the door. Over the chatter and sound of scraping chairs and desks, he shouts a reminder to get a good night's rest. Rose raises her eyebrow at me from where she waits near the exit, pausing there so we can walk together to our next classes. I grab my bag off the back of my seat and glance out the window one last time.

A guy in a black hooded sweatshirt, blue jeans, and black high-top sneakers is strolling down the sidewalk toward the bush I've been staring at. He slows for a second and I wonder if maybe he sees something the police missed. But he keeps walking.

"How did you do on the review?" Rose asks as we navigate the noisy hallway.

"Fine," I say. "A few things were wrong, but I understand enough to pass tomorrow's test." Which might not be good enough for Rose but is perfectly fine for me.

"Why don't we get together after school and study?" Rose offers, waving to one of her brother's friends. "Mom is working at home today, but she won't mind if you come over." Mrs. Webster can focus even when Rose and I are at our silliest. Rose's dad cares less about fun and far more about the rules. I never see Rose when she runs out of excuses and finally has to spend a weekend at his place.

When I hesitate answering, she smiles and adds, "Isaac will probably be around, too."

Which I know Rose thinks is a selling point. With his good looks and slightly crooked and adorable smile, Rose's older brother, Isaac, is the reason almost every girl we pass in the hallways would jump at the chance to hang out at Rose's house. Maybe it's the fact that everyone else has a crush on him that makes it hard to think of him romantically. Or maybe it's knowing how hard it would be to keep his attention that makes me not want to bother. I've tried to tell Rose that I'm not interested in dating Isaac, but somehow I always pick the wrong words and make it seem as if I might be. I guess there is no good way to tell your best friend that her brother is just too obvious a choice without sounding stupid.

So, instead of that truth, I tell another. "I'm in charge of making dinner tonight."

"Well, I can always come to your house," she says. "It's been forever since I've seen your dad."

That's a streak that I am determined to continue.

"I could even help," Rose offers in an overly cheerful tone that raises warning bells in my head. It's the one that she used after she convinced me to sneak away from our Girl Scouts campout when we were ten and she didn't want me to realize that she'd gotten us lost in the woods. "It would be great to—"

"What's going on?" I stop in the middle of the hallway. Someone bumps into me from behind and yells as they shove their way around me, but I don't care.

"We're blocking the hallway," Rose says as a guy brushes past and flips us off.

"I'll move if you tell me what you're up to. Because this isn't about studying."

Rose blows a strand of hair off her face and sighs. "It's nothing terrible," she says. "There's just something I have to talk to you about and not when there are a bunch of people around."

"Are you okay?" I ask.

"I'm fine. Honest." Her eyes meet mine. "It's actually a good thing, but I really have to talk to you about it today."

We go down another hallway, which is starting to empty out, and reach the doorway to my last class of the day. One that I am in no danger of failing—Advanced Studio Drawing.

"I'll meet you at the picnic benches after last bell," I agree. "We can figure out the rest then."

"Great! See you there." Rose bolts down the hall and I head into class wondering what plan my friend is hatching.

Mrs. Rudoren tells us that we can use the class period to work on our final project—a still life of a bowl of bananas, oranges, and apples. Really exciting stuff. I call up my work that I finished days ago so I can turn to it if Mrs. Rudoren comes by. Then I call up the file of my mother's unfinished work, careful to tilt the screen so no one can see the abstract image. I start drawing and, again, nothing feels right. So I clear the screen and re-create my work from this morning. My mind wanders to the would-be criminal with magenta- and-black-streaked hair. Then to the man in the gray suit and buckled black boots—his hand raised, ready to strike—while lights flash atop the police car next to the deep forest-green bush.

After school, I wait for Rose sitting on the scarred, faded wooden top of the picnic table. I balance my tablet on my legs and continue the work I started in art class. Laughter and shouts ripple the air as people head to buses or down the sidewalks toward home. The public screen behind me chirps about the storms that will be coming our way. I spot Isaac with a group of friends standing under a tree. He grins in my direction and all his friends turn to look at me. I wave, then stare down at my tablet, waiting for the buses to move.

While I wait, I draw the sidewalk and the grass. I add shadows and some patches of sunlight and am starting to draw the boy I saw out the window of my math class—the one who stood in the same spot where the magenta-haired man was arrested—when I hear Rose call my name.

"Sorry, Meri. I got held up. What are you working on?" Rose leans forward and I pull the screen up against my chest.

"Nothing all that great."

I don't think Rose saw the arrest this morning, and for some reason I don't want to mention it. So I change the subject to something else. "I'm starting to think there's no point in trying to complete my mother's painting. It's too late. No matter how much sleep I lose or how much I try, I know that I'm never going to understand what she was trying to create."

"Maybe you're trying too hard to do it on your own," Rose says, climbing up to sit next to me.

"Dad doesn't know what she was working on, either." He knows what I know—that in the last six months before she died, almost every night after dinner, she spent hours in her studio or taking walks alone. She told us that she had been inspired by some project she was involved in. Only none of the drawings or photographs we found on her tablet or the projects the other designers talked about her working on resembled anything like the completed abstracts or half-finished painting. "He told me there was no point in trying to figure it out."

Better to keep your focus on what is in front of you instead of trying to see things that aren't there, was his advice.

Rose shakes her head at her brother, who steps toward us. He makes a face at Rose before he turns away. "Sometimes," she says, "the best way to get to know someone is to walk a mile in their shoes. If you were part of the City Art Program . . ."

"We talked about that this morning," I say. "The deadline for portfolio submissions passed. I didn't send anything in. It's over. I've moved on."

"I know, but I didn't. Don't be mad," she says.

I blink. "I don't understand. Why would I be mad?"

"Because I submitted something for you."

Before I can decide if I'm mad or not, she rushes to say, "My father explained the situation to someone he knows in the City Pride Department, and they said they would take a look at your work. So my mom helped me put together a few things that you sent me when you were starting on your portfolio, and I sent them in. They haven't made their final decision yet, and they are interested in seeing more."

My heart jumps, then crashes back to earth. "You talked to your dad—about me?"

"Hey, I do what I have to when it's important," Rose says. "And this isn't just about your mom's painting, it's about your entire future. That's important, Meri."

Even when her parents were still married Rose didn't have to avoid talking to her father because he was rarely around. And when he was around he wanted everything to be done the right way— which meant his way. Rose says it is because he's so used to being in charge at work. Which could be true, but that doesn't make it any easier to deal with.

Some days, I'm convinced that Rose continues to be my friend because I am one of the few people who genuinely couldn't care less that Mr. Webster works in the Public Awareness and Outreach Office down the hall from the mayor or that her mother is the editor in chief of the most popular fashion magazine in the country. Almost everyone in school and most of their parents subscribe for the fashion spreads, feel-good makeover stories, and lifestyle tips. Just tap any picture and acquire what you need to brighten your own world!

When I was little, I had no idea how important Rose's mom's magazine was or where her dad's office was located—which is the reason we are friends now. Had we met in high school instead of knowing each other most of our lives, I would never even have tried to speak to her.

Not that she would have noticed. There are a million others lured into her orbit by her glamorous parents, her stunning beauty and smarts and stature. Rose has no lack of people who would be happy to go to parties with her and gossip about boys and clothes if I disappeared. Yet she puts up with my moods and withdrawal. She tolerates my obsession with my mother's painting and doesn't ask questions that I know she must have about why I won't let her near my father. She insists on being my friend even when I'm terrible at returning the favor. Thank goodness, because she's the only person I know I can count on, even when I find myself not wanting to count on anyone.

Taking a deep breath, I ask, "The committee—do they actually like my work or are they interested in seeing more because your father asked them?"

"Does it matter?" she asks. "You want to learn more about your mom so you can finish her work. The best way to do that is to talk to the people who might know what inspired that work. Do you really care if having connections is what got you through the door?"

Resentment bubbles thick and black because I do care. The idea that someone would pretend I am talented in order to curry favor with Rose's father makes my stomach turn. But I bite back my indignation because this is Rose. She wouldn't hurt me on purpose. And when I set aside my ego and think about her words, I realize she isn't wrong. If finishing my mother's work is important to me, then the only thing that matters is arriving at that goal. And having my work submitted means I might still have a chance.

"You have a point," I admit.

Rose's laugh rings bright like the sun. "Good. I like to be right. They have to make a decision on who gets into the program really soon, so—"

"How soon?"

"By tomorrow night."

"What?"

"Don't freak out," Rose insists, and waves to her brother, who nods back. "All you have to do is go by their office before then with your real portfolio. My mom told Isaac to drive us, and he said he could if we do it now."

"Now?" The word catches in my throat. Isaac strides across the grass toward us. His smile is teasing, and the wink he gives me says he knows what it feels like to be neatly trapped into doing something by his sister.

"If I'm going take Meri to Liberty Tower we have to get going. I have to meet Dad at his office later, and you know how he is about being late."

"If that's the case then maybe I should just—"

"No backing out." Rose grabs my arm and pulls me off the picnic table. "We can drop by your house for you to change clothes and download any files you need for your portfolio, then head over there. They said it wouldn't take long, so you should be back home in no time. And maybe you'll see or hear something inspiring to you when you're there. Like your mom did."

The mention of my mother gets me moving, just as Rose knew it would. We climb into the new black sedan Isaac's dad gave him earlier in the month. Isaac had wanted a sports car. Instead, he got the same model his father drove, but with bright gold wheels. Isaac mutes the National News Screen on the dash and cranks the music. Rose yells at him from the back seat to slow down.

"Not all of us drive like turtles. Right, Meri?" Isaac yells over the wailing of guitars, drums, and bass.

The trip to my house takes a matter of minutes. I jump out of the car and turn to Rose, who is starting to climb out. "You don't need to come in. I'll be out in a flash." I turn and hurry toward the brick bungalow before Rose can follow.

It takes me just a few minutes to change from my school uni-form into a pair of black pants decorated with large yellow and orange and white flowers and a white top. I tuck in the shirt, tie the belt, and slip on a pair of yellow high-top sneakers, knowing full well Rose will complain about my wardrobe choice the minute I get to the car. But when I tie an orange scarf around my neck and look in the mirror, I actually smile at the reflection. While I still see the fatigue beneath the makeup, for the first time in forever I see something other than the hurt I've felt since my mother's accident. I see me.

With a nod, I head to Mom's studio to transfer the few finished portfolio projects from her computer to my tablet. While I wait for the computer to boot, I glance around the sunlit room at the paint-ings scattered throughout the space. A large painting created just before I was born shows a gold-and-silver city stretching toward the sky. Sitting behind it—a lake of brilliant blue. Another from a year ago hangs near the hallway door and depicts a blue cobblestone path winding through a park filled with children of all ages. After I pull up the files I need, I step to a corner of the room where a group of small, unframed canvases leans against the base of the wall—out of sight so my father won't have to see them if he decides to open the door and step inside. These are the pieces she worked on during the months leading up to the accident.

Unlike all her other works, these are abstracts. A half circle of burnished red seemingly guarded by a fence of deep maroon against a background of silver. A heavy, dark-gray form that reminds me of a wrought-iron flower. A stiff beige ribbon that slashes from one corner of the canvas to the opposite corner on the bottom of the other side. What looks like the tip of a black boot on a block of light blue stone. A line of seven red rectangles marked with a strange winged figure painted in gold—and finally, the one that she had yet to finish.

A horn honks, reminding me that I'm supposed to hurry. Still, I take one last look at the group of paintings. While I didn't understand what drove her to paint them, I recognize the talent that made the images leap off the canvases. All my life I have worked to be as skilled an artist as my mother. I'm not. Even without the small headshakes of disapproval she used to give my screen, I knew that. But if *she* could take the risk of creating something this different, maybe I should take a chance on the unknown, too.

The horn honks again as I leave a message on the kitchen memo screen for my father in case he gets home before me. Then, clutching my tablet tight to my chest, I hurry outside.

The music has been turned down from deafening to bearable. The minute I get in, Isaac peels away from the curb and Rose begins a steady stream of instructions that cause me to rub my palms on my pants.

"Katy Mitchell runs the City Art Program, but Victor Beschloss is the one that you'll be meeting with. Dad says he is a good guy."

Which meant he probably never unbuttoned his collar and didn't smile a whole lot.

"Tell him all about your love of art and design and why you want to be a part of the program and how important you think the program is to our city and to our national identity."

"Maybe I should salute the flag while I'm at it?" I ask sarcastically. Although it would be easy enough to do, since every house and business was gifted a flag at the time the new star was added.

Isaac grins at me as he stops at a light. Rose continues her monologue as if I never interrupted her.

"Make sure you smile."

As if smiling is really my thing.

"Mention how your mother's pieces, created on behalf of the government, influenced your own creations."

So basically, lie.

"Tell him how you want to use your art the way she did—to celebrate our society and to do your part to keep the country safe and strong and prosperous."

Finally something I can say without feeling like an impostor. "Okay."

"And don't gnaw on the ends of your hair."

I drop the strands of damp hair from my mouth and put my hands back in my lap.

"Lay off," Isaac says as he steers around a cab that is letting a passenger out. "You're making her nuts, Rose."

"Meri knows I'm just being helpful."

"Meri knows you are pushy and is too nice to tell you that you sound like one of the spokespeople for Dad's office."

"I'm not *that* nice," I say, even though Isaac's right. Rose does sort of sound like the talking heads on one of the country's two news channels. They all smile in a way that, in recent months, totally grates on my nerves.

"But I am trying to focus," I admit. "That might be easier if I just have a little space to think."

"See." Isaac smiles at his rearview mirror. Rose sighs but is quiet for the next several blocks. We drive across the Chicago River, sparkling gray blue as it snakes through the city. Isaac honks to get the cars in front of him moving, and my stomach flips when I see Liberty Tower—the building where my mother used to work—come into view. A large screen shows the projects that the department housed inside has worked on throughout the year. It's a reminder to everyone how far we have come since the days when Chicago was the most dangerous city in the country.

Isaac maneuvers the car to the curb in front of the rust-colored stone building that Mom told me was one of the most historic in the city—built after the Great Chicago Fire on the site of the old City Hall.

"Good luck," Isaac says as he brings the car to a stop. "Call us when you are ready to be picked up."

Rose frowns. "But—"

"She can handle this part alone," Isaac cuts off his sister. "Right, Meri?"

I nod, hoping he's right. Rose shouts good luck to me and reminds me again about my hair as I walk down the sidewalk toward the arching stone entryway and gold doors that shine in the late-afternoon sun. Other than the required billboard-sized screen above the front doors, the outside of the building is stately and beautiful in its construction. But it is the lobby that once again takes my breath away. White marble columns and walls all etched with gold greet me. I clutch my tablet tight to my chest as I walk under the words "THE ROOKERY" toward a security official ensconced in a white-and-gold marble nook.

I give him my name and nervously wait as he calls up to the head of the City Art Program to see if I am expected.

"Mr. Beschloss will be leaving soon, but he says I can let you up." He pushes out of his chair with a wince.

"You don't have to get up," I say. "I know where the elevator is. My mother used to work here."

He shakes his head and ambles down the hallway. "Mr.

Beschloss is on the eighth floor." When the gold elevator door opens, he holds up a red-and-white identification badge marked "CSS," then waves it in front of a small black scanner. "The elevator won't take you to that floor without this. He's in suite 802. Good luck."

"Thanks." I look toward the atrium that Mom loved, before stepping onto the elevator. A week after she died, the guard on duty felt sorry for me and let me sit in the atrium, staring at the glass ceiling and the sweeping staircases. The building was known for them. The City Pride Department took over the building mainly because of the historically beautifully architecture. The head of the department claimed it was only fitting the group be housed in a place designed to inspire.

The elevator dings, and I exit. Unlike the floor where my mother worked, whose halls were filled with murals of their previous projects and displays of working models of redesigned buildings, the eighth floor is stark. It has bare white walls and metal-gray floors. Aside from the whoosh of the elevator doors behind me, everything is dead quiet.

The few times I came to the office with Mom, there was always the hum of conversation or music playing from someone's speakers, giving the place a sense of life. There are no voices behind the closed steel doors on this floor. It feels sterile. Vacant. Unwelcoming.

Clutching my tablet tight to my chest, I take three slow steps down the hall, then stop in front of a door marked "ARCHIVES." It has a black scanner box next to the handle of the door, similar to the one the guard operated in order for me to get to this floor. The high security was another difference from Mom's level.

"Merriel Beckley?"

I jump and spin at the sound of my name. A red-haired man with a fussy-looking goatee stands in the middle of the hall. He is wearing a dark blue suit with black shoes that shine as if they were bought at the store today. A door that was closed just moments before now stands open not far from him.

"You *are* Merriel Beckley?"

I swallow hard and nod.

"It is good to meet you. I'm Victor Beschloss. Marcus Webster explained to me your interest in the City Art Program. I'm glad you found the time to come by. It must be hard to be back in the building where your mother worked."

I shrug as if it's no big deal. "I've never been to this floor before. It's . . . quiet."

Mr. Beschloss smiles. "The offices on this floor are utilitarian by nature. We're not the creative types up here." His smile fades. "Your mother was very talented and very . . . driven."

Driven. It isn't the first word I would have associated with my mother, but I suppose that trait would be important to the people on this floor.

He sighs and turns toward the open door. "I'm sorry to say I don't have much time. So if you would please follow me . . ."

My footsteps echo in the hallway as I trail behind him into an office lined with windows on the far side. There are large tablet screens on each of the other walls—all displaying one of the two news channels with the volume muted. There is also a dark gray couch that runs along the wall next to the door. In front of it is a glass coffee table. If the decorator wanted to make this office look as intimidating as possible, he definitely succeeded.

"Have a seat." Mr. Beschloss steps behind the wide black desk that takes up the middle of the office and gestures toward the two high-backed silver chairs across from him. "So Marcus Webster informed me of your interest in the City Art Program and pursuing a career as a national artist. He said the trauma of your mother's death derailed your ability to focus on your application, but that you are still passionate about your work and your future."

He hits a button on the console of his desk, and the screens on the walls turn on. Drawings—my drawings—the projects Rose must have given to her father—suddenly surround me on three sides. One is a color portrait I did of Rose—her smile open and warm, but her eyes narrowed with the steely resolve I admire. Another is of Navy Pier with the Ferris wheel, the ride I went on at least a dozen times with my parents, soaring above the boardwalk, surrounded by the glistening lake that the country worked so hard to make fresh and clean again.

The final image looks nothing like the others. Most wouldn't recognize it as mine. The lines are thicker, darker, and more angular than the other two. The streetlight glows at the edge of the picture, but the illumination barely cuts through the shadows of the night that surrounds the sidewalk and building. It was the first picture I drew in art class after my mother's accident, for an assignment that asked us to paint a place we recently visited in the city. Everyone else created images of Wrigley Field and Buckingham Fountain. I drew the site of my mother's death. I didn't keep a copy, but Mrs. Rudoren must have saved the file after I turned it in and given it to Rose when she asked for it.

"Did you bring other samples for me to look at?" Mr. Beschloss asks.

I nod and click on my tablet. My fingers tremble as I call up the portfolio and hand it over the desk.

He strokes his little beard as he flips through the files. "Your mother must have been proud. Did she work with you on these or influence the subjects you chose to draw? Maybe nudge you to find inspiration by talking about locations she appreciated or ideas she thought should be explored?"

I try to ignore the dark sidewalk in the picture still being displayed on the tablet to the right of me. "She did when I was little. A few years ago, when I got more serious about my art, she took a step back and encouraged me to find my own way. And in the last year she stopped volunteering information about her own projects." I add the last because I don't like the insinuation that I drew only what my mother instructed me to draw. Whether the projects are good enough or not, they are mine.

"How interesting." The flat, beige color of his voice tells me he thinks my words are far less than interesting. "I would have thought with another artist in the house she would have been excited to share her projects and stories about the people she worked with."

"She used to, and when I asked she did, but my dad isn't an artist. Mom didn't want him to feel left out of the conversation, so she tried to make sure we talked about things we all enjoyed."

He studies me with a sad smile. "Well, I know how your father feels." He looks down at the tablet in his hand one more time, then stands and holds it out to me. "Thank you for coming in to show me your work. Marcus Webster is right. You have talent. I'm sorry you couldn't get your application submitted in the typical manner, but I can promise we will consider your work as we make our final choices for this class. We have your information, and if you're chosen you'll be hearing from us soon."

Just like that, I'm dismissed. There is no time to ask about the last

34

project my mother worked on or if her team finished it, because once I take the tablet, he is walking me to the door, talking all the while. He wishes me luck in my finals at school as he escorts me down the empty hallway and tells me to give his best to my father. He pushes the button on the elevator and within seconds the doors open.

"Keep up the good work, Merriel," he says as I step inside.

The elevator doors close. Disappointment settles in my chest. My hand feels heavy as I push the lobby button. As the elevator starts to move, I hit the number three, and when the doors open I feel my mother beside me as I start down the hall. If anyone asks what I'm doing here, I will just tell them I want to take the atrium stairs on my way out.

The design has changed since the last time I was here. Now instead of vibrant walls of lavender and blue, swirling ribbons of color snake along a background of yellow. Screens are scattered along the walls, all muted but tuned to various programs. One displays a report on the weather—sunny and warmer with no rain in today's forecast. On the second, a broadcast of the current president addressing a group of smiling workers. Two others flip through slides of a handful of upcoming projects—like a park with an arching, waterfall-like fountain and a new apartment complex in rose and white stone.

An unfamiliar blonde dressed in a bright green top and tight purple pants smiles at me as she ducks into a workroom to the left. A burst of laughter sounds from inside the workroom as I pass. People are standing around a large square table with a model of something in the center of it. I don't recognize anyone in the meeting space, and there aren't any familiar faces in the next, but I do spot one person I know in the workroom not far from the stairs.

Kacee Anderson's back is to me as she draws on a whiteboard. She's dressed in all black and taps her foot to old rock music that is pumped through the room's speakers. Her dark hair is pulled into a tight ponytail that sways as she works. Several other artists are working at the table or on graphic-design tablets along the wall.

Mrs. Anderson turns. I hover in the doorway and start to step forward as her eyes widen in recognition. But a small shake of her head stops me in my tracks and she turns back toward her project as if she never saw me at all.

For the second time today, the sting of rejection pricks deep into my heart. Still, I wait for several more seconds, hoping she will look back at me. When she doesn't, I hurry toward the staircase at the end of the hall. I blink away the tears I refuse to let fall, keep my head down, and make my way to the atrium. Someone bumps me. I grab hold of my tablet to keep it from crashing to the ground and walk on—through the atrium, past the elevators and the security guard, until finally I stand in the sunshine outside the gold doors and am no longer able to control the tears that fall.

Disappointment floods through me. No matter how hard I try to hold on to her, my mother is slipping further and further away, as are the dreams I once had for my future.

I swipe at my cheek and look up and down the street for Isaac's car. Isaac and Rose probably think I'm still discussing my work and that they have lots of time to kill before I need them to fetch me. And I'm glad. The short time spent in my meeting will give away how badly it went. Poor Rose. She worked so hard, and even enlisted her father—which had to have taken a lot of persuasion. It isn't her fault that my talent fell short. She shouldn't have to feel bad because she tried to help. So as much as I want to go home, I decide to walk around the block and get myself together before I call them to pick me up. It's the least I can do for all that she has done for me.

The light changes, and I follow a bunch of businessmen across the street. I start to turn down the block when I notice a guy standing next to a light post who stops me in my tracks.

I think I know him.

No. I take a step forward and squint into the sunlight. We have never met. But I have seen him before. And when he turns and I see him slide a piece of paper into the front pocket of his pants, I realize where I know him from.

Black hooded sweatshirt. Rich brown skin. Close-cropped hair. Blue jeans that fit like a second skin and red shoelaces that snake up his black high-tops. It's the guy I saw out the window of my math class, searching the bush after the cops arrested the magenta-haired man and carted him away.

But it can't really be him. It has to be a coincidence. Still, after going months without seeing any paper, I can't help thinking the two things are connected. Maybe that's why I find myself trailing him when he turns and heads down La Salle Street toward the river. His stride is long and quick, and I have to jog a bit to keep up with him. He pauses to wait for the stoplight to change, and I get close enough to see his profile.

He's younger than I originally thought. Isaac's age. Maybe a year older. It's hard to tell, but he's closer to being a boy than a man.

The light changes. A group of giggling girls in their school uniforms race in front of me, pointing up at a giant screen on a building that in between news programs is featuring highlights from the "USA Proud" pop boy band currently touring all fifty-one states.

I dodge around them and hurry forward, determined to keep the guy I'm following in view. He glances over his shoulder, and I try to pretend I'm just another tourist looking up at—what? I fix my eyes on a bronze statue of a man with his fist raised to the sky and wait several heartbeats before glancing back.

Damn. The black hoodie has gotten farther away.

Sweat drips down my neck as I zigzag through the people on the walkway. The boy crosses the street and heads for the bridge that leads over the river. I pick up my pace from a jog to a run.

A horn honks.

Fingers dig into my arm, and I'm yanked backward to the curb. I stumble and clutch my tablet as cars stream by.

A man in jogging shorts and a Chicago Cubs T-shirt helps me get my balance. "I'm sorry if I grabbed you too hard, but I didn't want you to get hit."

I stammer my thanks, then rise on my tiptoes and shift from side to side, catching glimpses of the sweatshirt as it gets farther and farther away. The light changes and I bolt forward. I push through people who are crossing the street in the opposite direction. My heart drums faster as I hurry toward the bridge, but when I get halfway across the expanse of the river I have no choice but to admit the obvious. The black sweatshirt and the boy who pocketed the paper have vanished.

How much time has passed in my wild-goose chase, I don't know, but Rose and Isaac are going to be seriously worried and probably a whole lot annoyed if I don't contact them soon.

Shaking my head, I turn and walk along the arching, rust-red iron bridge back to the side I came from, feeling foolish for having wasted so much time on . . . whatever that was. The light is red and I tap my foot, impatient for it to flash green. A seagull calls overhead. I look up and watch as the stretched white wings soar against the blue sky, then dip lower. The bird flies in front of the top of one of the large stone support posts that flank the end of each side of the bridge, and even though everyone else starts walking toward the crosswalk, I can't move. My feet are like stone.

On the top of each of the supports is a set of windows. Above those windows is an artistic iron roof. And in the center of it is a design that I know almost as well as I know my own face. I should. I've looked at it every day for the last three months. The hard curves and dark shapes.

It's an image out of one of my mother's final paintings.

THREE

What feels like an eternity passes before I can get home and assure myself I wasn't imagining things.

When I climb into his car, Isaac is irritated my meeting took so long. He huffs and snaps at me to get in and doesn't wait for me to fasten my seat belt before he hits the gas. Rose, however, is thrilled that Victor Beschloss talked with me for over an hour and wants to hear details.

"Did he love your portfolio? He must have, considering how long you guys talked. I knew you had nothing to worry about. Can I see what you showed him?"

Since the questions come in such rapid succession, there is no need to answer any other than the last. I bring up the portfolio images and put the tablet into Rose's outstretched hands. She oohs and aahs and makes all sorts of comments about the subjects and the bright colors. I smile as if I am listening, but in my mind I'm picturing the series of small canvases leaning along the wall of Mom's studio.

Isaac yells at another driver and steers the car onto a less congested street. Rose continues asking questions, seemingly unconcerned by the speed of her brother's driving or the quick succession of accelerations and stops. Rose pauses after each of her next questions, so I have no choice but to focus and answer.

No, I don't know when they will contact the people selected for the City Art Program.

Yes, I saw one of my mother's colleagues, but I didn't really have time to talk with her.

"Well, when you're working in the program, you and she will have lots of time to talk," Rose assures me as Isaac pulls the car to the curb in front of my house.

"No offense, Meri, but get out," Isaac says. His sister smacks him on the shoulder and he glares. "I still have to change before I meet Dad."

"I really appreciate you driving me, Isaac," I say, pushing open the car door. "Tell your father thanks and I'm sorry I made you late."

Rose yells that she'll call me as the car zips away from the curb. I wait until it is out of sight before I race into the house and back to Mom's studio. Could the picture really be the same as the design I saw today on the bridge?

I flip though the canvases leaning against the wall.

Air catches in my throat.

There. That picture *is* the same image that I saw today.

I pull up the photograph I snapped of the top of the bridge with my tablet, zoom in until just the sculpted onyx iron of the image is showing, and compare it with the one in front of me. One that I had once believed was an abstract floral.

The large round centers in the tablet photograph and the painting are identical. Both have three curved petals at the top. Neither has individual petals at the bottom. Instead there is just one rounded curve that spans from one side of the round center to the other.

This isn't some strange thing my mother saw in a dream and worked on despite it being a waste of resources. This is an identical representation of a small piece of the city I never thought to look closely at before.

I grab the other paintings from their perches on the floor and set them up on easels around the room. Now that I understand the images aren't abstract, I look at them with a fresh eye, searching for anything that appears familiar.

Yes. The last one in line has a hard, rust-red curve. That's the same shape and color as the supports of the bridge from today. The La Salle Street Bridge. And I think the one with bluish stone-like texture and a curved bit of burnished bronze could be the edge of the podium and statue that I passed today while following the guy in the black sweatshirt.

My mind spins as I look from picture to picture—at the unfinished work that has haunted me since my mother's death.

I don't see any other part of the La Salle Street Bridge reflected in the rest of Mom's other paintings. But I feel as if I might actually be getting closer to finally understanding. . . .

A door slams. Dad's home. And when I glance at the clock I realize how long I have been staring at the pictures. Dad is later than normal. Much later.

When I walk into the kitchen, it is obvious as to why. My throat tightens. His gait is unsteady, and when he turns toward me the pink in his cheeks and the dull, glassy sheen across his eyes make it clear he has broken his promise . . . again.

Whatever he sees on my face causes his tentative smile to fade and his shoulders to slump. "Meri . . ." He takes a step forward. "I saw a woman in the lobby at work who looked like your mother. The others invited me to get a drink and . . ."

His voice trails off. His eyes search my face, begging for forgiveness.

I want to scream.

I want to scream and yell and tell him that he wasn't the only one who lost Mom. I lost her, too. And every day that he drinks I lose *him*. I need him. He's all I have left. And he doesn't seem to care.

But I choke back the words bubbling to break free. I've said it all before. Dozens and dozens of times and nothing changes. He apologizes and promises to do better, and even though I don't believe him, a part of me desperately wants to.

A part of me still hopes, and I'm angry that I do.

"Go change," I force myself to say. "I'll make something for us to eat."

He crosses to me with a sad smile. "I promise tomorrow will be better, Meri." He pats my shoulder. I stand still as a statue as he passes by. When I hear footsteps on the stairs, I swallow the bitter taste in my mouth, go to the pantry, and take out two cans of tomato soup. I empty them into a pan and am grabbing stuff to make grilled cheese when I hear something thud upstairs.

That's when the frustration and anger and hurt finally bubble over.

There are no tears. I'm too angry for tears, which is good because tears never help. I dump the bread on the counter, turn off the stove, grab my father's keys off the table, and head out to the garage. It takes me no time at all to find the small bottle of vodka he has stashed in his glove compartment and the larger bottle still in its bag in the trunk. Before I can think too hard about what I am doing, I empty both bottles onto the ground, then throw them into the recycling container. The shattering of glass echoes in the night like the screams that I keep caged inside.

Will getting rid of the bottles change anything?

No. He'll just buy more. But when he finds them missing or sees the pieces of broken glass in the recycling container, he'll know I was the one who took them. Maybe that will make him wait a day or two before going to the store for more.

When he finally comes downstairs, I put food on the table and feign hunger. Dad makes a point of eating the soup and the grilled cheese with enthusiasm and asks if I am ready for my finals to-morrow.

"I need to spend some time looking over my geometry notes," I admit as I dump the last quarter of my sandwich in the garbage and place my plate and bowl in the sink.

"Do you want me to go over them with you?" he asks. "I'm good with numbers."

I turn back toward him. For a minute Dad looks at me like he used to before the accident. Interested. Excited at the prospect of helping me. He always said that math was the greatest thing in the world.

When I was little he used to tease Mom when she struggled with a design. He'd say she should have become an accountant because math was dependable in the execution. There was no worry over choices. The numbers just added up.

I know he was hoping, for a while, that I'd follow in his footsteps.

Dad was the one who saw the step in front of him. Mom had

dreamed of the steps people had yet to take. I can't help but wonder if things would be better between us now if I were more like him.

I shrug off Dad's offer. "I just need to read over some of the proofs one more time. That's easier to do alone."

And really, sitting in the living room with him talking about numbers would feel normal. There's nothing normal about either one of us, and I'm not up to pretending.

"Well," he says with a sigh, "I'll be just a room away if you need me."

If only that were true, I think as he brings his plate to the counter. We do the dishes in silence. There used to be laughter in the kitchen. Dad is probably thinking the same as we dry the plates and put them away. The quiet is painful, and as much as I want to hide in my room alone, I find myself suddenly saying, "I guess . . . we could go over my notes together, if you really want to."

The delight on my dad's face rubs me the wrong way—but I made the offer. So I get my school tablet, load my textbook and review sheet, and come back into the living room, where Dad is waiting for me.

It's awkward at first. After months of doing everything on my own, I'm defensive when I hand Dad my tablet. But he finds a bunch of ways to compliment me on things that I understand and finally gets around to talking about the stuff I'm struggling with.

After we get through a few problems, I find myself leaning closer as he scribbles on his tablet. The jokes he makes about congruency and tangents and chords are lame but still make me laugh. By the time we get through all the review questions, I'm feeling more confident about getting a decent grade on tomorrow's exam and Dad is smiling in a way I haven't seen in months. Instead of being colored by dull blues and grays, he's now shining with vibrant yellow. He's not pretending to be happy. He really is.

"So is there anything else you need your old man's help with?" he asks, picking up my tablet. His finger punches one of the icons and suddenly the image on the screen changes from mathematical problems to my mother's half-finished painting.

I watch it happen—like rain falling on a chalk sidewalk drawing. The melting of beauty into nothingness. The teasing glint in his eye disappears, and he leans back as if worried the image will jump out and bite him for real instead of just nipping at his heart. "Are you still thinking about that picture?" he asks.

"Not really," I lie. I take the tablet from him and tap the screen so the math book replaces Mom's painting. "Do you think we can go over one other thing?" I ask, trying to bring the brightness back into the room. "The cone problems are still giving me trouble."

He sighs and shrugs. "Sure, honey." And for the next ten minutes he tries. I can tell he tries. But the brief period of light we found blinks out.

Dad gives me another pat on the shoulder, tells me, "Just focus on the numbers the problem tells you to concentrate on. Don't get distracted by anything that doesn't apply. That's the trick. Follow those steps and you'll be fine." Then he leaves the room. A few minutes later I hear the back door in the kitchen close and I head upstairs.

I put on my headset and study for the rest of my finals. The volume is cranked up high. If the car engine revs to life and my father drives away, I can't hear it. I also won't be able to hear the sound of his return or his unsteady footsteps pacing the floor of his bedroom, although I can imagine them as I compose an essay on the National Communication Initiative. My stylus glides along the surface of the tablet as I write my conclusion: "Scaling back the number of television channels and publications helped heal an angry and divided country by reducing vitriol, and providing more points of commonality."

When that's done, I read through my chemistry notes, then try to memorize names and dates of people I couldn't care less about for my Modern American History class. When my head feels heavy and my vision swims, I burrow into my covers and pull them over my head to blot out the world. Then I will my mind into sleep.

The dream comes as it always does. And as always, I know it to be a dream. Suddenly, I'm standing next to my mother on a sidewalk in the fading early-evening light. Bright silver-and-stone buildings with sparkling glass reach into the cloudless sky behind us. A wide screen congratulates the neighborhood on winning a beautification award.

Her long yellow coat is buttoned up to the top. The blue scarf I gave her for Christmas is wrapped tight around her neck as she studies the street with narrowed eyes. Then she reaches into her matching shoulder bag for her design tablet and begins to draw. Her stylus runs across the tablet, but when I step closer, there is nothing on the screen.

"Look harder," she says in the clipped tone that convinced me she'd never think I was talented enough to be a real artist. Before I can tell her I can't see what isn't there, tires begin to screech.

She doesn't run. No matter how loud I shout, she never runs.

The car swerves onto the curb. It has no color—almost no shape as it crashes into my mother. She flies backward, and my eyes snap open before her head cracks against the ground.

My temples pound as I glance at the clock. The glowing red numbers tell me I have slept four hours. There are three to go before school starts. Knowing there's no point in trying to go back to sleep, I throw off the covers and climb out of bed. I take a shower and let the water wash the grain out of my eyes and swirl the memory of the dream down the drain. Once I'm dressed, I take my tablet to Mom's studio to work.

On the way I open my father's door. In the dark, I slowly cross to the nightstand and check the alarm. Dad remembered to set it before he passed out. Part of me wonders how much he had to drink. A lot, I'd guess, considering he caught sight of Mom's unfinished picture.

An incomplete picture.

An incomplete life.

But the painting isn't just about my mother. It's about how my father and I are now living. We're stuck in this place. Neither of us can move on until the empty spaces she left are filled. For months I've tried to add to Mom's work without a sense of what direction she was taking. But after finding the inspiration for at least two, maybe three, of her paintings yesterday, I feel like I might eventually be able to fill the canvas the way she intended.

I pull up a picture of the bridge, but no matter how much I zoom in or spin sections and try to see what my mother saw, I can't figure out how this final piece fits into the puzzle. After several attempts, I do what my art teacher told us to do when we are stuck. I stop trying to force the issue and begin to draw something else.

The outline of the guy I followed flows from the tip of my stylus. I picture the moment when I was only ten feet away from him and he turned toward me. In my mind I erase the rose gold of the newly refinished buildings near him and the half-formed impressions

48

of other people on the sidewalk so I can focus on the details that belong to him.

I fill out his hair—shaved at the back of his neck and just a bit longer on the top. The sharp lines of his face and his slightly off-center nose. A strong face. Older than me, but not by much. Not classically handsome, but increasingly compelling as my stylus fills out the shadows of his jawline and the texture of his eyebrows.

When his face is done, I move on to the black sweatshirt with the sleeves rolled up to the forearms. I picture something on his arm—peeking out from the edge of the sweatshirt. But I'm not sure what it is or if that detail is real or if my imagination has taken over. However, I am certain of the narrow shoulders and the long legs. By the time my father's alarm snaps my concentration, I know the image I have in front of me is as close to memory as I can make it.

The alarm goes silent almost as quickly as it sounded and I hold my breath and listen. Floorboards creak. A shower turns on. I let out a relieved sigh. One less thing to worry about.

Quickly, I slide off the stool and head to my room. I pull my hair into a low ponytail, grab my bag, and head back downstairs. The shower upstairs turns off as I take an apple and a can of Pepsi from the fridge. My body craves coffee, but I am not going to wait around for it to brew.

For once, I get to school in plenty of time. I slide into my desk and read over my notes for several minutes before our teacher tells us to hook up our personal screens. Along with everyone else, I grab the cord at the corner of my desk and plug it into my tablet port. My screen goes blue and the word "WORKING" appears in white as the school system locks the programs stored in my tablet so they cannot be accessed during the exam. Any attempt to do so will activate an alarm in the school network. Cheating is not allowed in any form.

While it seems like any sensible person wouldn't risk trying to beat the system, there are always a few who do. I remember the door to my biology classroom swinging open last year in the middle of the first-semester exam. Two of the school's security officers entered, and a freshman named Jeremy jumped up from his desk. His eyes darted around as he looked for a way to escape the two officers who approached. But there wasn't any way out, especially when Principal Velshi appeared. The security officials each took hold of one of Jeremy's arms and walked him out the door. Principal Velshi shook his head and apologized for the disruption. "Your fellow student thought he had found a new code that would allow him to access his own files without alerting anyone to his activities. There is a zero-tolerance policy on this campus for cheating. I encourage all of you to remember that."

As if I could forget the fear on Jeremy's face when he was led out of the classroom. I never saw him again. The no-cheating policy meant he received a failing grade for all his classes and was forced to repeat them at a different school. Two students were pulled out of their tests for cheating last December—a senior girl and a junior boy who ended up with the same punishment. I assumed they must have parents a lot like Mr. Webster, who forces Rose and Isaac to do extra work if they don't get perfect grades. Parental pressure can make some students do irrational things. But Rose disagreed.

"It's not just pressure to excel at school. Hackers are compelled to break codes that others say are unbreakable. It's just the way they're wired."

Maybe that was true, but it seemed crazy to risk upsetting their families and maybe screwing up their futures because they wanted to prove they could beat the school's examination program. I liked a challenge as much as the next person, but there was no point upending an entire life just to prove that you could outthink the system.

The word "LOCKED" appears on my screen. Once all the tablets display the same message, our teacher tells us we have an hour and a half to finish the test. She taps something on her computer and uploads the final exam into the network. A new image appears on our screens. Our teacher takes a seat and we get to work.

All around me, people shift in their chairs. Stylus taps against shatterproof glass echo through the room. We write in answers and select the correct bubble for what year World War I started, why approval is necessary and takes years for anyone who wants to travel outside the country, or when the green tax was put into place.

I answer most of the questions. My late-night cramming clearly paid off. My chemistry test is about the same. Not terrible. Not great. Good enough.

Rose waves when I walk through the door to geometry—my last test of the day—and mouths for me to wait for her after the bell rings.

Despite the emotional fallout, my study session with Dad helped. I stumble through the first two proofs, but by the time I reach the second screen I'm surprised at how fast I cruise through the test. I finish with almost twenty minutes to spare, and after reviewing my answers one last time, I hit the Complete button. The tablet asks for confirmation that I am ready to submit my work, reminding me that no changes can be made after I do so. When I tap the Confirm icon, I am certain that I have passed the test and the class. One day of finals down. One more to go.

I shift in my desk as I wait for exam time to expire. Rose is still hunched over her tablet, along with almost everyone else in the class, probably double- and triple-checking answers. I feel a stab of worry, then shrug the anxiety off. It's not like I can change anything now, so I turn and stare out the window at the bush on the other side of the street until the bell rings.

All our personal screens turn red as the tests are officially submitted. The screens go green to show the process is complete. Our personal data has once again been unlocked.

Chairs scrape against the tile. Everyone shoves their tablets into bags and bolts for the door, grateful to be done for the day. I sling my backpack over my shoulder and wait for Rose, who is asking Mr. Greene about one of the questions. She isn't smiling when she turns.

"Is everything okay?" I ask when we reach the hallway.

Rose shrugs. "I changed one of my answers and I shouldn't have. After I hit Complete I knew I had made a mistake. I have a feeling I didn't get full points on a few others. I hope that my score doesn't bring down my semester grade, or my father will use it as an excuse to make me take summer classes instead of working at *Gloss*. How did you do?"

"It could have been worse," I say, downplaying my performance so Rose doesn't feel bad. "I'm glad it's over. Now we just have to get through tomorrow and we'll be free for the summer. Or I will. You'll be busy working with glamorous people and playing with samples of new makeup."

Rose punches the combination into her locker. "Just because I'll be doing some work for my mother's company doesn't mean I won't be around. I will. And you'll probably have less free time than I will if you make it into the City Art Program—unless you want to come work at *Gloss*. Mom says the offer is still on the table." She opens the door, grabs her phone from the charging station, and frowns at the screen.

"What's wrong?"

"Isaac. He's going out with friends and isn't going to give me a ride home even though he promised Dad he would. He's still upset about yesterday—Dad reamed him for being late and threatened to take away his car."

"That was my fault," I correct. "If he is mad at anyone it should be me."

"He'll get over it." She gives a dramatic sigh and slams the door to her locker. "I mean, he just had to get an ID and a uniform. No big deal. Well," Rose says with a bright smile. "I guess the good news is that Isaac won't be around to annoy anyone, so we can go to my house and study."

"Um . . ." I had planned to return to Mom's paintings. "The only real final I have left is English Composition." My art and phys ed finals weren't exactly the kind you could study for.

"I have Composition tomorrow, too, and I really need you to read over my history paper. The information is all there, but I know there are places it could be better. I'd ask Mom, but she has to work late tonight, and I'm *not* about to ask my father." Before I can come up with a good excuse to turn her down, she adds, "Please? It's our last time studying together as underclassmen."

A couple of our friends we've known forever shout that they have to catch the bus but that they'll call us later so we can all get together. I wave back, even though I know that while they have included me, they really mean they are going to call Rose. Which is why, instead of turning her invitation down, I say, "You know what? Sure. I can study today."

The bridge will be there later, but unless I'm careful, Rose might not.

The clouds are thick and misty gray as we walk to her building. It sits on a block that has been completely redesigned by the City Pride Department. All the buildings and flowers and the occasional tree by the curb complement each other. Rose lives on the top two floors of a five-story building created out of off-white stone and rose-gold steel—a modern twist on the older architecture in this part of town.

Even with rain threatening, the colors chosen for the building make it appear as if it is almost glowing from within. The whole street has that same warm feeling. While I love my neighborhood, with its redbrick bungalows and cobblestone-edged sidewalks, this area helps me understand how effective the City Pride Department's work can be and how creating this kind of environment for everyone really does improve lives.

Rose uses her key to activate the elevator, which shines in metal of the same hue as the outside of the building. Rose pushes 4, and moments later we are walking into the beautiful red-and-white living room. Art screens filled with various covers of Mrs. Webster's fashion e-zine grace the walls, along with a colorful rendering of the Chicago skyline that I watched my mother create years before.

"I'm sorry," Rose says from behind me. "I should have come up first and shut that screen down."

"No, you shouldn't have." I shake my head and stare at the strokes that so vividly brought the city to life. My mother had given Mrs. Webster a canvas version of the same image. Part of me wonders whether she turned it in to the government-recycling program, the way most people have done with their old art. I hope not. I turn away from the screen and try to smile. "Can we study while we eat?"

For the next several hours I almost feel as if time has turned back. We make sandwiches and work at the sleek black kitchen table while we eat her brother's stash of corn chips that he thinks no one else knows about. And we study. Longer than I would like, but Rose is a taskmaster. She forces me to read her essay on how designating English as the national language helped foster cooperation and a sense of shared identity. Then she drills me with writing prompts for my English Composition class tomorrow. The slamming of the front door causes us both to look up. And when Isaac appears in the kitchen doorway and lets out an annoyed sigh, I am glad to tell Rose that I have to get home.

The sky is darkening when I arrive. I'm late enough that I am not surprised to see that my father is already there and has brought dinner home—sweet-and-sour chicken and rice. A favorite of mine. An apology from him. My stomach growls, and I decide I have no choice but to accept it.

The food is good, even if the conversation is stilted and my father won't meet my eyes. This is normal, but after yesterday, when we were able to talk and joke without the strangling tension between us, I notice it more. I think Dad does, too, because each time silence falls he fills the void with another question about my exams. I feign enthusiasm, even when he has run out of questions and starts repeating them, but eventually he realizes that neither of us is fooling anyone. He falls silent and we both pretend to focus on the food.

Dad pushes back his chair first. "I brought some work home. I'll be upstairs if you need me."

As he heads out I find my voice again. "Dad?"

He turns in the doorway and straightens his shoulders, trying to look upbeat, which makes me feel even worse. I want to tell him that it will all be okay and make us both believe it. But I can't, so all I can say is, "Thanks for dinner."

He sighs. "You bet, sweetheart."

I hear his footsteps on the stairs, the sound of his door closing, and then my father pacing his room above me like a Bengal tiger searching for a way out of its cage.

And I hate it. I want this horrible loop we are trapped in to end. And there is only one way I can think of to do it.

I empty my plate into the garbage, then grab my bag and head out the door. The sun has set and the moon is fighting to shove its pale yellow beams through the thick, charcoal clouds. Wind whips the trees as I cross the patch of grass to the garage and roll out my bicycle. It is dusty from disuse over the winter, but the tires are still inflated.

The approaching storm and the darkness have chased most people inside, so I ride on the sidewalks instead of on the streets, avoiding traffic entirely. The wind whips against me, making it difficult to pedal, but I push my legs harder and ignore the burning of my muscles as the buildings grow taller. The quiet of the North Side disappears into the bustle of the city, which will last until the city-wide street repair curfew begins.

I have hours before that, and even then I have nothing to worry about. The curfew applies only to motorized vehicles. People in our neighborhood walk their dogs or ride their bicycles or take out the garbage after curfew all the time.

My mother used to take walks after midnight several times a week. She said her best ideas came to her when the rest of the world around her was still. She said it allowed her to see beyond what was there into what could be. I wonder if in those final months she walked the same sidewalk that I now ride. I wish she had let me go with her when I asked instead of telling me I wasn't ready.

The sky rumbles as I finally reach Liberty Tower, where I started my journey yesterday, and climb off my bike. The building stretches up beyond the illumination of the streetlights. I ignore the ache in my chest and focus on the paintings, the shapes I studied over and over and couldn't find meaning for. I don't see anything in the structure that evokes those images, so I wheel my bike across the street and keep searching. What about the unusual lamp on the building on the next block? Could it be part of one of her paintings?

My heart sinks when I get close enough to see that there is nothing about the lamp that looks familiar. So I keep riding, studying every brick and iron bar and . . . there. I spot two white gateposts that lead to a courtyard several blocks away. When the lamp and the posts are combined, my artist's eye tells me they match one of the images my mother painted. I snap pictures and keep walking.

My heart pounds. A drop of rain lands on my cheek, but even as everyone around me picks up their pace, I don't rush for fear I will miss what my mother saw.

I see the blue-and-red columns on a building at the end of the block, put down my kickstand, and walk around, looking for what my mother painted. Finally, I find the right spot where the tree suddenly appears to be just small green specks behind the wide blue-and-red pillar.

Energized, I climb back on my bike and keep going—determined to find them all.

There! The corner of a concrete pedestal and the weathered bronze tip of the man's boot from the statue I passed yesterday match another of my mother's canvases.

Certain I am finally going to be able to finish my mother's work, I ignore the mist of rain that starts to fall and keep riding until I again reach the La Salle Street Bridge.

The streetlights that line the bridge are bright. Thunder sounds. People hurry around me as I stare up at the black iron flower design and then walk the bridge past the arched red iron to the other side, looking for the last two of the completed paintings and a hint as to what the unfinished one might be.

Wait. There.

I snap a fast photograph from a distance, then shove my tablet into my backpack so it stays dry and hurry forward.

Fat raindrops fall from the sky. Thunder rumbles. A man with a shoulder bag bumps against me as he struggles to raise his yellow umbrella. Those without umbrellas race for cover. I don't run, but I do wheel my bicycle faster as I approach a small courtyard area a half block away from the entrance to this side of the bridge. The rain soaks me, plastering my shirt to my body. My socks squish with every step until finally I get close enough to be certain that I've found the inspiration for Mom's fifth painting. There is only one more finished painting to find the source of and then I'll be able to search for the one she never got to complete.

"Here," a man's voice says. "I could be wrong, but I think you need this."

I turn and see the man who bumped me holding out his large yellow umbrella.

"Thanks." I smile gratefully and shake my head. "But I can't take your umbrella."

"Not the umbrella," the man says as he holds out his other hand. Clasped between his fingers is a folded piece of paper. "This is for you."

FOUR

The man thrusts the folded paper into my hand, then turns on his heel and hurries to the sidewalk that leads back toward the bridge.

"Wait! What is this?" I call, almost tripping over my bicycle as I turn it around to go after him. By the time I finally am ready to ride in his direction, the man and his brightly colored umbrella have disappeared.

Lightning streaks white against the sky, illuminating the heavy gray clouds. A crash of thunder follows. Rain streams down my face. My heart drums as I continue to search the street for any sign of the strange man.

Nothing. And he could have gone almost anywhere. Down the steps to the walkway by the river. Across the bridge. Into a building. There was no way to know. The page in my hand is the only proof that he was ever here. And even that will disappear if I don't get out of the rain, which is now coming down hard and fast.

Quickly, I fold the page into a smaller square and shove it into

my pocket. Then I turn my bike and, with dozens of questions swirling through my mind, pedal to my house.

Why would someone give me a piece of paper? Why would they
give *anyone* paper? Especially now when the city had joined the
national effort to buy back any paper that had not yet been recycled.
Technically, I should go to one of the centers and turn the page in.
It's what anyone who loves our city and country would do.

Instead, I steer toward home.

Several times I have to stop under a tree or an awning as water
pours from the sky in sheets. I am soaked and shivering when I
finally pedal up my driveway and lean my bike against the back of
the house. The windows of my father's bedroom are dark, and when
I step inside the house it is completely quiet. I strip off everything
but my underwear and use a dish towel to get the worst of the wet
out of my hair. Now that I'm not dripping, I dig the sodden piece of
paper out of my pocket and start to unfold it.

Damn.

The paper immediately starts to tear. There is no choice but to
wait until it dries out before I can see what the man handed me.

Frustrated, I dry off, change my clothes, then go to my mother's
studio and flip on the light. The paper has to dry. Obsessing about
it won't help me. Time will. So I try to focus on the other thing I
gained while I was out. I now know the source of almost all of my
mother's final mysterious paintings. Carefully, I rearrange the small
canvases in the order I saw them tonight, starting with the combination of the lamp and the white posts and ending with the arrows
and diamonds. At the end of the line I place a canvas of deep red con-
toured rectangles all lined up next to each other. Gold lines divide
each of the shapes. Shimmering gold images—which look sort of like

winged trees—are lined up like sentries at the top.

Finally, I place the unfinished canvas with the red stars at the corners on the last easel to complete the set.

I know so much more about what my mother was painting before she died, and yet I still have no idea what any of it means. And now I have another mystery to unravel—the wet folded piece of paper. The man with the umbrella was unfamiliar but not exactly forgettable. He had a line of hooped earrings in one ear and a small diamond stud above his left eyebrow. No, I didn't know him, but he seemed to know me.

I go to the kitchen to retrieve the tablet from my bag, glad that it was waterproof or I would be totally screwed. Then I curl up on my bed and draw what I can remember of the man in the rain.

Taller than me, but that's not saying much. Yellow umbrella. Dark stubble against slightly olive skin. And sunglasses. Despite the rain and the dark, he was wearing black sunglasses. Maybe if I had seen his eyes I would recognize him. But looking at the image I have created, I find nothing about his face that pulls at my memory.

Rain pounds the roof as I turn and stare at the paper sitting on the nightstand. *I'll give it another hour to dry,* I think, just before my eyes close.

I dream that I am lost in a forest of silver metal trees—hungry and tired and desperate to find a way out. When I see a crust of bread, I race toward it and cram it into my mouth before I can even think about who might have left it on the ground or why. I find another crust fifty feet away. The trees start to change color—bronze and wrought iron, then gold—as I follow the trail of crusts to the edge of a rickety bridge that spans a gaping hole that I can't see the bottom of. I am just about to step onto the first wooden slat when I hear someone call my name.

"Meri—wake up. Your alarm didn't go off. You have to get up. . . . Meri!"

I snap open my eyes. My father's face comes into focus above me, and for a second, I don't understand why. I am still standing at the bridge past the forest of metal trees, looking for more bits of bread, trying to find my way out. Then the words sink in. The bridge and the bread vanish as I sit up straight and glance at the clock. For the first time in months, I slept for six hours straight.

"I'm going to be late," I say, leaping off the bed.

"I can drive you," my father offers. "And I'll put some coffee in a go cup just in case you decide you want it."

It takes me just minutes to put on my uniform, brush my teeth and hair, and grab my things.

Wait.

I hurry back into my room, snatch the now dry paper off my nightstand, and shove it in the side pocket of my bag so I can open it later. Dad has the coffee and a toasted bagel ready for me when I reach the kitchen. I grab both and am glad he suggested the ride because I am just walking into the gym for my physical education final as the second bell rings.

Thankfully, the test for gym class is pretty simple. We have to either run a mile or take a fourteen-page written exam about the rules and history of the various team sports we participated in throughout the year. It's not a surprise when all but four of us change into shorts and a school logo T-shirt and head outside to the track.

On my best day, I'm not a fast runner. Today was not even close to my best day, which means I end up jogging with a bunch of other students I've known forever. They keep up a running conversation about the end of finals and their excitement about summer break. And for some reason they insist on asking me questions.

I force myself to answer in between panting breaths. It isn't until the test is over and I am getting back into my uniform that I think about the dream and realize what it meant.

Bread crumbs.

Mom's paintings were like the bits of bread. Her trail led from Liberty Tower down La Salle Street to whatever the last painting represented. That was where something went wrong. The trail wasn't complete. But logic dictated that it had to pick up somewhere on La Salle Street—the street where that man with the yellow umbrella found me.

I dig the paper out of my bag and duck behind an open locker so no one can see as I unfurl the fragile page. The paper is stuck to itself in several places. I have to keep reminding myself to go slowly. Not to rush as the page tears.

"Coach Kay wants everyone in the gym now," someone yells.

Several lockers slam shut and someone calls my name to hurry up.

"I'm coming," I yell back, but I don't move as I finally pry the page all the way open.

The paper is wrinkled and torn, but the one word written in the center of the page in red block letters that are faded by the rain and partially washed away still is readable.

VERIFY

Or is it an N in the middle? V-E-N-I-F-Y?

Either way, is it a word? A name? Maybe a product or a place?

If VENIFY is some kind of new business, then handing out pieces of paper with the name would certainly get attention. People could turn in the papers for the recycling incentive money.

I fold the paper and carefully stash it away, then head to the gym to listen to Coach Kay's last-day speech before the bell rings. She gives the screen in my hand a deliberate look as she reminds us all to stay active this summer and not to spend all our time with our tablets.

As soon as the bell sounds, I bolt to the door and hurry to my next final. I am one of the first to arrive at English Comp, which gives me time to turn on my tablet and open up a search window. Do I think the word has an N or an R in it?

I type "VENIFY" first and hit Enter.

NO INTERNET CONNECTION AT THIS LOCATION.

Ugh. In my excitement, I forgot that the school turns off all wireless connections on final-exam days.

The letters on the paper haunt me as I hunch over my tablet for my composition test.

Thankfully, after English, my last final for this year is art, which means all I have left is to answer a few questions about the importance of celebrating American culture through realistic artistic expression, which I do in a matter of minutes. I hit Complete on my work and now I have nothing to do for the next hour.

I think about the page tucked deep inside my bag. I could wait until I go home to look for information on the strange name or . . .

I raise my hand and wait for Mrs. Rudoren to notice me and wave me toward her desk.

"Are you having trouble with your final?" she asks.

"I'm finished, but I'm not feeling well," I say, putting a hand on my stomach. "Can I get a pass to visit the nurse? I think I just need to lie down for a few minutes."

"You know, I thought you looked pale," Mrs. Rudoren says, opening her desk drawer to pull out a small blue-framed e-memo screen. "Why don't you take your backpack and tablet with you just in case he keeps you for the rest of the period. I can get the pass back from Mr. Hayes after school is over." She glances at her watch, uses her stylus to key in the information, then hands the pass to me. "If I don't see you before the end of the day, have a great summer, Merriel."

I thank her and collect my stuff on the way to the door. As soon as I am out of Mrs. Rudoren's sight, I hurry down the empty hall, past rooms filled with students hunched over tablets or staring off into space. Quickly, I head not to the nurse but to the Technology and Research Center to use one of the research computers.

On test days, the technology specialists are typically running from classroom to classroom helping fix tablet connections or making sure exams download properly. Today is no different. As I had hoped, the center is completely empty when I slip inside.

I hear a humming sound coming from the office in the back. Someone could be in there, but the blue door is closed and this won't take more than a few seconds. I can be gone before whoever is in the office notices I am here.

I cross to a computer that's behind a large blue-and-white column, out of the sight line of the office.

Heart pounding, I click on the Search bar and enter the word "VENIFY."

THERE IS NO ENTRY FOR THIS QUERY.

The humming in the office grows louder. I shift the bag on my shoulder, hit New Search, and try the other combination of letters: "VERIFY."

The screen in front of me changes from black-and-white to blue with red writing.

ERROR CODE 253

REPORT TO ADMINISTRATOR IMMEDIATELY.

Unless I want to explain what I'm doing here, I don't think so.

My foot catches on the leg of the chair as I jump up. The clatter of the chair hitting the desk rings in my ears as I hurry toward the door. I close it carefully behind me. As it latches, I hear short, high-pitched beeps sounding from behind the doors.

"It's coming from the Technology and Research Center," someone calls down the hallway to my left, so I hurry toward the one to the right. I hold my breath as footsteps echo against the linoleum tile of the hall behind me. I slow my steps as I approach the white door with a plaque that reads "Bryan Hayes, RN" on the wall beside it.

One look at me—breathless and sweaty—and Mr. Hayes directs me to sit down so he can take my temperature. It's not until he declares my temperature normal, has asked me a half-dozen questions, and checks on the four other students who are camped out in the office that he even thinks to inquire about my pass. He logs the information into the computer without questioning the time Mrs. Rudoren signed me out of art class.

I let out the breath I didn't realize I was holding and close my eyes. My heart beats loud in my ears as I think about the red error message on the computer screen—the beeps that started as I left the Technology Center and the voices that had been approaching it as I left.

The message appeared as soon as I searched for the word

"VERIFY." The beeping and the voices came seconds later.

That could be coincidence.

After all, it was just a computer search . . . for a series of letters on a piece of paper that had been given to me by a man I didn't know, but who seemed to be waiting for me. In the rain. On the path of bread crumbs my mother painted.

This was all crazy. And yet . . .

The bell rings. The others sitting in the nurse's office bolt for the door, but I take my time swinging my feet over the edge of the cot.

"How are you feeling?" Mr. Hayes asks. "Your color looks a little better. Do you want me to call your father to pick you up?"

"No, I'm okay." I push to my feet as if to prove it.

He watches me as I walk to the door. When he seems satisfied that I'm not going to keel over, he wishes me a good summer. I repeat the sentiment as I go out the door and into the hallway. It feels like a party. Spare uniforms and T-shirts are being shoved into bags, lockers are being slammed shut, and people are streaming toward the door that leads to several months of freedom from school. I start toward my locker, but when I reach the hallway for the Technology and Research Center, I turn down it instead of going straight. Through the long glass window in the door, I see Principal Velshi arguing with several security officials. Mr. Velshi looks frazzled. The guards don't. They seem—

"Excuse me!"

I jump at the sharp voice and whirl around. Mrs. Haberman, the head Technology and Research Center specialist, has her arms crossed over her wide chest and gives a fierce frown. "Is there something I can do for you?"

"I was looking for Rose Webster," I lie. "I said I'd meet her here."

"Well, you'll have to meet her somewhere else," Mrs. Haberman snaps. "The Technology and Research Center is closed."

I step back and she pushes the door open. Just before it latches closed I hear Mrs. Haberman say, "Well?" and Principal Velshi reply, "Someone did a search on that computer seconds before the alarm went off. We need to report this problem and find whoever is behind it."

I stumble back from the door. Principal Velshi is a nice man. When my mother died, he wasn't one of the ones who told me that he was "always here" if I needed to talk and then never mentioned it again. Like it was a box to check—act sympathetic and then move on. He dropped by my lunch table or found me in the hallways every couple of weeks just to chat. If it had just been him in the Technology Center, I might have opened the door and told him about my search for VERIFY. I could have showed him the water-stained paper and asked what he thought it was.

But he isn't alone and I just want to get out of here.

Two officers pass me as I walk to my locker with my head down. It takes only minutes to punch in the combination and empty out my space. I snag a school hoodie from a hook, shove my extra pair of sneakers into my bag, and fish out a sequined hat my father gave me for my birthday (and I pretended to have lost). I slam the locker shut and head for the closest exit, all too aware of the tattered paper in my bag. I'd love to throw it into the trash, but I'm scared someone will notice me doing it and realize I am the one who tripped the alarm.

Despite the warm sunshine, I am shivering when I step outside. The buses have already left. Two police cars with their lights flashing are parked in the rounded school driveway in their place.

"There you are!"

I spin and spot Rose strolling down the sidewalk in my direction.

"I thought you'd blown me off." I must look confused because she says, "I sent a message to your phone and your tablet—asking you to meet me. You didn't get it?"

I shake my head as several police officers come out of the main doors. One is on his phone. Another is squinting into the sunshine as if she is looking for someone.

Rose follows my gaze and frowns. "I wonder what the police are doing here."

"I think it's . . . because of me," I whisper.

Rose snaps her head back toward me. "What are you talking about?"

One of the cops looks in our direction. I grab Rose's arm and pull her toward the parking lot. I need to tell someone what's happening. If anyone can make me feel less freaked by all of this, it's Rose. That's when I spot a gray-haired woman in a black hoodie standing across the street. She's next to the shrub where I saw the man arrested two days ago. The man who had a piece of paper.

My steps slow as Rose asks, "Meri, where are we going?"

The older woman meets my eyes with dark ones of her own and nods.

And I know I'm not imagining it. She isn't standing there by coincidence. The way she meets my eyes tells me the woman is waiting for me.

FIVE

The woman in the black sweatshirt lifts her right arm. Then she turns. I see the flutter of a paper in her hand as she walks toward the corner of the tan stone apartment building and disappears out of view.

"Meri, what is going on? Are you feeling okay? You look really pale."

I pull my eyes from the spot where I last saw the woman. Rose says my name again and tugs her arm out of my grasp.

"Sorry," I say. Rose is looking at me as if I have lost my mind, and maybe I have. I glance back across the street. The woman has not reappeared. I shake my head, take a deep breath, and say, "Something happened today during last period. I think I might be in trouble."

"What kind of trouble?"

The policewoman starts in our direction. She isn't looking at us, but . . .

"Can we talk somewhere that isn't here?"

Rose glances back. A bright red car pulls up behind the police cruisers. "Sure," she says, falling in step beside me.

"How did your finals go?" I ask as we cross the asphalt of the student parking lot, which by now is mostly empty of vehicles. I look for Isaac's car. It's not there.

Rose sighs. "My finals went fine, I guess. You know about geometry already. I think my essay for Comp was really good. There were two questions on the history final that I wasn't positive about, but there's no point in worrying about it now, right? How about you?"

"My essays were good, thanks to you, and gym was mostly painless." I glance behind me as we turn down the block. The police cars are still parked in front of the school. No one is close enough to hear us talking. So I swallow hard and admit, "Things got strange after I turned in my art final. I got a pass for the nurse even though I wasn't really feeling sick. . . ."

Rose says nothing as I tell her the story of going to the Technology and Research Center and doing a search for the string of letters. I leave out the part about where I got the paper. It all sounds weird enough without admitting to taking something from a stranger I encountered on an artistic scavenger hunt that my dead mother left behind.

Instead, I say that I found the folded, rain-soaked paper after my father dropped me off in front of the school. But once I get through that, I am honest about every detail of what happened from when I sat in front of the computer until now.

"I can't imagine why anyone would call the police just because you did a computer search," Rose says. "It has to be a coincidence, but . . ."

"But what?"

"But you're right about it all being really strange. Do you still have the paper?"

"No." I pull my backpack close to my side and turn down my street. "I tore it into a bunch of pieces and threw it in the trash on my way to the nurse's office. It was falling apart after being in the rain and with the alarm going off—I don't know. It just seemed like a good idea to get rid of it."

Rose stops walking. "Are you crazy? First of all, you know we have a duty to recycle. Second, the word on that paper may have alerted the police. How could you just throw something like that away? It could be important!"

I look down at the line in the sidewalk as guilt burrows deep in my chest.

"Sorry," Rose says before I can come up with some kind of explanation. "I get it. I do. You're freaked out. I would've done the same thing. Still, I wish you had hung on to the paper long enough to take it to a recycling center. Then I could have read the writing for myself." She starts walking again and I fall in step beside her. After a few seconds, she asks, "What did you say the letters were again? The version that set off the error message?"

"V-E-R-I-F-Y."

Rose scrunches up her nose. "Ver-i-fee? I don't think I've ever heard of it before. What do you think it is?"

"If I knew that I wouldn't have done the computer search."

We walk in silence for the next few minutes. The glow of the sun against the red and orange flowers makes them appear as if they are on fire. There are almost no clouds in the sky. It's a sea of perfect blue that would be hard to replicate on my screen. It's bright, but it has depth.

My mother could have captured it. I wish she were still here to tell me what to do next. Because even though I don't know why I'm in trouble, I know that I am.

They will check the list of students who weren't in class.

They're going to figure out I was the one who did the search and set off the alarm.

"What should I do?" I ask the question of Rose instead.

"Okay." She purses her lips. "Well, you shouldn't have taken a detour to the Technology Center, but other than that, you didn't really do anything wrong. The best policy is to tell someone what you did so they don't think you are trying to hide anything."

"Okay." I press a hand to my stomach to still the churning and stop walking. "Then I should go back to the school and confess everything to Mr. Velshi."

"I don't think that'll work," Rose answers. "This isn't just a school matter."

This is why I need Rose. She can ruthlessly assess almost any situation.

"So I just keep quiet and hope for the best?" I ask, shifting my weight from foot to foot.

Rose unzips the front pocket of her bag and pulls out her phone. "I'm calling my father. You'll tell him what you told me and he'll clear this up."

Before I can voice an objection, Rose hits her dad's number on speed dial. Her father must answer on the first ring because she almost immediately starts talking while pacing up and down the sidewalk. Her voice is low so I can't hear everything she tells him. When she pulls the phone away from her ear, she gives me a thumbs-up and says, "He'll meet us at your house in fifteen minutes."

It is almost fifteen minutes exactly when I watch a dark sedan pull up to the curb. Mr. Webster climbs out from the back seat, says something to whoever else is in the car, and then starts toward the house. He's about the same height as his son, has the same rich skin as his daughter and the identical wide smile that can light up a room. But there's no smile now. Mr. Webster has no interest in lighting up anything at present.

While his children are lean like their mom, Mr. Webster is built like a football player, with big, broad shoulders and a chest like a barrel. In his dark blue suit and crisp white shirt he looks stern and unapproachable. He gives his daughter a hug and asks how her finals went. Then he turns to me. I swallow hard as I lead him into the living room and take a seat on the couch.

Mr. Webster removes his glasses, deliberately folds them, and slides them into his front jacket breast pocket. Then he focuses his sharp brown eyes on me. "Rose said there was some trouble at the school today that you wanted to talk with me about. I made a few phone calls on my way here to learn more. Would you like to tell me your thoughts on what happened?"

If he called the school, he already knows about the computer search, the resulting error message, and the police. He probably knows more than I do about whatever they think I did wrong—and the punishment they want me to face for it.

My mouth goes dry. I slowly repeat what I already related to Rose—about finding the paper, and my curiosity about the unfamiliar letters on the page, and how I stopped on my way to the nurse to see if I could find out what it meant. His expression never changes as I tell my story. His eyes never stray from my face, which makes my stomach squirm. But I do my best to appear calm as I explain everything up to the point where I met Rose outside the school.

"Meri told me right away what happened." Rose sits down

next to her father as she makes her point. "She wanted to go back to the school and tell Principal Velshi everything, but I convinced her it was better to talk to you first since neither of us understands what's going on. I know she's scared. I would be. I mean, why would a search for a word on a school computer set off alarms and make people at the school call for the police?"

Mr. Webster answers his daughter, but his eyes—clear and steady and searching—stay focused on me. "I can see why Meri would have been upset by what happened today. It would upset anyone." He folds his hands and taps his thumbs together as he studies me for several long moments. "Neither of you are supposed to know this, but I am going to trust you both to keep this information to yourself."

He pauses long enough for both of us to nod. "The paper Meri found outside the school had a code word written on it. It's a word used by a gang of known criminals to help them identify each other. They've been causing problems around the city—breaking into buildings and encouraging violence."

"I haven't heard about any gangs causing problems," Rose said.

Neither had I, and that would be news even I would have noticed. Since the pilot City Pride Program began, Chicago's crime rate had dropped to the lowest of any major city in the country—something that was touted on all the public screens at least several times a week. A gang wreaking havoc in the city would be *the* featured story on both public news channels.

As if reading my thoughts, Rose's father continued, "The authorities have been careful to keep this quiet. To do otherwise would give the gang the publicity they need to recruit new members and quite possibly inflict even greater harm on the city. We've been mostly successful, although we haven't been able to cover up all of it. You might have heard reports of an explosion near the lake or the Blue Line train going off the tracks. They were reported as accidents, to keep the city calm. Public panic is something the mayor would very much like to avoid," he explains in the cool tones he is known for when he gives interviews on behalf of the mayor. "It is easy for this kind of thing to get out of control."

Everyone is required to take American history as freshmen and one of the units is about Chicago. According to the history text and my teachers' droning lectures, not all that long ago Chicago had the reputation of being the most dangerous place in the country. Gangs ran rampant. People were scared to step out of their homes for fear of being shot. Thousands of Chicagoans were killed every year just walking down the street. People began to flee the city in droves until finally the government stepped in and order was restored. Once a year, the news runs a special on the city Chicago used to be and how much we've grown since those dark days of just decades ago. Still, it's hard to imagine that kind of chaos and fear now that the murder rate is the lowest in the country and the only gangs on the streets are people working with the city to keep neighborhoods welcoming and prosperous.

"That's why all known code words for the group send up an alarm when they are entered into a computer search," Mr. Webster says quietly. "We've set up a system that combs the internet for specific words and phrases to stop this gang of troublemakers from recruiting new members who don't understand what they are getting themselves into. We're also exploring options about how to shut them down for good. Hopefully, the authorities will get a lead on how to do that before they cause far greater trouble. It took time for our city to become the safe, thriving place it is today. We don't want all that hard work to be destroyed. I'm sure you can agree with that."

Now that he has explained the problem, I guess I can understand how the search triggered an alarm and why the school called the police. But that answers only one of my questions. I swallow hard and ask the other: "So now what? What happens to me?" Compared with gangs trying to destroy the safety of the city, that probably sounds a bit selfish, but I never claimed to be generous.

"They can't blame Meri for being curious," Rose insists, shifting on the sofa so she is now facing her father. "Had I found the paper, I probably would have done the same thing."

No. Rose doesn't bend rules the way I do. She would have immediately asked a teacher what the letters meant. But I appreciate her support.

I feel like I am going to jump out of my skin until Mr. Webster lets out a sigh and says, "I will talk to Principal Velshi. Then I'll contact the chief of police and inform her that you set the alarm off by accident. The task force always knew this kind of thing could happen."

"So you know this isn't Meri's fault. Right?" Rose's voice is like steel. "It wouldn't be fair if she got in trouble for a mistake made by the city."

Mr. Webster purses his lips, and I hurry to pull his attention away from her before one of them says something that will strain their relationship even more. "I honestly didn't know what the word was, Mr. Webster. It was a mistake not to turn the paper in the minute I found it."

Finally, he pulls his gaze from his daughter and looks back at me.

"Rose is right. It wouldn't be fair if you got in trouble because you were curious." For the first time he smiles, which warms his eyes. "I would have wanted to know what an unfamiliar word meant, too. It is the nature of active minds to search for answers. Don't worry, I'll see that you don't get in trouble for what happened today."

I let out a relieved sigh as Rose matches her father's grin. "Thank you."

"But," Mr. Webster adds as his expression dissolves from positive to stern. "Now that you know about the gang and the things they've done, I'm certain you can see the value in putting a stop to this group's activities sooner than later. We would like to keep any other innocent people from setting off the alarm and being questioned."

I nod. I'm lucky Rose could ask her dad for help. What would happen to someone who didn't have a city official to call?

"That's why I have to ask, are you sure you don't still have the paper you found, Merriel?" He leans toward me. "There is a chance something about the paper could help us track them down."

"Dad, she said she tore it up and threw it away," Rose answers.

Part of me considers going to fetch the note where I stashed it after we arrived at the house. Rose went to the bathroom and I shoved it in the back of the freezer under a box of frozen peas that have been in there as long as I can remember. But Rose's defense had taken away any chance of my turning the note over. I wasn't about to make her look foolish while at the same time turning myself into a liar. Not when Mr. Webster was going to make all of this go away. "I'm sorry, Mr. Webster. I'd like to help, but I don't have it anymore."

My heart beats hard, and I force myself not to wipe my palms on my uniform. He stares at me like he knows I am not telling the truth and is waiting for me to admit it. Finally, he slaps his hands on his legs and says, "Well then, that's that. I will call your principal on the way back to my office, and if you want me to, Merriel, I can call your father later and let him know that this has all been cleared up."

"It's probably better if he hears about it from me," I say. Which means he won't hear about it at all.

"Very well." He stands and walks to the door. Turning, he adds, "In the future, I advise you both to come directly to me if you run across anything you have questions about. No matter how insignificant you think it might be."

Rose nods. "Of course we will, right, Meri?"

"Right," I agree automatically.

"Good." He smiles again, then turns to Rose. "I'll drop you at home on my way back to the office. Your mother told me you have some details for your summer job that you have to see to."

Rose leaps for her bag as her father heads to the door without a backward glance.

"I totally forgot!" Rose shoots me an apologetic look. "Do you want to come with? My mom would love to see you. I showed her some of your recent work and she really wants you to take a crack at the new logo. Maybe after Mom and I finish our stuff, you could—"

"You go on without me." I want to make sure I destroy the paper I hid in the freezer before anyone can find it. The sooner it's gone, the sooner I can put all of this behind me. "I'm good," I insist as Rose gets that fighting look in her eyes. "Thanks for helping today. I'm not sure what I would do without you." My voice cracks.

Rose's eyes soften and she lets out a small huff. "Fine, I won't push about today. But next time I'm dragging you along," she says as she heads down the hallway to the front door. When she reaches it,

80

she turns back and adds, "I'll ask my dad about the City Art Program while he's driving me home. I'll call you if I get any news."

"Don't—"

The door bangs shut, cutting off anything else I might have said.

I watch through the window until their car pulls away from the curb. Once it is gone, I go to the freezer and dig behind the frozen foods for the page with the word "VERIFY." Everything I've ever been taught tells me to take the paper to a recycling center, but I don't want the money or, more important, the recognition that might come from turning it in. I just want it and all the problems the gang tried to cause me gone.

I turn the dial on the stove, watch the burner ignite with a circle of blue-and-orange heat, and touch an edge of the fragile paper to the flame. It takes two tries before the orange flicker glows and begins to consume the page, leaving a curling trail of black in its wake. I dump the paper into a large pot and watch as the faded red letters slowly turn into black-and-gray char. When there is nothing left but smoldering remnants, I put the pot under the sink and run water until all evidence of VERIFY and the page on which it was delivered are washed into the pipes and carried away, leaving behind only a campfire smell.

When the pot is dried and stowed in the cabinet, I take my backpack and go upstairs, determined to move on. Mr. Webster said he was going to talk to the school and the police and make all of this go away.

There was nothing left to worry about. It was all over.

I pull off my uniform, glad that I don't have to wear it again for the next few months, and change into faded yellow shorts and a white-and-red shirt. With several hours until my father comes home and no homework or studying to do, I pull out my tablet and sit on the bench next to my window to work on my mother's painting. But no matter what I try I can't seem to focus. All I can think about is the gang Mr. Webster talked about and the way the flame consumed the water-stained page.

Guilt snakes through my chest and squeezes.

Could my destroying the note prevent the police from finding the gang that's causing so many problems for the city?

The idea that there's a group out there threatening people is scary, mostly because, until Mr. Webster told us, I had no idea. I'd heard about the explosion near the lake. A faulty gas line was the explanation. And the train going off the tracks stopped travel on the Blue Line for a few hours. Some of the teachers had trouble getting to school, but otherwise it wasn't a big deal, which makes this all hard to believe. No one I know thinks things are more dangerous in the city. Riding around on my bike yesterday didn't feel any different from the way it had before. And the guy who gave me the slip of paper was more surprising than threatening. He certainly didn't seem like someone who would be capable of any kind of violence.

I shut down my art application, call up my history text, and jump to the chapter on the end of city violence in the United States of America—starting with Chicago—and the rise of a new doctrine of Pride.

The photographs are as terrible as I remember. Buildings burning. Children sprawled like broken dolls on cracked asphalt—rusted chain-link swings sitting empty in the distance. Face after face of people of all ages terrified to go out of their homes because of the people who robbed and sold drugs and murdered. All of the gang members pictured in the history text look intimidating—especially when smiling at the camera. Their grins are cocky and belligerent—as if they are daring someone, anyone, to try to stop them.

I look at the dates under the photos: May 25, 2017. December 17, 2018. This was what the city—the whole country, really—was like just a few decades ago. The country was at war with itself while our armed forces were scattered in wars around the globe. If they hadn't returned in order to set our country free from the unpatriotic who were determined to terrorize it, who knew what the city would be like now?

Only, the guy in the rain last night didn't fit in with the images in front of me. He didn't have an assault rifle or a sharp, bloodstained knife. Just the yellow umbrella, a couple of earrings, and the folded paper he handed to me.

But according to Mr. Webster, the man I met is dangerous—not just to me but to my family and friends and even the entire city.

I lean my head against the window and watch Mrs. Johnson and her toy poodle, Bruiser, coming down the sidewalk. The fluffy white dog stops every few feet to sniff at a tree or a plant, then yips at the car parked at the curb. Still barking, he lifts his leg and pees on the car's gold-and-silver back tire rim. Mrs. Johnson tugs at Bruiser's leash and yanks him away. The dog continues yapping at the car until he and Mrs. Johnson are out of sight.

I slide off the window seat and pace the room. Mr. Webster had listened to my problem, promised to fix it, and given me an answer about it that made sense. Part of me just wants to forget the whole thing. But the longer he and Rose are gone, the more questions I seem to have.

Like why did the man with the umbrella give me that paper and then disappear?

Why did it seem that my mother's paintings were leading me to that exact spot?

And why had the woman been standing across the street from the school waving at me to follow? Was that what she was doing or did I just imagine it? And if she had been signaling me, was there a chance she was still in that area?

Waiting?

If so, then it's possible the woman across the street from the school could have answers to some of my questions. Answers I need if my father and I are ever going to move on, but suddenly I'm not sure if I want them. Suddenly, I realize there's a chance I don't know my mother at all. If "verify" is some sort of code used by a violent gang . . . if the man who gave the paper to me was a member . . . and my mother knew him . . .

I walk across the room and look at the picture screen on my wall as it scrolls through the images I've uploaded over the years. Mom with her hair pulled back in a knot and secured with her tapered paintbrush—her screen balanced on her lap as she sits on a rock, staring out at Lake Michigan. I took the picture the previous summer. It was the last time I remember all three of us going to the lake together, only Mom said she was tired and that she just wanted to sit in the sun and draw while Dad and I walked on the beach. I offered to draw with her, but she said watching me struggle would just be a distraction from her own work and I didn't think twice about walking away.

For years she said I was talented. She applauded even my worst efforts and told me, when I got frustrated, that all artists had to learn to walk before they ran.

Then something changed.

Mom grew distant. She brushed aside my work or suggested I should try to draw easier subjects. The stool in her studio—the one she bought for me to use—was put in the back corner and she asked about my work less and less.

Dad said the change was because I was getting older. Mom knew how hard it was to get accepted into the university programs and hired by the government. Her friends at work were seeing their own kids get crushed because they were turned down. Only the best of the best made it into the university arts programs, and those who didn't were forced to put their art aside and find a new vocation. Mom wasn't sure I was improving enough and didn't want me to be left adrift because I wasn't talented enough to be selected.

But what if Dad was wrong? What if there was more to it than that? What if Mom was trying to hide who she had become and the things she was doing from both of us? There are so many things I clearly don't understand.

A hollow ache builds in the center of my chest. I wrap my arms tight around myself and stare at my mother's face—eyes pinched close together—mouth pursed tight, but turned up slightly on the edges, as if amused by something only she could see. Did I lose my mother in that car accident or was she already gone long before she died? Not knowing is like losing her all over. I shouldn't have to feel that kind of loss again. And yet . . . here I am.

I turn my back on the pictures scrolling on my screen and pace across the room. Mr. Webster made me promise to come to him with any questions I have, but I can't risk telling him about my mother's paintings. Which means the only way to learn exactly who I lost in that accident is to find the answers on my own.

I grab my phone and retrieve my bicycle from where I had leaned it against the house. Before I can let my doubts about what I'm doing stop me, I climb on and start to ride.

My leg muscles complain as I pump the pedals. Today's mile run and the ride yesterday are more of a workout than I'm used to. But even though it's been two hours since I spotted her there and the chances of her still remaining are slim, I push the pedals as fast as I can.

The sun is bright orange yellow against the cloudless sky as the school comes into view. I allow myself to slow down so I can get a better look at what is happening there.

The police cars are gone. A couple of guys shoot hoops at the outdoor courts at the far end of the building, and a handful of people are standing on the sidewalk not far from the faculty parking lot with their backs to me. I keep my head down as I coast along the street and turn up the inclined drive where I saw the gray-haired woman disappear.

There is a tan brick garage behind the three-story apartment building. It has a white, slightly chipped door, a patch of deep green grass with some reed-thin trees, and a fenced-off area for a vegetable garden that looks as if it was recently planted. But no gray-haired woman in a black hoodie.

I didn't really think she would still be here. Still . . .

"Atlas was certain you'd return. I was not as optimistic."

I spin around as the woman I saw hours ago steps from the side of the garage and nods. Up close she looks younger than I had originally thought. The gray hair is streaked with hints of brown. Her eyes are clear blue and flash with impatience. "Had you taken five minutes longer it wouldn't have mattered because I would not have been here."

"Who are you?" I ask. "Who is Atlas? And why—"

"Hush!" she snaps, and steps toward me. "You have questions. Had you come immediately I could have given you the answers you seek, but it's no longer safe. You have to leave immediately."

"Leave? Why?"

"Because you didn't come here alone. You were followed by city detectives, and if you don't show yourself to them soon, they'll grow curious. If they start to search for you they might find me, and I'm not interested in outrunning Marshals today."

I shake my head. "No one followed me."

"Just because you believe something doesn't make it true," she warns. "If you wish to continue this conversation, be on the La Salle Street Bridge at twelve thirty tonight. Make sure you aren't followed or no one will be there to meet you."

She turns toward the garage.

"Wait—" I wheel my bike after her. "I can't just go out after midnight to meet some stranger." It was crazy enough that I came here in the middle of the day!

"Then don't." She glances back. "Come or don't come. The choice is yours. You won't be given the opportunity again."

Panic flutters in my chest as I recall what Mr. Webster said about how the gang was creating unrest. "If you're trying to scare me, I'm not scared," I say. "There isn't anyone following me."

"If you are so certain of that, why are you whispering?" she asks.

She's right. I am. I was. I straighten my shoulders and at a normal volume say, "The police are looking for you. I can turn you in."

"You can try." She gives me a sad smile and shakes her head. "Twelve thirty. If you don't come, we'll understand that you wish to live your life as it is now. You will not be judged." She disappears around the garage, and I drop my bike and follow in time to watch her run toward the chain-link fence beyond, leap, and gracefully vault over the five-foot-tall barrier. She lands in a crouch on the other side, and when she comes up, she winks in my direction before racing down the alley and out of sight without my saying another word.

For several heartbeats, I can do nothing but replay the exit in my mind. By then it is too late to chase her. And really, there's no point. The woman isn't going to tell me anything that will answer my questions. Instead, she and whoever is behind this group want to lure me away from my neighborhood back to the heart of the city—alone.

Which is insane. All of this—the paper, the woman, the insinuation that someone followed me here, the vault over the fence—is unbelievable. I climb on my bike and pedal home, zigzagging down different streets from the ones I used on my way. Every few seconds I look over my shoulder, and while there are cars driving along and people on the sidewalks, none of them pay me any special attention.

I was right. The woman had been trying to freak me out. This was all designed to upset me and my life. My mother would never have wanted this. Whoever this gang was, they had gotten me to trigger an alarm at the school with the mysterious word they found a way to put in my hands. They had made me doubt. That had to have been part of their plan all along, and I fell for it. How stupid was that?

I stash my bike behind the house and head back upstairs, frustration building with every step. Mr. Webster warned me that the group was looking to cause problems. Who knows what would have been in store for me if I had bought into what the gray-haired woman wanted. . . .

From my window, I spot a dark blue car parked across the street.

It was the one with the gold-and-silver rims I'd watched Mrs. Johnson's dog pee on earlier. I'd never noticed that car on the block before today. It hadn't been there minutes ago when I returned home.

But it is there now.

I tell myself it means nothing.

But when I check an hour later, the car is still there, and this time the driver's-side window is lowered an inch. Maybe two.

Even though I have vowed not to think about the gang again, the woman's warning about my having been followed to meet her replays in my mind. I find myself going downstairs to the living room to get a better look at the car. Slowly, I walk to the edge of the front window, careful not to rustle the curtains.

I'm just trying to prove the woman wrong once and for all, I tell myself as I peer out the edge of the window. There's no way anyone was following me then and no way anyone is just sitting in that car now.

I spot a pair of eyes staring out the lowered window. There's someone in that car.

When the man in the driver's seat shifts, I can see another shadow behind him.

My heart trips. There is more than one person parked in the blue car. The car has been there for over an hour with the engine off.

That's . . . really strange, I think as the driver's eyes flit along the street before returning to the one house he seems to be the most interested in watching.

Mine.

SIX

My heart beats loud in my ears as I jerk back from the window.

This is stupid, I tell myself. *I'm overreacting.* After everything that has happened today, it's no wonder I'm spooked. The alarm . . . the police . . . Rose's dad telling me about the gang . . . it's enough to spook anyone.

I glance out the window again. The car is still there. The men are still inside. The engine is quiet, and the men are very definitely watching my house. Who are they and how did the woman know about them?

Pushing down the fear that has burrowed deep inside my stomach, I hurry upstairs and grab my tablet. I cast looks out the window to make sure the car is still there as I pull up Mr. Webster's office number at City Hall. Then I dial, hoping he's still at work.

It takes ten minutes to convince the woman who answers the phone that I know Mr. Webster and that he told me to call him. Finally she puts me on hold. I pace the room and catch a glimpse of a police car cruising down the street. The Chicago Police Department vehicle slows and then stops a few feet in front of the car of the men who have been watching me. I hold my breath as I watch the uniformed police officer climb out of his car. The driver's-side door to the car that's been watching my house opens and a man in brown slacks, a white shirt, and a navy-blue jacket gets out. Sweat glistens off the top of his hairless head as he stands with his hand on the top of the car door and nods at the officer who approaches.

I lower my phone and step closer to the window as the bald man shifts his jacket. Sunlight glints off the gold shield clipped to his belt. The uniformed officer says something, and the bald guy points back at whoever else is sitting in the car.

The officer nods and heads back to his own vehicle.

"Merriel? . . . Are you there? . . . Merriel."

I blink at the sound of my name, then look at the phone in my hand. Mr. Webster!

"Sorry." My hand holding the phone shakes. The man watching my house knows the police. It seems like he might even be one of them—perhaps some kind of detective. And he's tailing me—just like the woman said. "I was looking out the window while I was on hold and got distracted."

"When my assistant told me you were on the phone, I was worried something else might have happened."

"Nothing happened." My mind races. Why would detectives be watching my house? The only answer I can come up with is because Mr. Webster told them to come here. "I just wanted to thank you again for helping me today and to ask . . ."

"Yes?"

"Just . . ." Thoughts trip over each other. "I know you told me not to worry, but is there any chance that the gang you told me about could figure out who I am? Is there any reason the police or someone should be watching my house in case they try to contact me?"

I wait for him to tell me about the guys in the car out front, but instead he says, "The gang is looking for people who want to become members. They aren't going to come looking for you at your home. Trust me. No police protection is necessary, but if you feel uneasy or remember anything more that could help us find whoever the code word came from, I want you to contact me immediately. My assistant has been instructed to put you right through."

I picture the gray-haired woman who'd waited for me near the school. She said a guy named Atlas was certain I'd come back to find her. That's exactly the kind of thing Mr. Webster wants me to tell him about. But the words stick in my throat when I look at the car sitting on the opposite curb with the driver's-side window cracked open.

Mr. Webster has to know the detectives are sitting outside my house, but he isn't telling me about them. Maybe he's doing what he has to in order to keep me safe. Maybe he doesn't trust me not to flip out if I learn there is a chance I'm in danger. Maybe . . .

"Is there anything else you need to talk about?" Mr. Webster asks. "I have a number of important matters that require my attention before I leave the office today."

My eyes stay glued on the car sitting outside. "I guess I just need to hear you say that you'll tell me if you think the gang might come looking for me."

"If I thought there was any chance they would seek you out or that you or your father were in danger, I would tell you, Merriel. Does that set your mind at ease?"

"It does," I lie, because there doesn't seem to be anything else I can say. "Thank you, Mr. Webster."

"You're welcome, Merriel. And don't worry. The police are clos-ing in on this gang as we speak. They won't disrupt the peace and safety of the city much longer. Good day."

The call goes dead before I choke out a good-bye. I stand at the window for several minutes watching—waiting for the dark blue car with the two men still inside to move or for something to happen.

Nothing does. That should make me feel better. Instead, I feel trapped.

I pace the living room, then turn on the screen and flip through the channels. *There have to be a dozen logical reasons why Mr. Web-ster didn't tell me about the detectives stationed outside the house,* I tell myself. But as much as I try to keep calm, I can't help but wonder and worry about everything I have seen and heard.

Had I found the paper on the ground like I told everyone, I wouldn't have so many questions. But I didn't find the paper on the ground. I'm aware of far more than I have admitted.

I know my mother's paintings are the reason I was standing in the very place the man with the umbrella found me. He handed me that paper because I was there. That's the reason I learned the word "verify." While I want to think that is a coincidence, I can't make myself believe it.

Mom's paintings lead straight to that bridge for a reason. But why? If she had wanted me to learn the word, she could have just told me about it. Right?

And what does my mother have to do with a bunch of strangers who are being hunted by the government? Who was she really? And what had she hoped for when she created those canvases?

I ask those questions of myself as I prepare dinner, walking back to the living room every few minutes to see if the blue car has moved from its spot next to the curb. It's still there.

By six o'clock the meatballs are out of the oven, the spaghetti is cooked, and I have decided to tell Dad about everything. Maybe he knows something, anything, that can help me make sense of what's going on. But when my father comes through the door, he holds his right arm tight to his side and hurries past, saying that he will wash up quickly before dinner.

He's hoping I didn't notice the bag in his hand. I wish I hadn't.

When he comes back downstairs, I tell him about my finals first, not mentioning Mr. Webster's visit. Before I can do that, I have to ease the conversation toward the topic of my mother. I use my art final to broach the subject. "It's hard to imagine Mom ever being happy drawing a bowl of fruit." Maybe not the greatest transition, but it was the best I could come up with. Dad flinches. His fork stills, and I force myself to forge ahead. "We never talk about her," I say quietly. "We should talk about her more."

Dad looks down at his plate. "What do you want to talk about?"

I take a deep breath and ignore the ache growing in my chest. "Did she stop loving us? Did she stop loving me?"

Dad looks up. "Of course not. Your mother loved you more than anything!"

"I guess I feel like, when she died, I didn't really know her anymore. She didn't seem to want me around. She was always thinking about something else."

"She was under a lot of pressure at work."

"Did she tell you what kind of pressure? Did she show you what kind of things she was working on? Did you ask—"

"Damn it, Meri!" Dad's fork slips from his hand with a clatter. "Of course I asked her about it and she told me she would explain everything when she had it all worked out. She was on edge and said she needed space and I didn't push her. Maybe I should have. Maybe if I had insisted she tell me what she was working on instead of turning my back on her when she went out that night she'd still be alive. But I didn't, and now I have to live with that for the rest of my life."

He picks up his mostly full plate and takes it to the sink. Without turning, he says, "Your mother loved you, Meri. But the truth is I'm not sure if she still loved me. I have to live with that, too." When he turns his eyes are clouded with pain and anger and the hollow hopelessness that I remember from the weeks immediately after my mother was killed. I have pushed him as far as I can. Any further and I'm not sure if he'll ever forgive me.

"I'm sorry, Dad," I say quietly.

He shakes his head and looks like he is going to say something else but changes his mind and sighs. "Leave the dishes. I'll take care of them after I watch the game."

Shoulders slumped, Dad goes into the living room. I run the water full blast, hoping he'll hear it and come back to help clean the dishes. But he doesn't. And I don't go into the living room to keep him company the way I know I should. Instead I go upstairs and stand in front of my father's closed bedroom door. He has a bottle hidden in there, and after the questions I have asked I know he'll crack the seal on it tonight. This is my chance to search for the bottle. To keep him from drinking himself into oblivion. Because he will. After that conversation I know he will.

For one heartbeat, I wish I could, too, because I still don't know if the mother I lost is the person I thought she was—or someone else entirely.

I don't think I can sit here day after day waiting for something to happen. That is my only choice unless I take the option that was presented by the woman who waited for me across from the school. If I go tonight, I will have to be brave enough to face people who want to do this city, and maybe even me, harm. I'll have to face learning the truth about my mother.

Am I that brave? Am I willing to walk down that path no matter where it might lead?

I shift my weight from one foot to the other. My stomach churns. My heart tightens as I make my choice.

I turn my back on my father's room and the bottle hidden there. If my father drinks, he drinks. And if he passes out, he won't be able to hear me slipping out of the house.

The minutes crawl. I change into a black T-shirt and jeans and pull my ratty green robe on top of them. Then I sit in the window seat and gnaw on the inside of my lip as I listen to the sound of my father coming up the stairs. He calls good night and waits for me to respond before closing his door. A half hour later, the weeping that always comes when he drinks too much too fast rings loud in my ears. I pull my knees up against my chest and try to block out the sound. Eyes closed tight, I bite my cheek and taste blood. Finally, after what feels like forever, the house goes mercifully quiet. The silence says Dad has fallen into oblivion. If I'm going to go, I need to move.

I walk by the window one more time in my bathrobe, giving anyone outside a good view of me. The car with the gold rims is gone, but a new silver one with tinted windows has parked in the same spot. Here's hoping if someone is still watching the house they'll think I've gone to bed when I turn out the light.

With careful, quiet steps, I slip out the back door and am grateful for whatever dog is barking as I grab my bicycle and wheel it to the alley behind the garage. Every crackle of gravel under my feet or snap of a twig makes me jump and look over my shoulder, certain someone is moving behind me. I feel both relieved and foolish when I reach the deserted alley without incident. Shaking my head at my unnecessarily dramatic exit, I climb onto my bike, adjust my backpack, and, before I talk myself out of going, ride.

After several blocks, I zigzag out of the alley. I pedal down the asphalt through scattered pools of streetlight, toward the skyscrapers with their windows shining bright against the dark sky. The number of cars dwindles as I ride, which tells me the midnight road-maintenance vehicle curfew is fast approaching. Unless there is an emergency, vehicles aren't allowed on the roads between midnight and four. The curfew was first put into place as a step to curtail the high volume of crime, since the middle of the night was the time that behavior was most likely to occur. When that was successful, the ordinance was kept in place by the City Pride Program so they could use the time to repair streets and signs without interrupting traffic or daily life.

A few years ago, I stood with my mother as the head of her department gave a news conference about the success of the City Pride Program. He showed picture after picture of the roads before the curfew was put into place. The images of yawning black holes several feet deep, ever-lengthening cracks, and the perpetual traffic backups caused by the gaps and the feeble attempts at repairs made everyone agree that the late-night driving restriction was both necessary and effective.

Since it is currently summer and Friday night, the lack of cars means more pedestrians and carriages and bike riders are wandering the popular city streets around the La Salle Street Bridge when I arrive. I come to a stop before the bridge near a man sitting on a bucket playing a dull silver saxophone. The low notes color the air with melancholy as I look around for whoever it is I am supposed to meet.

There is no one who seems to be watching me, and no one I see strolling in the clear night looks dangerous. I take several deep breaths, secure my bike to an iron rack not far from the street musician, and start across the bridge. As I walk, I study every face that passes. Couples of various ages holding hands. A large group of men wearing blue-and-red baseball attire. Groups of three and four laughing and telling jokes and slapping high fives as they stroll to whatever their next destination might be.

Twelve thirty finds me standing in the center of one of the pedestrian walkways holding my breath. I turn in a circle, waiting for someone in a black sweatshirt to appear. Only no one comes.

Each minute feels longer than the last. Five minutes pass like an hour. The next ten are an eternity. The woman who sent me here is screwing with my mind. These people are just trying to hurt me, and I'm letting them. I should go home.

But I don't. Not quite yet, because I can't let go of the idea that my mother was hiding a huge truth about herself and this could be my only chance to learn it.

I jump at every voice. Still nothing. A girl in a flirty red dress and sparkling heels laughs with abandon as she comes my way. Her date calls for her to wait up as I turn and lean my forehead against the cold iron of the bridge to stare at the dark water below. *It's over*, I tell myself. No one is coming, and I'm not sure if I'm angry or relieved.

"Excuse me, miss. What time is it?"

Turning, I see a boy a few years older than me in a black shirt and red tie standing several steps away. His face is cast in shadows by the brim of a black fedora. Behind him is the girl in the red dress, whose laugh has been replaced by an annoyed frown.

I glance at the time on my phone. "It's twelve forty-nine." It's time for me to go home. I slide the phone into the front pocket of my bag and turn to go back to my bike.

"Are you certain?" the guy calls to me. "Or do you think I should ask another?"

"My phone says twelve forty-nine, but you can do whatever you want." I glance at the guy in the black hat, who is now standing just a single step behind me with his head cocked to the side. The girl in the red dress has vanished.

"You really don't know." The whispered words brush the shadows. He removes his hat and I finally get a better look at his face. It's one I recognize. The sharp-angled cheekbones, and deep-set dark eyes. I've drawn this face. He's the one I followed from my mother's building to this bridge just two days ago.

"Who are you?" I demand. "I was told to be here at twelve thirty. Are you the one who is supposed to meet me?"

He looks over his shoulder. I peer behind him, but neither of the people I can see in the distance appears to be looking this way.

"Answer me!" I snap. "Who are you?"

"I thought when you followed me here to the bridge that you knew." He takes a step backward. "I'm sorry. This was a mistake." He sets his hat low on his forehead and turns. "Go home."

"Go home?" I shout. He doesn't acknowledge me, so I chase after him to the edge of the bridge—back in the direction my mother's paintings sent me yesterday.

"What do you mean this was a mistake? Hey! Stop!" I yell, and almost run right into him before I notice he actually followed my command.

For some reason that makes me even angrier. "Is this your idea of fun? Screwing with someone's life? I basically encouraged my father to drink himself into a stupor tonight so I could get out of the house without any chance of him hearing me. I did that because I was told to come here by someone from your group—a group I was warned was dangerous by a person I have known all my life. You owe me answers!"

He removes his hat again and stares down at me for several long seconds before finally nodding. "Fine. Ask me one question. I'll answer it as honestly as I can."

One question? I have dozens of them. I should ask about my mother since she's the reason I'm here. But what exactly do I ask?

I wrap my arms around myself to ward off the cold wind whipping from the river. "I've been told you're part of a gang that is determined to undermine the city and harm the people in it and that 'verify' is a code word you use to create trouble."

"Is there a question in there?"

"There would be if you waited for it to be asked," I shoot back, wishing I were taller. I crane my neck upward to meet his eyes, which are shining bright against the charcoal blanket of night. "Is 'verify' a way of terrorizing people and causing trouble for the city? Or does it mean something more?"

"What do you think?"

I clench my fists at my sides. "If I knew the answer I wouldn't have asked the question."

"If you really thought your mother was associating with criminals would you have come to meet me?"

The mention of my mom steals my breath. I go over every single word I've said. I didn't mention my mother. He did.

I swallow hard. "You said you'd give me an answer, not ask more questions."

"You don't know what you're asking."

"I'm asking for the meaning of one word. Why is that so hard?"

He glances over his shoulder, again. Then he grabs my arm and pulls me deeper into the shadows where the lights on the bridge don't quite reach. "Words have more power than you can imagine. Your mom understood that. They can give you strength, but they can also put you in danger. They can change your entire world. Do you really want that?" He shakes his head as I open my mouth to respond. "Don't answer without thinking. Once you know something, you can't unknow it. Because you're young—"

"And you're an old geezer?" I mock, yanking my arm from his grasp.

"You're still in school," he shoots back. "You want to finish, right?"

"Yes, *Mr. Geezer*. I do."

"Then walk away now, Merriel, while you still can." He runs his hand over his short-cropped hair and replaces his hat. "I can tell them you never showed up. They will never know any different, and you can forget that any of this ever happened. Life will go back to normal as long as you never tell anyone any of this happened."

Normal? I don't know who my mother really was. Nothing will ever have the chance to be normal again.

"And if I refuse?" I ask.

He meets my eyes with his own dark brown ones and I realize I didn't get them right in my drawing. There is a fierce intensity shining from them that I failed to capture. It transforms every feature—makes it impossible to look away. "Then I guess we're both going to have to live with the consequences."

"I don't understand—"

"You've got to the count of ten to decide."

Before my mother died, I understood what I wanted. I knew what to expect from the world. I am not sure what "verify" means or what I am stepping into, but I know what waits on the path behind me. And I can't go back. If I do, I will slowly lose my mind. The only way to stop feeling stuck in the unfinished moment is to follow the crusts of bread past the bridge to wherever they might lead.

My stomach twists. My heart is an unsteady drumbeat as I place my hand atop his warm fingers and in a voice more confident than I feel ask, "Do I get to know your name?"

For a second he just shakes his head at my hand in his. Then he smiles. "Don't come whining to me if you regret this. Because chances are that you will." He closes his fingers over mine. "You're going to have to move fast if you plan on keeping up."

He's not joking. One second we are standing just beyond the bridge. The next I'm being yanked to a set of steps that leads down to an area right next to the river. I almost miss a step and have to let go of his hand to grab the rail. He doesn't turn to help or slow his steps and I struggle to regain my balance before racing after him.

"My bicycle is on the other side of the bridge!" I yell. "I have to go back and get it." My parents gave it to me three years ago for my birthday and it was my mother who picked out the color—the exact shade of the sun when it starts to set. I don't want to lose it or the ability to get away quickly if I change my mind about Geeze here and wherever he's leading me.

"I'll see that your bike is taken care of," he shouts back, never losing a step. "This way."

He zigzags through a brightly lit area filled with silver tables and chairs and heads down another set of steps that are less well lit. The river slaps against the black iron footings below. The sound accompanies our footsteps and the faint rattling of a jackhammer somewhere in the distance. The water. The rattling. The darkness. The path we take through shadows and around iron barriers. Together they create a symphony of sound that, combined with the lack of people anywhere in sight, makes my throat go dry and my shallow breath come faster.

Instinct screams for me to turn around and bail, but I ignore it and keep going.

Another iron bridge rises out of the darkness. I know there are many bridges that cross the Chicago River, but I've never seen them from this vantage point and I am not sure which one we are facing. The lack of orientation only adds to my bubbling anxiety as Geeze heads to another set of stairs and begins to climb.

My legs are tired, and I'm breathing hard by the time we reach the street above.

"Wait up," I gasp.

Geeze doesn't say anything, but he does stop next to the first building as I grip my side and wipe the sweat off my forehead.

He seems to be watching the darkened shadows of the staircase where we just emerged. Then, slowly, he scans the street. There is a jogger running across the bridge. A group of people are standing in a huddle outside a doorway at the start of the next block.

Whatever Geeze sees must be fine to him because he takes my hand and says, "This way."

He doesn't comment on my sweaty palm as we walk down the sidewalk beside the empty street at a normal gait. I pick up my pace when I spot a man with a scruffy beard, tattered clothes, and a hat pulled low standing in a darkened doorway to our left. Geeze, how-ever, stops walking, and the viselike grip he has on my hand means I have no choice but to stop, too.

"Do you know what time it is?" Geeze asks the guy in the door-way, who clearly couldn't care less about the time.

I pull out my phone as the man in the doorway says, "It's one twenty-one."

"Are you sure?" Geeze asks. I go still as he continues with words like those he spoke to me not long ago. "Maybe I should ask someone else?"

The guy in the doorway doesn't get annoyed at the question like I did. Under the scruffy dark beard, the guy's mouth spreads into a wide grin. He pushes away from the wall, shoves his hand into his pocket, and with a flourish holds out a dull gold key. "I always verify things that are important."

The bearded guy turns and unlocks the door behind him. "I was starting to think you weren't coming tonight." He steps to the side so Geeze can lead me into the darkened doorway.

"My passenger is new to the train," Geeze says, nodding to me. "Did the other passengers arrive?"

Hat Guy jams his hands into his pockets. "Two passed this way. They should be in the station now. You should get going." Then the guy looks at me. "Getting on the train isn't easy. I'm glad you're here to take the trip."

Geeze ushers me through the doorway, so I don't have to figure out how to respond. The minute we step across the threshold, the door behind us shuts. I hold my breath as my heart pounds hard against my chest. The click of the lock sliding into place echoes loud in the darkness.

No way out.

I swallow hard and fight to keep the building fear out of my voice. "What train are we getting on?"

"It's not a real train." He takes off his hat and moves deeper into the shadows while beckoning me to follow. "At least not the way you mean. We go through here."

"I have a flashlight on my phone," I say. "We don't have to stumble around in the dark."

"It won't be dark in here." He leads me through another doorway, and the illumination he promised flares to life.

The light is soft, but I still have to squint as my eyes adjust. There are two worn, mismatched armchairs in the middle of the room. I am about to ask Geeze to explain the train again when the walls of the room catch my attention and my heart squeezes. Hard.

The walls are filled with old-fashioned books.

Not real ones. Paintings of them. Stacked together. Strewn across the ground. Red. Blue. Yellow. Black. All with pages of white. Open. Closed. And flying out of the open books as if being set free into swirling air are carefully printed words that shimmer at the edges as if by magic.

The truth is found when men are free to pursue it. —FDR

The truth is incontrovertible. Panic may resent it, ignorance may deride it, malice may distort it, but there it is. —WC

Trust, but verify. —RR

Verify.

That word jumps out at me first among the words and sentences painted throughout the room—all of them drawn by a hand that I know as well as my own. Maybe better.

My mother was here. She was a part of this.

Whatever *this* is.

I ball my fingers into fists. My nails bite deep into my palms as I turn in a circle. "My mother painted this."

She must have been in this room for hours. It would have taken days, if not weeks, to create this entire scene.

Geeze nods. "Your mother had some help, but, yeah, the design for this train station was hers."

"This is a train station?" It wasn't like any train station I'd ever seen. For starters, there were no trains.

Geeze smirks. "The term was chosen by my grandfather and his friends to honor the Underground Railroad."

"The what?" I ask.

Geeze shakes his head. "Sorry. I forgot that was edited out of your history. We'll get to that another time. All you need to know for now is that this is what we call a station, and what happens next is what we refer to as 'getting on the train.'" He takes a seat in a faded red chair and nods to the one across from him. "For this little adventure, I will be your Conductor."

"My Conductor?" I step cautiously toward the raggedy yellow chair. Next to Geeze is a round end table with a box sitting in the center. There is no table next to the chair designated for me. "You're going to tell me why my mother painted these walls and what she was doing before she died."

"I'm going to tell you the truth."

The truth.

I glace at the words snaking along the wall next to me.

He who knows nothing is nearer to truth than he whose mind is filled with falsehoods and errors. —*TJ*

"I promise I will answer all the questions about your mother I can, but I have to admit that I only met her once and just for a few minutes. My father was your mother's Conductor. This was her train station. It was her experience almost two years ago that inspired her to create the design on the walls. Since then a number of our stations have undergone transformations to help make the transition onto the train a bit more . . . pleasant."

"You make it sound as if we are going to do something dangerous."

"Sometimes the most frightening leap is the one we make in our minds," he says sternly. Then he shakes his head and laughs. "Sorry. It's something my grandfather liked to say and my father repeats—a lot. Dad's really good at this Conductor thing. I'm new to it, so I'm still working out the kinks. Developing my own style, you could say."

"Maybe I should wait and talk to your father. Is he one of the other people the guy outside the door said is here?" I look back at the walls and the dozens of books pictured. Each one has a title on the spine. Most I've never heard of.

"My dad isn't . . . available right now. If you want to do this, you're stuck with me." The tension in his voice is less than reassuring. "Once you sit down we can get started."

I place a hand on my stomach and take the seat across from Geeze, who still hasn't told me his name. If he thinks I'm going to call him Conductor, he's dead wrong.

Geeze flips his hat onto the table next to him. Then he places his hands on the chair's armrests and says, "I thought you already knew a bunch of this because of your mom. However, since she followed the rules, I'm going to have to start at the beginning—the paper you were given and the word written on it."

"Verify." Clearly, by the quotes on the wall, the word has a meaning.

"Have you ever heard it before this week?"

I want to say yes, since my mother clearly knew the word, but I am honest and shake my head.

"Don't feel bad," he says, which irrationally makes me feel worse. "There's a reason for that."

"So what does it mean?"

He takes a deep breath and then carefully says words he has clearly taken the time to memorize. As if they are part of the Conductor instruction manual or something. "The word 'verify' means to establish the truth, accuracy, or reality of something. As far as my grandfather could tell, it was first used in the fourteenth century. It was one of the first words banned from use by certain government agencies back when they started 'cleaning up' the streets and making the country 'safer.' Little by little, they removed crime and poverty, but they also removed words. Ones that would encourage people to question what they were told. And by doing so, they changed this from a country that believed in facts to one built on lies."

SEVEN

Removed words? "Words don't just disappear," I snap.

"That's a reasonable assumption." He leans forward. "But if you don't know the words they removed, how would you know if they've vanished or not?" He lifts the lid of the wooden box next to him and pulls a tablet out. "What did you do when you were handed the word 'VERIFY'?"

"I looked it up."

"Did you find out what it meant?"

"No," I huff. "I set off some kind of alarm on the school computer. The police think you and your friends are part of a dangerous gang threatening the city."

"And what do you think would happen if you searched for another word—one that was removed and not flagged as *dangerous*?" He turns on the tablet, opens a browser to the dictionary website, and hands the screen to me. "Try searching for the word 'corroborate.'"

He spells the word, and I punch in the letters, then turn the screen to show the message that appears.

NO SEARCH RESULTS FOUND.

"Try 'vulnerable.'"

We go through the same process with him spelling out the strange word and me typing it into the tablet.

NO SEARCH RESULTS FOUND.

"'Entitlement.'"

Still no results.

"'Diversity.'"

Nothing.

"This is stupid, and just because I'm not finding these words doesn't tell me what you're claiming it does," I say, holding out the device for him to take back. "They could all be gibberish. I mean, how do I know you aren't just making up these so-called words?"

"I'm glad you asked." Geeze doesn't take the device. Instead, he grins in a way that transforms the sharp lines of his face into one that is softer. More approachable. His eyes fill with excitement as he once again lifts the lid of the wooden box. This time he pulls out a book. A paper one that looks like the ones painted on the walls of this room and not the virtual ones I read on my tablet or on the computers at school.

"Here," he says, passing the book to me. "Try this."

The faded red and white with blue book feels heavy and thick and awkward in my hand. I run my thumb along the rough edge of the pages as I read the title.

Merriam-Webster's Collegiate Dictionary.

"It's the hard-copy version of the website you just used," he says. "Why don't you start by looking for 'verify.' The words are listed in alphabetical order, so it'll be near the back."

"I know how a dictionary works," I snap, even though I don't. Not really. On the tablet you just have to search for the word and it comes up automatically. If you don't spell it correctly, the program will give you various options about what you might have been trying to look for. This is going to require me finding the right spelling of the word on my own.

Slowly, I flip open the cover and turn the thin, almost brittle pages until I reach the section for V words. I run my finger down the page until I land on the one I'm looking for.

ver•i•fy \'ver-ə-ˌfī\ *vt*
-fied; -fy•ing
to prove to be true; to confirm; to establish
the truth, correctness, or authenticity of.

I skim through the rest of the entry for the variations of the word, then flip to the front of the book to check the date. According to what I see written there, the book in my hands was printed in 2003. Decades before my parents were born.

"Try 'diversity' next."

I find the *D*'s as he once again spells the word for me.

di•ver•si•ty \də-'vər-sə-tē, dī-\ *n, pl* **-ties**
state of being diverse; contrariety, variety.

"You can look them all up if you like," he says, leaning forward. "Every word you tried on the tablet is in that book, and a whole lot more."

Pressure builds as I methodically search the book for each of the words I typed earlier. I find them all surrounded by words I have known for years. As if they belong there. As if they have *always belonged* there.

"How do I know you didn't do something to your tablet to make the words not appear in the online search?"

"Do you have your own screen in that bag?"

"Yeah, but—"

"Then go ahead and use it." Geeze flops back against the padding of his armchair, sending a small cloud of dust into the air. "It's not like I have anything better to do."

The smirk on his face tells me what I'm going to find before I type the first word.

NO SEARCH RESULTS FOUND.

Every single time.

I stare at the tablet, then at the heavy book on my lap. When I glance back at Geeze, the superior expression is gone. Instead, the only emotion I can describe in his eyes is sorrow.

"They took those words away, Merriel."

I shake my head and scoot so I am sitting on the edge of my slightly sunken seat—my knees so close to his that they are almost touching. "Okay, so maybe a few words were removed from the dictionary. There's a news story every year about what words are added to the online dictionary and which ones are too old and unused to be in it anymore. But a word not being in the dictionary doesn't pluck it from people's minds or from their speech or from books or articles or whatever. Just because the word isn't written down in one particular place doesn't mean people wouldn't know about it."

Yet I can't shake the doubt that's creeping through me, because I *didn't* know these words. And the book in my hands says they are— or were—real. "And it's Meri," I correct. "People call me Meri."

Geeze leans forward so his elbows are resting on his knees. His eyes—clear and unwavering—are even with mine. "You're right, Meri, people don't immediately forget words and ideas. But this started almost seventy years ago. The government created lists of words and banned them from use by anyone who worked in the government. Just a few at a time, but enough to change how people dealt with their work and eventually how they thought about their lives.

"Once that transition was made, the government quietly took those words away from everyone else in the country. No announcement was made. Just one day a bunch of words were suddenly unavailable for searching on tablets and computers. Green taxes were placed on paper goods. Suddenly paper books became far more expensive than electronic ones. A few people complained, but most barely noticed. Bulky school textbooks fell out of use first. That change alone affected the future in hugely important ways. Once the textbooks were gone, print books of every kind were abandoned in favor of electronic ones. Can you guess what happened next?"

His eyes lock on mine and I can't look away.

"The words vanished from the screen versions of books." He picks up his tablet and turns the screen around for me to see. The word "VERIFY" is written in block white letters against a background of blue. "Words on paper are forever. But the ones on screens can be altered or removed with just a push of a button." The word on the screen shimmers as if it is alive. Then, suddenly it blinks away. "And no one even remembers they were ever there."

He pauses as I stare at the blank screen. When I finally look back up at him, he says, "People who weren't part of the government still used the words at first, but when they weren't used on television or in the news or in anything they read, fewer people came across them. One by one the people who knew the words best died and those who were left started to forget they existed. With no one using the words, kids never had a chance to learn them. And now, seventy years later, it's as if those words never were used at all."

I swallow hard. My mind fights to keep up—to see the picture he is painting.

He leans in. "Bit by bit the world changed—like ants moving grains of a mountain from one place to another. The difference is so gradual that no one notices the landscape has changed. Not until it's too late. They changed everything about our world—they took the words and the ideas that those words define and with it the freedom to make our own choices—and they did it without anyone noticing."

I shake my head, trying to clear the gray fog of fear. Do I believe Geeze when he says the government eliminated words? The searches I performed and the book I hold say he's telling the truth. Do I hate that possibility? Of course. Censorship isn't what our country is supposed to be about.

But I also know that the paper tax was instrumental in spreading the use of renewable energy sources and reducing the country's reliance on fossil fuels. It was an important step toward battling changing climate patterns as well as reducing our reliance on other countries. Our history teachers have all said it was possibly the most important step our country had taken in decades. It was *necessary*. All the history books said so.

Another part of my brain whispers, *You mean the books that you read on a screen? The books they—whoever they are—can change without out anyone knowing about it?*

I squirm in my seat, wishing for the first time that I hadn't come here tonight. That I didn't know the little that I have come to understand.

I thought I understood how things worked and why. Now . . .

"But why does it matter?" I say to Geeze. "There are *other words*."

"Don't you see?" he presses. "Words have power. They are the way we pass along history and knowledge and thoughts and ideas. Sometimes conflicting ideas about the same subject. Books—real books like the one in your hands—give everyone equal access to those ideas. Limit the words people can see and you limit their power. Limit the words heard on the news and you shrink people's understanding of the world to what you want them to see.

"Get people focused on other things while you limit their choices in ways they don't think to complain about. Only so many television channels—that way the ideas in them can be controlled. Only certain artists are allowed to display their work—because others might provoke different thoughts and viewpoints. You limit immigration and say it's for safety and insist that other countries have made it harder to travel to theirs. Little by little, piece by piece, lives are controlled—*minds* are controlled—even as people still believe they are free."

"No one controls my life," I say. "No one controls any of us. We make our own choices—lots of them—every day."

"Really?" he asks. "Is it really a choice if you aren't able to see all the options? Think of a magician who tells you to pick a card. Is it really a surprise that you select the same one he's thinking of if all of the cards he's holding are the same?"

"I—I don't know," I admit. I'm unsettled, because I've never once given something like that a thought. And Geeze . . .

"What's your name?" I ask again. "I can't just keep calling you Geeze. It's distracting."

His left eyebrow arches. "Geeze? As in geezer?"

"You were the one who said I was too young." I shift against the faded fabric of my chair and stare down at my hands. "I had to call you something."

"Geeze." He sounds baffled. Then he starts to laugh. "I think I actually like it better than Atlas."

I look up. This is the Atlas the gray-haired woman from across the school said I would speak to?

Still grinning, Atlas answers, "As to how they control us? Well, what did you just do with the tablet and the book?"

"I searched for the words you mentioned."

"Why?"

"Because I wanted to know if you were telling the truth."

"Have you ever done anything like that before?"

"I look up the meanings of words all the time for school."

"Not that. Have you ever *verified* what someone told you before?"

Verify.

To prove to be true; to confirm; to establish the truth.

"I've never had to," I say, feeling dumb and defensive even as I say it.

"Really?" Atlas mocks. "Are you just that smart that you miraculously know everything, or is it because it never occurred to you to question something that you've been told is true?"

Insult and uncertainty twist inside me as Atlas gets up and starts to pace the length of the room.

"You've never questioned whether what your instructors teach you in class is the truth or whether what you hear on the news might not be real?"

"Of course not. Why would I?"

"Why wouldn't you?" He walks to the wall and places his hand next to a line that reads:

Truth will ultimately prevail where pains is taken to bring it to light. —GW

"I suppose you believe the midnight-to-daylight curfew is to prevent people from being inconvenienced by pesky roadwork and vice versa. That the City Pride Department's work miraculously caused crime to disappear with a fresh coat of paint? 'Verify' isn't just a word they've pulled out of use, Meri. They've taken away people's ability to question what is real and what is something they want you to believe. And the sooner you admit that it's the reason you don't know anything, the sooner we can get out of this room. Your mother—"

"My mother did important work!" I leap out of my chair. The book on my lap falls to the scarred wooden floor with a loud thud. "And crime did disappear. Otherwise they would have never taken all the cameras off the streets." We still have a day off from school to celebrate Civic Liberation—the day the country removed the last of the cameras.

I look at the walls around me. My pulse thuds like steel drums in my ears. If I believe Atlas, I also have to accept that my mother kept a giant secret from everyone she claimed to love. That she didn't trust us with something so important.

Suddenly, I'd rather live with the lie.

"You're wrong," I insist. "Whatever this is, you're wrong about it and her and I'm not staying here and listening to you make fun of me or destroy my mother's memory anymore. I'm going home."

I shove my tablet into my bag and stride across the room.

"Meri, stop. Wait!"

I throw open the door of his "station" and step into the blackness of the anteroom. Atlas can chase after me if he wants, but I'm done listening. I'm not getting on his stupid train-that's-not-a-train. I'm going to go home and recycle my mother's paintings and any hint of the life she never cared enough to tell me about. Then I'm going to forget all of this. Every bit.

I feel my way to the door we came through and grasp the handle. Locked.

"Meri, I'm sorry."

"Give me the key," I yell as Atlas stops beside me. "I want to get out—now."

"I'm not a stationmaster. I don't have the key," he says in hushed tones. "This is my first time being a conductor."

I yank on the door. It won't budge.

"I'm sorry," Atlas continues. "I can't even imagine how hard it must be for you to accept all of this. That your entire world is a lie. I've grown up my whole life surrounded by books—real books. I heard my father and grandfather speaking the words that your mother painted on those walls—talking about history and the way it's changed over the years. How they—the government—shape lives without almost anyone understanding what they have done. I've never seen the world that you thought you lived in. It makes it harder for me to explain things to new people."

The regret in his voice pulls at me and I shake my head. I'm not going to listen to any more. "Let. Me. Out!" I pull at the door again and kick it when it doesn't open.

Atlas lets out a frustrated sigh and runs a hand over the back of his neck. "Look, your mom was involved in something—something important. She didn't tell you about it, because that's the Stewards' policy. There are good reasons for the rule, but it hurts. I can see that, and I'm sorry. You can leave. I promise you can, but not just yet. A passenger can't go until they have heard it all. You have to ride the train at least that far before you make the next choice. I can't let you off in between stops."

"Maybe your father should be the one to talk to me about the rest since his son seriously sucks at it."

"He can't."

"Why should I believe that?"

Atlas snaps, "Because he's *gone*."

We stare at each other as his words settle like a blanket on the darkness.

"He's missing, and no one knows where he is or even if he's alive."

Atlas's voice cracks and I let go of the door handle.

Atlas shoves his hands into his pockets and looks up into the black above us. "My father and your mother were working with someone on an important project before her accident. I have no idea what it was or who they were working with. They kept it secret from almost everyone—including me. So when I saw you following me the other day, I thought your mother told you about Verify, like my father and grandfather told me. That you were like me and maybe because of your mother and what she told you, you might know something that could help me figure out where he is."

The rest of my anger fades. If my mother had gone missing, I would have done the same. I stare at him in the darkness. A sliver of light from the next room casts a shadow across his face, but it doesn't hide the hurt and the hopelessness that I know far too well. We're both alone. Both trying to find someone. We both need something to hold on to. Quietly, I ask, "What's your dad's name?"

Hope flickers in his eyes. "For safety, we all have code names. Your mother would have known him as Atticus. That's a character from an important book I guess you never read and . . ." His expression goes blank as he studies my face. "Atticus. You've never heard of him, have you?"

I wish I could say yes. But I would have remembered a name like that. "I'm sorry."

He shakes his head and turns so I can't see his face in the shadows. "It's not your fault. The Engineers told me to leave it alone." There's a pause. Then, "I screwed up everything tonight."

My heart twists. I don't want to feel for Atlas. He's irritating and self-important. There are so many reasons for me to question whether he's telling the truth—and yet, I recognize the hopelessness in his voice. And maybe it's foolish, but I feel as if I know him because of it. Rose would tell me to be logical. She would warn me not to trust the connection I feel, but I do.

I step away from the door and turn my back on the exit. "So I'm a disappointment because I didn't know anything about Verify and you screwed up everything about my 'train ride' in order to learn more about your father. Does that about sum it up?"

He stares at me and there is a moment where it feels like time stands still. Then relief fills his eyes and the corners of his mouth twitch. "You forgot to say that I'm a pain-in-the-ass know-it-all who acts more like he's two than eighteen."

"Wow. Eighteen. I'm only two years younger than you." More like one year and a handful of months, but who's counting.

"Yeah, I know," he says, waving me back toward the light of the station room. "There's a reason why your age matters. This might sound simplistic, but it's hard to hide what you know once you know it. Because of what has happened to other resistance groups, the Stewards have been incredibly careful. No one under eighteen has been allowed in from the outside. We have had hundreds of our members arrested or gone missing because they unintentionally revealed too much about what they know to the wrong person. And the new recycling push that will be launched next week is going to cause us to lose members even faster now."

"How?" I ask.

"People have been convinced they are doing good by calling the Earth Protection Group when they see a neighbor or friend with books or newspapers they don't want to get rid of. Instead, they're helping the government ferret out people who know too much while fulfilling their goal of eliminating all records that dispute their claims."

I think about the man with the magenta-streaked hair who was arrested just days ago near the school.

"Look," Atlas says. "Going back into the world after stepping onto the train . . . it's not as easy as it sounds. You're different in ways now you don't even understand. My dad's friend Quixote once told me it felt like he had to pretend he didn't know two plus two equals four and agree with everyone when they told him the answer was really five."

"I'm sorry that your dad is missing," I say honestly. I can imagine how screwed up he is over it. Hell, I know how messed up I am still. "But I don't understand what you're doing here or what my mother was a part of. You talk about missing words and train stations and people getting arrested, but how do I know any of it is real? How do I know you're not trying to harm the city, like I've been told?"

"So you want to *verify* what I'm saying." Atlas flips open the lid on the box and picks up a red spiral-bound book. He fingers the edges as he studies me. "The Engineers have a long list of all the things I'm supposed to talk to you about and rules about how much to say and when. That's supposed to take weeks, then after that you decide if you are ready to take the train to the next stop."

"Weeks?"

"Yeah." He gives me another bright, white grin. "I think we can both agree that I suck enough at this that no one will be surprised if I skip a few of the steps. I don't think we have time for that, and I certainly don't have the patience."

"Why don't we have time?" I ask.

"The government has been making a big push to find anyone who knows what we know. My dad and over a dozen of our people have disappeared in the last few days. The new recycling program I mentioned is going to make it worse, and the Engineers in charge are looking to shut things down before that starts. Dad was against pulling back, but now that he's missing, I don't know what will happen."

I yawn. "Sorry," I say. My body aches and is heavy with fatigue. It feels like finals happened days ago. So does my talk with Mr. Webster and Rose. If I sit back in the armchair, I'll probably be asleep in a matter of seconds. If that. Everything Atlas is saying about the recycling program sounds like it's important, but I just don't understand why. I shake my head to clear away the fog. "I promise I'm listening. It's just been kind of a long day."

"Yeah, I get that." He stoops down to grab the dictionary from where it fell and returns it and the spiral notebook to the box where he found them. Carefully, he places the wooden lid back on and runs his hand over it. Then he looks up at me and says, "Is there anything

I could say in the next few weeks that would make you trust what I've already told you?"

I am torn between wanting to believe Mr. Webster, who I have known all my life, and Atlas, who has related a story that paints my mother in an altogether different light. I can't imagine what he could tell me that could tilt the balance. Slowly, I shake my head.

"I didn't think so. So there's only one thing left to do. Follow me."

He crosses to the far wall and presses a small wavy gold design that's located on a painted book's burgundy spine. I jump as a door in the left side of the wall slides open. He grabs a small lantern off a hook inside and hits a button on the top, and it flickers to life. The bright illumination chases away enough of the shadows that I can make out a set of stairs beyond the doorway. The stairs lead down.

"Come on."

"Where?" I don't move a muscle. "To talk to someone else who is going to try to convince me to accept that everything you're saying is real?"

"Who said anything about talking?" Atlas arches an eyebrow. "I'm going to jump a few chapters ahead of where we are now in the notebook and do what I'm not supposed to do. I'm going to show it to you."

He steps through the doorway. The gold flickering of the lamp catches every sharp angle of his face as he turns and waits for me to make a decision about what I will do next.

"Are you scared, Meri?"

To walk into a dark stairwell with someone I met just a few hours ago in order to go God only knows where? Logically, I should be terrified. But while there is much that I don't know, I can't make myself believe that Atlas would intentionally cause me harm.

"No, I'm not." I cross the room, trying to shake free of the foggy tentacles of fatigue. "No more talking."

He nods with approval. "Then let's go."

Atlas heads downward, taking the golden ray of light with him. His footsteps echo as I step through the doorway and follow.

The stairs are steep. The rail I grab for support shifts and rattles. A musty smell envelops me like a damp fleece blanket and I shiver at the chill that seems to have materialized out of the chipped, pocked walls.

"Be careful of where you put your weight on those last steps. The wood is rotting," Atlas warns from the bottom.

He holds the lantern up high. The shadows undulate. I feel the soft sections of wood move under my feet and leap to skip the bottom step. I smack into Atlas, who lets out an "Oof!" The lantern clatters to the ground, taking the light with it. I start to push away, but Atlas's arm wraps around me and squeezes me against his chest. He stumbles, hits the wall, and swears when he kicks the lantern and it scrapes against the hard, cold ground. But he doesn't let me fall.

"You okay?" he asks as he steadies us both. Without the light I can't see his face. I can only feel the warmth of his chest and the strength of the arms that didn't let me hit the ground. It reminds me of the only other embrace that I couldn't shake loose and made me feel secure and safe.

When I was a toddler, it was a game to try to slip out of Mom's arms. Her laugh would shimmer in the air, and she would hold tight and tell me that no matter how much I tried, I would never be able to shake her free. When I got to middle school it was more something I had to put up with, like taking the red cough medicine that is supposed to taste like cherries but never fails to make me gag. I tried to explain my feelings to her. I yelled. I complained. I gave her the silent treatment. I stepped back whenever I could to keep her at arm's length. I'm not sure when she stopped trying to close the distance between us or why I didn't tell her that I never wanted her to.

"I'm fine." I shrug and step away. "No damage done."

"Not to you, maybe. The lantern wasn't as lucky." The moist chill returns full force as Atlas retrieves the lantern from the ground and holds it aloft to display the large dent in one of the bottom corners. "I did warn you those steps were rotten."

"You should probably get someone to fix that."

"I'll put it on the list right under find my father and hoard the resources that will someday rescue a country that doesn't understand that it needs rescuing."

Well, when he put it that way . . .

"The problem with running an underground movement like this is that a lot of what we do needs to happen in areas the city has lost interest in or forgotten about."

There can't be a lot of those places left. Not with all the work the City Pride Department has done. Everyone says the reason the program is so successful is that it focuses on places that had been neglected by the government for so long.

Clearly, the City Pride designers had never stepped foot into this place, I think as we wind through two more hallways. Atlas leads me into a large room filled with what can only be called old junk. From the reach of the light, I can see a couple of old saws, a rusted claw-foot bathtub, a bunch of ratty paintbrushes, and dozens of old wooden crates and rolls of plastic.

Well, I can certainly understand why someone forgot about this room. "Are you sure we didn't go the wrong way?" We had taken so many twists and turns I would struggle to find my way back to the staircase.

Atlas's grin is bright even in the low light. "Follow me."

I stick close behind him as we snake around the tub and weave a path to the back corner. Atlas squats and reaches for a thick loop of rope. Something skitters on the other side of the room. I spin toward the sound as Atlas laughs. "Don't mind the rats, and they won't mind you."

"Rats?"

Atlas yanks open a trapdoor. A ghostly glow comes from somewhere below.

"We'll have to be quiet from here on out. Unless of course you want to stay with the rats."

Someday, I vow, I'll get even with him for the amusement in his voice. But that'll have to wait. I scurry down uneven steps—these made of weathered gray stone—and spot the source of dim light. A narrow doorway waiting for us at the bottom of the steps.

I lean my forehead against the cold concrete wall as the lack of sleep pulls harder. Atlas closes the trapdoor behind us, then he takes the lead again. We duck through the glowing narrow doorway and Atlas turns out his lamp.

"Are we there yet?" I ask.

"Almost," he whispers. "We take a right here."

He picks up the pace as we walk down a hallway with soft dirt floors that is wider than it is tall. How Atlas walks without stooping is beyond me. There can't be more than a couple of inches between him and the ceiling in some places. I am about to ask again when I see the glow from ahead that shines so bright it seems like the sun after you look at it too long. I hear the low hum of voices. The tones of someone singing. A tapping sound like insects beating their wings against the cool glass of my bedroom window on a hot summer night.

The floor slants downward. My gym shoes make a sucking sound as I pull them out of a patch of mud, and I'm about to tell Atlas what I think of this hallway when he stops next to a set of stairs at the edge of the brightly lit opening.

My breath catches as Atlas leans toward me and whispers in my ear, "Welcome to Lyceum Station—home of the Stewards."

EIGHT

Lyceum Station.

I'd assumed from the name it would be another room like the one my mother painted. Part of me had even hoped that it would resemble the unfinished painting in her studio. I couldn't have been more wrong.

If I stood here for days with my tablet and stylus—or a canvas and easel and every color imaginable—I would never be able to capture what I see in front of me now.

Lights.

Those are the first things I focus on when I blink and my eyes adjust from being out of the darkness of the corridor. Hanging from the soaring ceiling are dozens, maybe hundreds, of mismatched lights. Single, illuminated, naked bulbs dangle next to stained-glass domes. Elaborate chandeliers gleaming with thousands of crystals sending prisms of color across the dark ceiling and onto the ground far below. The fixtures all sway slightly, as if pulled by a gentle current of air, making the shimmering glow appear as if it's alive—like dozens of luminous moths circling overhead. The effect lends a magical quality to the space, which is already hard to accept as reality. The sight is accompanied by the faint clicking I heard before—only the sound is slightly louder now and interspersed with a soft bell-like chime. This whole room makes me feel like a character stepping into a fairy tale. Despite recognizing the objects in my sight, I see nothing familiar.

I pull my eyes downward and try to take in the rest. Low wooden walls fill much of the space, lined up like oak and ash and mahogany dominoes throughout much of the front and center of the room. There are freestanding walls that edge the large area and stretch at least two stories, maybe more, into the air, as well as another dozen or so on the side opposite where Atlas and I now stand.

The taller walls have stairs and ladders and platforms to make sure people can reach the top, because each and every single one of the walls and dividers in the room is stuffed full with books. Thousands and thousands of them. All colors. All sizes. I never dreamed there could be so many books left in the world, let alone in the city of Chicago. They are in every crevice and even stacked atop some of the shorter walls. I blink, but they are still there. The books—all of this is real.

Someone in a dark sweatshirt and a baseball cap takes one of the books off a low shelf and then disappears through an exit far to the left. Someone else races through an aisle in the center of the shelves to our right carrying a large blue duffel bag. He places the bag on a counter, rolls out his shoulder, and hurries off again into the maze. Counting the doorway I now stand in, I see four exits from this cavernous space.

"Mind-bending, right?" Atlas's tone and smile are smug. "Wipe off whatever mud you got on your shoes and follow me."

He swipes his feet on a tan grass mat to the right of us. Next to the rug are two small racks—one contains dirty boots and running shoes. The other has a stack of beige towels and a number of slippers in various sizes and styles.

I clean off my feet and realize as I walk in Atlas's wake that there is something different about this room compared with the hallways I just traveled. The smell of mildew and wet has disappeared, traded for the faint scents of citrus and bleach. The dirt and mud under my feet are also gone. Instead, they have been replaced by an array of tile.

Squares of blues and slate grays. Rectangles of various tans and rust and black. They stretch across the floor in a patchwork quilt of hundreds of different colors and textures. Artistically, they should be displeasing, yet somehow they aren't. Each area of the room seems to be dominated by one or two particular colors, or a single shape. And winding through all the patches of various colors and sizes are ribbons of glistening white and silver. These tiles swirl around large wood support pillars and through the sections of the room that hold a tangle of tables and chairs.

"The Lyceum is the main station of the Stewards." Atlas's voice is low as he leads me down an aisle toward the center of the room, along a path of glacial white. Beside us on either side are shelves as high as my shoulders. "My grandfather and his father collected as many books as they could when they first realized what was happening. My great-grandfather was a historian. He warned my grandfather before he died about the danger of destroying books, because, no matter the justification, the action is always meant to eliminate the ideas and the history those books contain. History can only be rewritten if no one remembers the way it existed before. The Nazis did it in World War Two. The Spanish when they discovered the Mayans. The Mongols destroyed libraries in Baghdad. In ancient China, they not only destroyed the books, but killed the writers who penned them."

"Wait . . ." I shake my head. "This is just stuff your grandfather told you about?"

"No," he says, turning toward me. "These are things I've read about in books—*these* books—that my grandfather and some of his college friends worked to save."

His eyes shine with an intense passion as he explains, "One by one, public libraries modernized to all-electronic collections and sent their books to be recycled. My grandfather intercepted them. When he and his friends ran out of room in their homes, they came up with the idea for this place. Between the five of them, it took them decades to create this."

Decades. For my entire life this place has been under the city streets that I walk. And I had no idea.

I run my hand against the long, rough-textured spines of the books on the light oak shelf closest to me.

George Washington's Rules of Civility & Decent Behavior . . . and Other Important Writings
The Federalist Papers
The Autobiography and Other Writings by Benjamin Franklin

"None of the books are in alphabetical order," I say. When I catch Atlas watching me, I jerk my hand away like I used to when I was little and my mother caught me putting my finger in one of her paints. "Sorry. I'm probably not supposed to touch these. They look pretty old."

"Old or new, books are for reading. At least that's what my grandfather has always said. There's a group of Stewards whose job it is to repair or reinforce bindings or record the contents of damaged parts just in case any of the pages go missing, and a bunch of others whose job it is to collect the supplies to do it."

"What was this place?" I ask. "Before your grandfather found it, I mean."

"A network of forgotten streetcar tunnels."

"Chicago never had streetcars."

"Sure about that?" He smirks but must see my annoyance because his expression turns sympathetic. "Don't feel bad. Even before the government started taking books away most people didn't know the tunnels were here. And from what I've read, the city could never really use them. In a lot of places the builders made the inclines too steep and the ceilings too low for them to be useful. The whole project was scrapped. Bad for trolleys, but good for us, since my grandfather and his friends not only knew they existed, they were able to swipe all copies of the plans. Most of the entrances have been walled up with concrete over the years, but they found a few that weren't and that discovery led them here."

Atlas starts walking again, and I hurry to keep pace.

I shake my head, trying to clear the haze of disbelief and wonder. "I can't believe this room was just waiting here all these years."

"Actually, it wasn't," he admitted. "According to old newspaper articles the tunnels were created around the 1900s, but this room is a whole lot newer. As best as my grandfather and his friends can guess, this space wasn't made intentionally. Walls caved in during a major flood back in the 1990s. The force of the floodwaters carved out this area and it was just waiting for the Stewards. Although it took a lot of work for them to get it ready to move in. My grandfather is lucky he had friends who understood architecture, construction, and drainage or were able to learn what they needed from the books they saved. Moisture is seriously bad for paper."

"I guess that explains why the floor is tiled," I say.

He nods. "They picked up scraps of tile where they could and laid the floor. They added pumps and dehumidifiers and a ton of other stuff that's been updated and expanded over the years. There's also a gigantic mechanism attached to thick steel-and-stone doors that can be triggered to lock down the tunnels that lead to the Lyceum. The Stewards thought of everything. They made what you see today."

My mind races as I try to reconcile where I am with everything I've ever been taught. It's—

I yelp as something brushes against my leg, certain it's a rat like the one I saw in the basement room earlier. Atlas starts to laugh. Really laugh. A full, rich, contagious sound that makes me want to join in. But I am not going to give him the satisfaction as he squats and holds his hand out near a gap in the books on the bottom shelf.

"I think you scared him," he says quietly.

"You're worried I scared a rat?"

Atlas's laugh warms the silence again as a furry red-brown face and curious hazel eyes emerge from the bookshelf crevice. "Now you've offended George—a very valuable, albeit slightly hairier, member of our team. He and Margaret make sure there aren't any rats in the Lyceum. Right, boy?"

The long-haired, fluffy cat gracefully hops down from the shelf and winds like a ribbon in between Atlas's legs. He lets out a plaintive meow that melts my heart.

Atlas scratches the cat's ears and gives him a pat on the head. "Lucky for you, George isn't the type to hold a grudge as long as you pet him and put up with his longing stares while you're eating. One hard-and-fast Lyceum rule is that no one is allowed to feed George and Margaret no matter how much they beg. And they *will* beg. Especially George here." George lets out another loud meow as if to verify Atlas's claim, and I can't resist stooping down to let George inspect my hand. He gives several curious sniffs before head-butting my palm—a surefire signal he wants the strokes I give him.

"Why can't anyone feed the cats?" I ask.

"Everyone on this train has a job, even George and Margaret. If they want to eat, they have to hunt. Keeping the Lyceum vermin-free is imperative."

George arches his back in a long stretch and gives us one last meow before sauntering off. "What exactly are the Stewards? How many of them are there and what are you trying to do with—" I look up at the lights high above me. "With all of this? What do you think you can possibly change by hiding books?"

I'm tired, and the tiny clicking noises mixed with bells are beginning to sound like Irish step dancers inside my head, making it hard to focus.

"Hiding books? That's all you think this is?" Atlas shakes his head as if I am deliberately missing the point. He unfastens his tie, shoves it in his pocket, and starts unbuttoning his black dress shirt. "This is everything. It's our history. Our lives. Our futures. The only way anyone will ever know these things existed is if we safeguard them."

"I get that part." At least, I think I do. "But what good is it doing if it is all just down here and no one knows about it?"

"Eventually, everyone will know. But we have to wait for the right moment. Until then, we protect it." He takes a deep breath and lets it out slowly before speaking again. "The government shrank our world and the lives we live bit by bit and we let them because it was easier for people to believe what they said than to fight. Our government taught people not to question what they were doing. There used to be a dozen places to find news. Now there are two. They took away the words first. Then the people who voiced doubts and the people who resisted vanished. Most people never objected because their lives seemed just fine. It's easy to just keep putting one foot in front of another. It's harder to stand up and fight, especially for something that doesn't seem to affect you. Right now people still don't see how affected they are. They don't know it's hurting them. The Stewards have vowed to be here waiting when they do."

Atlas peels off his dress shirt, revealing the off-white T-shirt underneath. I catch a glimpse of a design on his upper arm as he wads the dress shirt into a ball. But I can't make out what it is before he turns and starts walking.

"I still don't understand," I say, and trail after Atlas as he weaves around several taller bookshelves. Finally, we enter an area that is filled with a large silver-and-black metal machine. It has massive rollers that appear to be made of rubber. Situated around it are a dozen or so desks. A few desks have computers sitting on top of them, but most have old-fashioned typewriters colored black and gray or dusty blue. Two of the desks are currently occupied—one by an older man and another by a younger woman with a swath of dark hair. Warped bound books are stacked on one side of their desk. Sheets of white pages are balanced on the other side, while metallic *clickity-clacks* and dull chimes strike the air. "What do you think is going to change if people realize they are missing the information from these books?"

"Maybe fair elections where anyone can run for office instead of those who are *approved*. Open travel to other countries. A free exchange of ideas where people get to decide what to believe instead of being told to agree."

"Yeah, but it's just . . . words."

"Words have power. They change minds. They inspire and create fear. Words shape ideas—they shape our world—and the words down here will someday be the ammunition we need to change it all back."

"Back to what?" I ask. "Back to when there was crime on every corner of Chicago and no one cared about the people who lived in the city with them? That's what happened when people who weren't qualified were elected into office in your 'fair elections.'" The words come out in a rush, and I keep going before Atlas can tell me I'm wrong. "Look at how beautiful the city is now. How safe the country is. Almost no one has guns anymore. No one needs them. Is it any wonder that everyone in the world wants to be like us? The ideas we've been using are working. People are happy. Why would we want to change any of that?"

"*Some* people are happy," says Atlas. "The people who aren't have a habit of disappearing. And other people just don't know any better. In other countries, anyone can be an artist. Did you know that? You don't need to work for the government, or create designs that they have to approve. And despite what you've been told, other countries don't want to be like us. We've fallen behind—in art, technology, science, and medicine. Competing ideas can be messy and chaotic, but better ideas—and huge leaps forward—come out of them. The safety and prosperity government leaders tout now is their way of convincing everyone they should be grateful for what they have and scared of anything that is different. Fear of change is a powerful force."

I want to understand. I try to imagine what it would be like to not need to get a government degree—or how things would look if any images could be used in news reports or on murals around the city. The city wouldn't be as beautiful as it is now. Some things we look at would be unsettling or upsetting. People might complain or feel unsafe.

And yet . . . the idea of expressing *any* idea through art is—

"Atlas!"

He spins toward a woman with thick black hair piled high on top of her head. She's standing behind a typewriter desk not far from us.

"This is Renu," he says, closing the distance between them. "Renu joined the Stewards six years ago."

"And has been wondering when I'll get a decent night's sleep ever since." Renu gives me a tight smile that doesn't quite reach the dark eyes staring at me from behind angular red frames.

"It's nice to meet you," I say. "I'm Meri."

Atlas gives Renu a small shake of his head and explains, "She just hopped on the train tonight."

"Really?"

Renu removes her glasses. The sleeve of her gray T-shirt shifts and that's when I see the design on her upper arm. The dark strokes of ink pop against her lighter skin. Three lines on each side form a V—*no, not just a* V, I think as I look at the shelves around me. *A book.* A book as it is being opened. Licks of curved lines rise from the opening—like flames. And in the very center of the open pages is a small swirl. When I step to the side and look at Atlas's arm, I can see that the design he wears is the same and that it isn't a decorative swirl in the middle. It's an S.

Renu frowns. "I didn't think we were giving out any more tickets until all current passengers were accounted for."

"We're not . . . technically," Atlas admits.

Renu looks over her shoulder and says quietly, "I know you're worried about your father. We all are, but even if we weren't running on yellow, the Engineers would flip. She's what? Fourteen?"

"Sixteen," I correct.

"Sixteen." She shakes her head. "Get her out of here before they see what you've done."

"They aren't going to blame me for looking for my father. If the Engineers aren't trying to find out what happened to him—"

"Telegraphers have arrived," Renu cuts him off.

"There are Telegraphers here?" Atlas's grip tightens on the shirt balled in his hands.

"Two. I didn't get a good look at them. Holden and Scarlett hurried them through the Lyceum faster than I've seen them move before. You'd think they were Stokers."

"Stokers?" I ask.

But Atlas doesn't pay any attention to me. "How long ago did they arrive?" he asks Renu. "Where did they go?"

"They got in about an hour ago. The Engineers took them into the back room."

Atlas turns on his heel and hurries toward an opening in the bookshelves that goes back even farther in the room. I have to run to keep up as he zigzags through the shelves, which are so tall and so narrowly spaced that the bright white lights from above can manage to push only part of the darkness away.

"Atlas," I call as he ducks through another hallway. The murmur of voices comes from somewhere nearby and is getting louder. Not knowing who else is here or what's happening makes my heart punch against my chest. "Where are we going?" I ask, to remind him I'm still here. "Hey, Geeze!"

He glances back at me. The intensity of his eyes—the fear, the worry, the *need* that I see there—causes me to stumble. "Be quiet and stay right here." The words are like sandpaper—scraped and muted. "Can you do that?" His gaze shifts behind me. "Can you see that she does that?"

I turn and see Renu coming down the aisle of books after me. "I've got her," she says, taking hold of my arm. She digs her nails deep into my forearm when I try to yank free. She nods to Atlas. "I've got this. Just fill me in later. I have an investment in all of this, too."

Without another word, Atlas disappears around another bookshelf.

The murmur of voices grows louder. Loud enough to hear, but not enough to decipher the words.

"Stand still," she hisses as I lean forward. "He doesn't need more trouble. Not now."

"I'm not going to stand still or stay quiet if you keep trying to draw blood."

Renu releases her grip, and I step out of easy reach. She smiles at me in a way that says she knows I want to rub at the aches but won't give her the satisfaction. "I keep forgetting my nails have gotten so long. For the first few years, I kept breaking them on typewriter keys."

"Not a very quick learner?"

Renu's smile flattens into a tight-lipped frown.

"Sorry," I mutter. I'm not, but it would be stupid to antagonize her. I'd most likely get lost if I had to find my own way back out. Wandering dark spaces with the rats isn't my idea of fun. So I use the excuse the guy at the door of the station gave to me. "Getting on the train isn't easy."

"It's not supposed to be. Truth is hard at any age." She shuffles her feet and sighs. "And having the Conductor in charge of sharing that truth bail on you in the middle of the night isn't exactly easy, either. Atlas wouldn't have left if it wasn't important."

"So this is all about his dad?" I ask.

She gives me a long look. "If he wants to tell you what they're talking about in there, that's his business. But since we're both stuck here waiting, I can answer any other questions you might have."

"Are you a Conductor?"

She laughs. "Hell no. I don't have patience for that kind of thing."

Well, that was something she and Atlas had in common.

"I'm a Porter," she explains. "I create tickets for potential riders, make lists of supplies that are needed here in the station, sort papers, and help the archivist keep a running list of what books have been sent to what stations and which ones have ridden the rails to the Lyceum to the north. That kind of thing."

"Why were you working on a typewriter?" I ask. Computers have spell-check. I'd think that would be useful.

"I asked the same question the first time I saw them and got seriously annoyed each time I was asked to retype lists because I had to make just one change." She adjusted her glasses. "Since then, I've learned low tech is reliable. It can't get hacked or traced. We use the typewriters for the official day-to-day stuff because it's safer for everyone involved. In the early years, a lot of Stewards got caught because they were connected to the internet. We learned the hard way that the only chance we have to survive is to stay off the grid. There are too many Marshals out on the streets looking for us. We're determined to avoid them and to stay alive."

After what happened at school, I sort of understand the concern. "But you still have computers and printers."

She shoves her glasses up on her nose. "The computers that are used here in the Lyceum are old models. They don't have webcams and they can't be hooked up to any networks. They are as safe as they come."

"Well, if they aren't on networks, why not use them for everything?" I ask.

"We siphon off power for the lights from the buildings on the street above us. The rest of the Lyceum is powered by generators. Conserving that energy is high on the Head Engineer's priority list. So . . ." She looks at her hands and sighs. "Smudges from re-inking ribbon are a small price to pay in the fight for freedom."

"Fight for freedom." Those words are stirring, but I still don't understand how what the Stewards are doing will change anything or even if things really should be changed.

"Renu?" I ask quietly. "Atlas said you've been doing this for six years. If it's dangerous, why are you doing it? Was your life that bad?"

"I get why you'd think that, but no. My life . . . the life I thought I had . . . was good," she says. "I was a history teacher at DePaul University, which means I got to teach the classes most of the other faculty weren't interested in. World History 101. That kind of thing. I loved it even if my students weren't always enthusiastic. One of the more established professors came and observed me teaching. He was a legend in the department and I was really nervous. After the class was over he waited for the students to leave and asked me if I thought about whether the words chosen for our texts were as important as the information they conveyed." She laughs. "I could have given him an honest answer and said not really. Instead I wanted to impress him, so I did some song and dance about how history is always told by those who write the books and the words they chose were clearly of importance to them, but that the information they convey is far more important than the turn of phrase they use. He smiled at me and shuffled away.

"A few weeks later I was coming back to my apartment and saw him standing on the sidewalk. He asked me if I had given any more thought to how words shape history. If I had said no, I'd be living a very different life right now. Instead, I learned the meaning of 'verify.' I became a member of the Stewards, and now my life is down here. And no offense, if I'm ever going to get back out to a real life instead of one that involves paper cuts and a lack of sunlight, I have to get back to work. So why don't we—"

"No!" The word cracks like thunder in the cavernous room.

Renu and I both move at the same time down the corridor of bookshelves and around the corner as Atlas shouts, "No way in hell!"

"Atlas," a woman snaps. "Stop being emotional and think about what we are saying. You father would want you to think like a Steward instead of a son."

"Don't tell me what my father would want," Atlas shouts as we step into a room in the back of all the shelves . . . a real room with a long, silver-and-black table spanning the middle of the space and with a high ceiling and walls that are covered with maps and whiteboards. Atlas stands at one end of the table with his back to us. He is ignoring the half dozen people standing along the walls and appears to be directing his anger at the short but sturdy woman with a cap of white-streaked dark hair and the tall, lanky blond man at the room's other end.

"I understand you're upset." The woman's voice is cool and controlled. "We don't know how the Marshals learned of the Granville Station or whether your father is among those that were captured. None of them have turned up dead, yet."

Yet?

I take a step closer to Atlas and get jerked back by Renu and her killer nails.

"The Telegraphers think they were targeted," the woman says. The looks exchanged by three older, gray-haired men say that they believe it is more than possible. "It could have just been someone who turned them in to the Environmental Department, or someone could have been attempting to get at Atticus in order to learn the location of the Lyceum and the rest of our network. Regardless, after losing a dozen members in the last week, we have to assume the worst. We have to implement the Lyceum's lockdown protocol before the new recycling program goes into effect and we lose even more."

"Which is what Dad *didn't* want you to do," Atlas shouts. "He could be hurt somewhere. He could be in a hospital or hiding out and that's why he hasn't returned. And even if the Marshals took him, they don't know who he is. He'll never tell them what he knows."

"You don't know that."

"If the Marshals really had forced Dad to talk, they would already have come for us. We wouldn't be having this debate right now!"

"Our sources have told us that when the stepped-up recycling program starts next week, government agencies will be raiding the homes and businesses of anyone even suspected of having books or paper. It's impossible to believe this is anything but a direct attack against us. They are determined to destroy the Stewards and the truth we've been protecting." She takes a deep breath and clasps her hands. "Atlas, your father was against locking down the Lyceum, but I have spoken to the rest of the Engineers and we are all in agreement. The Stewards' mission must be adhered to and protected. The doors will close and we will wait out this storm as Stewards have always done in the past. If there is no one left in our numbers to read the books we have stored here, or to preserve the truth of what we have lost, we will have failed ourselves, the city, and the entire country."

"If they've taken my dad, we can find him and get him back. We can . . ."

The woman shakes her head. "I know you want him to return, Atlas. We all do, but we have done what we can. Anything else could jeopardize everything the Stewards have worked for. Your father would never want that. If your father has been captured, we can only hope he has done what all of us have sworn to do if they come for us. For the sake of the Stewards and all the work we have yet to do, we have to hope your father is dead."

NINE

Atlas throws his balled-up shirt on the table and lets out a choked sound. His shoulders slump as the black fabric skids across the dull silver top and then unfolds, revealing the slash of red tie.

Nails dig into my arm and Renu hisses, "Let's go" in my ear, but I don't move. The words I hear every night in my dreams echo in my head. *We're sorry. Your mother, Gillian Beckley, is dead.*

The blond man steps forward. "You have to accept that he's gone, Atlas. That's what your father would want."

"No!" I shout, yanking free of Renu's iron grip. "You can't mean that."

Atlas whirls around. "What the hell? You aren't supposed to be in here. Renu, get her out. Now."

"No one is going anywhere," the woman with the white-and-black hair snaps. Renu steps away from me as the woman sweeps around the table in my direction. "Atlas," the woman says in a quiet tone that sets my nerves on edge, "who is this girl? What is she doing here in the Lyceum? Who authorized this?"

"She's no one, Scarlett. I've got this," Atlas says.

"I'm Merriel Beckley," I say. "My mother was Gillian Beckley. She was one of you—one of the Stewards."

"Gillian?" The woman Atlas called Scarlett shifts her gaze to him.

"Folio." Atlas glances at me. "Here in the Lyceum your mother was called Folio."

Folio? As in a portfolio of artwork? Before I can ask, Scarlett crosses the room and stops a foot from where I stand. "This is Folio's daughter?" She's shorter than I am, but the way she stares at me— as if she can see the thoughts swirling in my eyes—makes it seem as if she is the tallest one in the room. "I wasn't aware Folio had a daughter old enough to be introduced to the Stewards or that any Engineer granted permission for a ticket to be issued in her name."

"She's not old enough, and the Engineers didn't grant her a ticket. I did." Atlas steps next to me. "I had reason to believe her mother might have shared information with her and that she might be exposed and . . ." He sighs. "Screw it. You weren't giving me any information, and I thought because Folio and Dad were working together that she might know something."

Scarlett stares at him with unblinking eyes. "And did she?"

Atlas straightens his shoulders. "No."

"So you risked the mission and everyone in the Lyceum to bring this child where she doesn't belong."

"I'm not a child," I shoot back.

The woman doesn't even bother to glance in my direction. "The rules are in place for a reason, Atlas. The Stewards have survived because we avoided the mistakes other, similar groups have made throughout history. Your father understood that—even if people like Folio were causing him to doubt our true purpose. The Stewards only choose members who are wise enough to be able to handle the choices we are forced to make—"

"My dad is missing. I couldn't just wait around and do nothing. I need him! We *all* need him. I know we are losing more members every day to the Marshals. I know the Stewards have to be protected at all cost, but I can't just assume Dad is dead. Would he use the deadman's switch if he thought he didn't have any other choice? Yes. But if he did, I have to think the Telegraphers would have found a record of his death by now. So don't tell me to hope he's gone. Unless one of the Telegraphers verifies that my father is dead, you can't make me believe he isn't ever coming back."

The air crackles as Scarlett shifts her gaze to study him. Finally, she says, "I understand your position, but our decision has been made. The rails are set to yellow. In two days at midnight, they will be turned red."

"For how long?" he demands.

"For as long as it takes for the government to stop hunting for us," Scarlett says, cutting Atlas off. "That's the protocol our grandfathers helped create, and all elevated to the position of Engineer, including your father and me, promised to uphold. All Stewards who wish to get into or out of the Lyceum will have the weekend to do so before we initiate the lockdown. Those who want to leave the city can go to the exit station up to a week after the lockdown and a Conductor will see they are relocated safely. If your father or the other missing Stewards are alive, they will anticipate this. They will do what they can to get back to the Lyceum or an exit station within that time frame. Otherwise, they will have to take their chances with the Marshals on their own."

She turns and adds, "From now until the lockdown, all stations will be manned around the clock. Telegraphers have already
started to spread word to those on the outskirts of our network. As
of now, all operations will be designed to help those who need to go
underground or who wish to be relocated out of Chicago. Under no
circumstances will new tickets be dispensed or new riders allowed.
Anyone who disobeys the signals will be confined. There will be no
exceptions. I don't care whose son someone might be."

Atlas silently stares at Scarlett, his hands balled into fists at his
side.

She straightens her shoulders and asks in a steely voice, "Does
everyone understand?"

A chorus of murmured assents tumbles in the air. Several sets of
eyes shift to Atlas and then dart away.

Atlas looks down and shoves his hands in his pockets.

Scarlett gives a satisfied nod. Her tone turns warm as she says,
"It's late. Anyone not on the night shift should get some sleep. We
need everyone working at full power to prepare to close the doors
and wait out this storm. And, Atlas . . ." She glances at me and back
at him. "I hold you responsible for this new rider. You broke the
rules. You brought her in without clearance. Now that she's here, it's
up to you to make sure her ride does not put the Stewards in deeper
jeopardy. If you fail, I will have no qualms about ripping the ticket
you gave this girl right out of her hands."

The flat, calm tone streaks an icy finger down my spine as Scarlett slowly turns and strolls back to where the tall blond Engineer
and several other Stewards are waiting for her. They begin to speak
in low voices as Atlas snatches his shirt from the middle of the table
and snaps, "Let's go."

I wait until we wind our way through the bookshelves to a small sitting area filled with fuzzy throw rugs, faded overstuffed armchairs, and worn couches before I speak. "What's happening?" I ask. "What did Scarlett mean when she said the Engineers would remove the ticket from my hands?"

My head is ringing. My eyes burn. Every muscle begs me to fall into one of the chairs and to stay there for days. I must look as tired as I feel because Atlas answers, "Why don't we talk about that after you get some sleep?"

"I can show her to the women's sleeper car," Renu volunteers. I jump because I hadn't realized she'd followed us. "There's a bed next to mine that's free."

"Thanks, but I'm awake enough to get home as long as someone shows me how to get out."

Renu points to two poles of stacked lights. They're flanking the entrance of the Lyceum we originally came through. All the lights are glowing a brilliant shade of yellow. "You heard what they said, Atlas. You're responsible for whatever she does if she leaves."

"I'm not staying here." I take a step back. I don't know these people. I don't know what to think about everything that they've said and what they claim to want to do. I don't understand half of it, and I haven't had time to really think about the half I do understand.

Renu turns to Atlas and crosses her arms in front of her chest. The light catches her forearm, illuminating the black-inked design. "There are more Marshals on the street this week than last. Stewards are failing to report in. People are being careful and they're still disappearing. Who knows how many will be left by the time the lockdown is initiated."

"Maybe they just got tired of being a part of this group," I jab back. "Maybe they just want to live in peace."

"Hey! If you screw up, they could find me here," Renu snarls. "They could find all of us. All it takes is one word to the wrong person and everything we've worked to protect will be destroyed."

"Meri . . ." Atlas says my name in a quiet way that raises the hair on the back of my neck. It's the same tone people use to coax skittish animals into cages before taking them to the vet. "The Stewards have a rule . . ."

"I don't give a damn about the rules, and don't pretend you do, either." I look to Atlas. His face is unreadable, and panic sizzles in my throat. "Atlas, please. I have to go home. My father . . ."

I grab Atlas's hand and squeeze tight. "When he stumbles out of bed he's going to worry if he can't find me. I can't just disappear. He can't think—he can't think that I've left him, too." I blink to keep the tears stinging the backs of my eyes at bay, but that only causes them to burn more. This strange place, the lack of sleep, and discussions about my mother have all laid siege to my defenses. "Please."

Renu shakes her head. Behind her eyes there is frustration and fear.

Atlas puts a hand on her arm. "I've got this, Renu. You should get back to your desk. Nothing will be ready for a lockdown if the Porters don't get to work."

"Don't do anything stupid," she warns before disappearing into the maze of walls and books.

Atlas puts his finger to his lips to still the argument hot on mine and watches the opening Renu disappeared through.

Finally, Atlas holds out his hand and says, "There are a few things we have left to do here. Then, I promise, we'll leave."

For the second time tonight I give my trust by following him through the bookshelves, this time to an older man in a dusty brown hat sitting at a desk crammed with papers and shelves filled with red books. He shouts orders about an assessment of essentials to several people stacking books on tables behind him. He glances up from the battered ledger he's scribbling in and spots Atlas. Without a word he reaches under the counter and comes up holding a black bag with a dark green stripe on the side. "I had just about given up. I'm breaking the rules if I hand this over to you."

"Since when do you care about the rules, Dewey?" Atlas asks.

Dewey goes still as he studies Atlas. Then his eyes flit to me. "There are certain rules I care about very deeply. She looks nothing like her mother."

I take a deep breath and calmly say, "Sorry to disappoint."

His deep blue eyes stare at me unblinking, as if waiting for me to break eye contact first. When I do, he says, "If you give in that easily about all things you will disappoint more than just me. A great deal was put on the line to bring you here. I very much hope you were worth such a risk."

Before I can blink, Dewey tosses the bulky canvas case to Atlas as if it weighs nothing. Just as deftly, Atlas snatches the heavy bag out of the air. As Atlas turns to me, Dewey calls, "'What we obtain too cheap, we esteem too lightly.' There is always a price, Atlas. I'm just sorry yours is already so high."

Atlas's jaw tightens. Dewey's eyes swim. Then, in a flash, whatever sympathy I saw is gone as Dewey flips a page in front of him and grunts, "Get her out of here before Scarlett and Holden start wondering if they should take her ticket now. And make sure you keep her from doing anything stupid."

"Hey—"

"Leave it be," Atlas warns. "Come on. Let's go." I shoot one more look at Dewey, who has pulled his hat low as he crouches over a book, and follow Atlas as he heads through another set of shelves.

Once we are out of earshot, I ask, "Why does he have a problem with me?"

"Your mother's death hit him really hard. She spent a lot of time reading whatever Dewey handed her. Seeing you . . . it got to him. We go this way."

I follow Atlas almost blindly through the maze. He claimed Dewey was my mother's friend, but I never knew the man existed before today, so it seems impossible. Yet so much that should be impossible has happened already.

It isn't until I see flickering images that my attention returns to my surroundings. We enter a small area where several Stewards are reclining in chairs watching large screens, which are tuned to various channels. On one screen a video of an accident filmed from far overhead plays. Emergency workers dressed in orange-and-yellow jackets scramble through a twisted pileup of a half dozen cars and a smoking semitruck pulling people out of the wreckage.

"I didn't know the news was on at this time of night."

"It's not," Atlas admits as we duck through another passageway lined with books. "They're watching recordings of broadcasts from the last twenty-four hours."

"Why?"

"The most convincing stories are the ones that people want to believe or have a hint of truth woven in with the lie. It used to be the news was all about reporting the facts. Then things changed. It's part of how the words were taken to begin with.

"According to the *news*, a truck driver fell asleep and caused the pileup. What we know is that the Marshals were trying to arrest a Steward and the passengers he was transporting out of the city. A car tried to get out of the way of the chase and pulled in front of the truck driver, who couldn't slow down in time to avoid hitting it."

"And you know this how?"

"The Steward and one of his passengers got to safety."

One? "How many passengers were there?"

"Three. A woman and her two children. The oldest girl survived."

A shadow of unease slides into my chest and settles like a lead weight.

"These Stewards are in charge of letting us know about any lies being reported." He doesn't seem to notice my anxiety as he heads away from the news broadcasts.

I shake my head. The news is *real*. It can't be changed like words in a book. And yet . . .

"Have you seen Atlas or that girl?" a woman's voice echoes from somewhere in the maze of shelving, and Atlas picks up the pace through a narrow opening between bookshelves. We go through a door, which leads into another low tunnel that slants steeply upward. Finally, after at least twenty minutes of walking we reach another doorway and the stairs that lead up.

More than once, Atlas glances behind us. Twice, he stops and cocks his head to the side. Each time he does, I hear Engineer Scarlett in my head saying she'd remove my ticket. Those words keep me climbing the three flights of stairs despite the way my legs burn and my head aches. After what seems like forever, Atlas opens a thick metal door. The air is crisp as we step into the shadow-lined alley behind a tall brick building. The dewy, fresh breeze washes away a layer of fatigue as if I have just woken up from a long, very strange dream. A quick glance tells me the street curfew expired almost a half hour ago. The sun will soon be on the rise.

"I have a car parked a couple blocks away. Can you make it?"

"Do I have a choice?"

"You could go back and become roomies with Renu."

"Not a chance." And we start walking.

Atlas's hand is warm and strong as it holds tight to mine. I start to draw away but realize the connection makes it look like we are a couple instead of near strangers. And, while I'd deny it if asked, I'm exhausted enough to admit to myself that his fingers are like an anchor keeping me from being swept into a current of dark, swirling thoughts. And maybe I'm anchoring him, too, because I know what he's feeling—the empty loss and uncertainty. And I wonder if maybe what he feels is worse, because winding through it all is a current of hope that the loss isn't permanent.

"He's not that bad, you know."

"Who? Dewey?" I give my head a small shake to wake myself up.

Atlas nods. "He's a good guy when you get to know him."

"He doesn't like me." I shouldn't mind. The man's a complete stranger. Only, the fact that he was my mother's friend means that I do mind, which sucks.

"Dewey is interested in two things, books and the truth. He's sacrificed a lot for both of those. It's made him . . ."

"Irritating?"

"I was going to say impatient, but that works, too. When he was a boy he found a bunch of old books in an attic, read them, and noticed the information he was reading wasn't the same as the things he was being taught in school. Along the way a teacher realized he had a photographic memory and put that fact in his file. She thought she was helping him. Dewey's parents died in a fire that was somehow started when the Marshals came to take him away. He spent years outsmarting the Marshals on his own until he met my dad. When he joined the Stewards, he donated all of the money he'd inherited to help keep things going. He's barely left the Lyceum during the last thirty years."

I can't begin to imagine thirty years underground.

"If he's helping fund the Stewards, couldn't he talk the Engineers out of locking things down?" I ask. "At least until you know what happened to your father?"

Atlas shakes his head. "Dewey has never wanted to lead. My dad tried to change his mind, but Dewey isn't interested in working with others. So he was put in charge of cataloging and circulation. He's much better with books than people."

That wouldn't be hard. "So Dewey's job is to keep track of the books?"

"That's what the Engineers believe. Dewey would tell you that his job is to find the answer."

"The answer to what?" I ask.

"How to make people care more about the truth than themselves."

I'm trying to decide what to say to that when Atlas pulls me into the entryway of a brick building. He whispers for me to stay completely still and shifts his position so I am hidden from view.

Footsteps slap against the pavement in the quiet of the night. Someone is there. Is it one of the Stewards looking for me? One of the Marshals Atlas claims is searching for them? I don't know what the danger is, but standing this close to Atlas, I can feel the rapid pounding of his heart as he holds his breath.

The footsteps fade, then disappear, and after what feels like forever, Atlas steps back.

"What was that?" I ask as he leads me down the sidewalk, glancing back every few steps.

"I'm not sure. Maybe nothing, but I promised I'd get you home. I don't want to take any chances."

Atlas leads me to a bright red Mustang that Isaac would kill to own. He drops my hand and reaches under the car. When he stands upright he is holding a small silver box. He flips the lid and pulls out a key fob, and the rear lights flash red as the car unlocks. "Get in."

The car engine roars to life as I buckle into the black leather passenger seat. "I would think if you were trying to avoid notice you'd want a car that isn't quite so flashy."

"We have those, too." He grins as he steers the car onto the street. "But any car driving around at this time of morning will attract notice. If you were a Marshal and spotted this car, would you think we're trying to sneak through the city without gaining unwanted attention? Or would you assume I was a guy taking his girl home after a successful date?"

"I hadn't thought of it that way."

"That's because you've never had to wonder if the police officer standing at the corner is looking for you."

He's right. I haven't. "Are the police really looking that hard for the Stewards?"

"Us and anyone ready to resist the truth they want people to believe. The original recycling program was designed to help them eliminate words and ideas so people would accept the reality they have crafted. The new version that encourages good citizenship by asking neighbors to report people who need additional information and encouragement to recycle is designed to eliminate anyone who still knows what they are doing. Anyone searching for words that aren't part of the world that they want us to accept suddenly has Marshals at their door. Hundreds that we know of have been taken off the streets in the last months. Thousands over decades."

I shake my head. "How is that possible?" People should have noticed if hundreds or thousands of people just vanished.

He raises an eyebrow. "Where do you think the homeless went after the City Pride Program started their work?"

"I just assumed—"

"They rounded them up and sent them away. Just like the ones that dared ask the wrong questions or learned the truth. One day they are here and then the next—gone."

Gone. Like my mom. And maybe now his dad.

"They've created a world where no one realizes anyone should verify what they've been told. No one doubts a text saying a friend got a new job, or questions if a moving van just shows up on their block one day and starts hauling stuff away."

I think about the moving van I saw just days ago on our block. How many moving vans have been on our block in the past few years?

He looks over at me. His dark eyes lock with mine. "And no one questions the police when they come to your door to tell you there's been an accident."

The knots in my stomach pull tight.

Car tires squeal inside my head. The screams from my nightmares scrape against my mind.

Black ice.

Out-of-control car.

Everything changed because of one driver's mistake.

I was told it was an accident. I never once wondered if the police at the door were telling the truth. Why should I?

Atlas pauses for several heartbeats, waiting for the question he must guess his words have sparked.

Only I can't bring myself to say the words. Too much has happened tonight. Too much is new. Fear of what is still waiting in the unknown stills my tongue and the question dies on my lips. I'm not ready to know the other secrets he has to tell. Not yet.

So I ask something else. "If all of this is true, why are you hiding down in the Lyceum with stacks of books instead of doing something about it? How can you just sit by and let it all happen?"

If my mother's accident wasn't an accident—how could the Stewards let me and my father go on with our lives thinking that it was?

Atlas's hands tighten on the steering wheel. "We have no choice."

"I thought you said words give you choices."

He takes a deep breath and stares out the window. "A lot of us want to do something—but we can't. Not now. Not if we want to survive. We're outnumbered."

"Yeah, but—"

He grabs the bag from Dewey out of the back seat and shoves it at me. "Open it."

I unzip the bag and find two books inside: a thick history textbook and a dictionary like the one Atlas had me use earlier.

"Read the book. Pay attention to World War Two. Read it. Then tell me how you think we can survive if we come out into the open. Trust me, I'll be all ears."

The streetlights through the windshield reflect off Atlas's eyes. They illuminate his pain, desperation, and resolve. Then he turns the wheel and heads down a street two blocks over from mine.

"You'll have to walk the rest of the way."

"Someone was watching my house today."

"Of course they are." He pulls next to the curb and cuts the engine.

The matter-of-fact way he says it, as if it isn't any big deal, freaks me out more than almost anything else I've heard tonight. Maybe because the men in the car and the threat they might pose feel tangible. The rest . . . I'm still working on. "So what do I do?"

"Cut through the yards. Hop over the fence behind your house. Go in through the back. Act like things are normal even when you know they aren't. Trust me, that's not as easy as it sounds." Atlas shifts in his seat to face me. "One wrong word could alert the Marshals that you're working with us."

"Then why?" I ask quietly.

"Why what?"

"Why did you bring me home instead of keeping me at the Lyceum, where you could make sure I didn't screw things up?"

His eyes stare out the window at the sky that is beginning to streak with a pale, pink light. "I didn't tell you the rules before showing you the Lyceum. I didn't give you that choice. The Stewards are about restoring choices, not taking them away. Besides—" He turns to meet my eyes. "I made a promise, and I don't break them. Give me your phone number."

"What?"

"I need your number so I can contact you. Just because I'm bringing you home doesn't mean you're done. You climbed on, and you don't get to jump off until this train comes to a stop." He punches the numbers I recite onto the screen of his phone, then slides it back into his pocket. "There's a lot for you to learn before the rails go red. Once that happens, you and all the Stewards who aren't on lockdown will be on your own until the Engineers deem it safe to open the doors again. The last lockdown lasted years. Anyone who screws up won't be around by the time it's over. I'm not going to let that be you. So don't talk to anyone you don't have to or leave your house until you hear from me. Okay?"

I'm still not sure what I believe, but I say, "Yeah. Okay."

That must have been what he wanted to hear, since Atlas leans over and reaches across me—his arm brushing my shoulder as he grabs the door handle and shoves it open. "Get some sleep. Read. Then think about what you knew before you saw the word 'verify' and what you know now. That should keep you busy until I can get back to do the Conductor thing with you."

The trembling of my legs and the floating fog weaving through my thoughts tell me I need sleep more than just about anything. Still, I don't move when Atlas sits back in the driver's seat.

"What?" he asks.

Get out of the car now, I tell myself. *Go home and go to sleep and forget about all of this if you can.* But I don't, because there is something I have to know and it can't wait until tomorrow. "What's a deadman's switch?"

His eyes look into the lightening sky. "On a train it's the fail-safe device that stops the engine and keeps the train from crashing if the operator is unable to do so."

That much I knew. "What is it for the Stewards?"

His jaw tightens. "It's a small capsule filled with several types of poisons. From the time it passes through the lips, it takes less than ten minutes before the switch is activated and the Steward is dead."

TEN

My bike is leaning against the side of the garage when I return home. Someone from the Stewards had taken care of it, just as Atlas had promised hours ago when we first stepped off the bridge and into the shadow-filled rabbit hole from which I have yet to fully emerge.

Everything is quiet as I slip through the door and soundlessly shut it behind me. I peel off my shoes, dump my bags at the foot of my bed, and climb under the covers, hoping to find refuge in unconsciousness. To escape the day and the questions swirling in my mind.

The dream comes as it always does. Mom standing on the sidewalk. The headlights shining bright as the car streaks down the street. Only this time the car doesn't hit her. This time the vehicle screeches to a stop at the curb.

Two men in dark coats jump out. They slam their doors shut and shout, "Are you Gillian Beckley?"

I scream for her to stop, but she is already placing a small pill on the tip of her tongue and swallowing.

"Mom! No!"

The men running toward her freeze in place. The sidewalk and the buildings and the headlights fade into nothingness until only Mom and I are there in a cloud of white.

"An artist's job is to look at the world and share the truths they see. I had no choice but to look, and I couldn't ignore what I saw." She holds out her hand. "Truth can be dangerous, but it is more dangerous to pretend it's not there. Be careful."

My eyes snap open.

Sunlight streams bright through my window as I shove the covers off and glance at the clock.

Nine twenty-two. I slept later than I have since the night the two officers came to break the news about the accident. The smell of coffee wraps itself around me like a warm blanket. Dad is not only awake, he's also functioning. I blink away the haze of sleep and look down at my clothes, which are damp with sweat, and that's when all that happened last night comes rushing back.

Dad drinking. Atlas on the bridge. The paintings on the station walls. The Lyceum and the books. My mother's hidden life and all that it implies.

I slide out from under the covers and check the foot of my bed. Two bags. The red one is mine. The green-striped black one has the two books Atlas told me to read.

I jump at the light rap on the door and shove the bag and the books under the covers as it swings open.

"Hey." Dad gives me a tense smile. "I heard you moving around and thought you could use this." He holds out a tall green mug with outlines of paintbrushes pictured on it.

An apology.

"Thanks," I say, taking the mug. "I didn't set my alarm."

"You needed sleep. We both did. It was a long week." He slides his hands into the front pockets of his khaki pants. "Do you have big plans for today?"

He doesn't want to talk about last night, which is probably for the best, since I'm not sure what either of us would say.

"I plan on showering and hanging around the house." I think about the books buried under the mound of covers and Atlas's instructions to stay inside. What would my father do if he saw the books? He always tried to get Mom to stop painting on canvas out of civic responsibility. Would he report the books, thinking he was doing the right thing? "What are you going to do?"

Dad shrugs. "I thought I might go into work for a few hours. My boss wants to meet on Monday morning. There are some problems. . . ." He shakes his head. "It's no big deal. I just want to be prepared. And I was thinking that maybe tomorrow morning I'd go for a run."

"A run?" Something he hasn't done since Mom died. Something that once was normal.

"What? You think your old man can't run anymore?" He rakes a hand through his still slightly damp hair and looks down at the floor. "Last night I really let you down. I let us both down."

My stomach twists. "It's fine, Dad."

"No," he says firmly, putting a hand to his temple—probably trying to calm the throbbing. "Nothing has been fine for a long time. We should be able to talk. You should feel like you can come to me about anything. You should never have to think you have to deal with things alone."

No, I shouldn't. But that doesn't change the fact that I do.

When I don't respond, Dad gives me a hint of a teasing smile. "Maybe you'd like to come with me when I go for my run?"

Those words, so like the ones he used to ask before Mom died, twine around my heart and tug.

"Have I ever wanted to come running with you?" I say, echoing the past routine.

"There's always a first time. Maybe next weekend." His smile widens.

"Yeah," I answer. "And maybe pigs will fly."

"They will if you draw them." And for that second he's the dad I used to have. The one I trusted with my heart. The one I want to trust with everything I've learned now.

But what if Atlas is right about anyone I talk to being put into danger?

Of course, Dad could know some of this already. What if Mom did share some of her secret life? What if keeping the secret is part of the reason he continues to drink despite his promises to stop? Maybe he needs to talk to someone as much as I do.

Before I can stop myself, I ask, "Do you think you should *verify* that?"

Dad cocks his head to the side. "Should I what?"

I wait for some kind of reaction—fear, recognition. Something to tell me he's heard the word before. But he just blinks twice as he looks at me. Disappointment stabs deep as I shake my head.

"It's nothing," I lie. "Just something we say at school to give each other a hard time."

"Well, you can give me an even harder time when I'm barely able to move later." He gives me a smile. "I'm headed to the office now. Let me know if you need me to pick up anything for dinner on my way home." As he heads down the stairs, I can only stand there holding the coffee-mug peace offering, listening to the back door slam shut.

I change into tan shorts and a T-shirt that swirls with colors that remind me of the sunrise. Then I take the bag with the books Atlas gave me and go downstairs to the kitchen. Armed with another mug of coffee and a bowl of cereal, I pull out both books. The dictionary I set to the side. The other I place on the table.

United States History, Colonial America through Modern Day.

The faded mustard-yellow cover is slightly dented and the edges of the pages are warped. From the printing date I find inside it seems the "Modern Day" in the title is almost sixty years ago. Reading the table of contents page makes my eyes start to glaze over. Having just been through finals, I have zero desire to wade through dense paragraphs filled with events that happened before I was born. Since I'm certainly not going to read the whole thing without knowing what I'm looking for, I flip to the final chapter of the book, figuring that's probably the most relevant. Shoving a spoonful of cereal into my mouth, I start reading the chapter titled "The Modern United States and the New Doctrine of Isolationism."

The chapter is the shortest in the book. It takes up only a handful of slightly worn, occasionally torn, discolored pages. I chew as I read the dull words detailing how worry for national security caused the government to limit internet access to certain websites that the intelligence agencies flagged as suspicious. About the push for Congress to pass a new constitutional amendment declaring English to be the national language and laws that required all applicants for immigration to demonstrate an acceptable proficiency of the language in order to have their request considered.

None of that seems all that shocking. After all, it makes sense that everyone in the country should speak the same language and that there should be only one internet portal to make sure service is reliable and equitable. But the words I'm reading aren't detailing the same history I've been taught. The book details how instead of a unifying language that brought the country together, the law denied citizens who spoke other languages driver's licenses, jobs, and the right to vote. I flip the page and drop my spoon.

The best art delivers an emotional punch in one glance. The photographs I look at now stop me cold. They're a series of images— pictures of two tan-skinned men being attacked on the street. One man has fallen to his knees and is covering his head with his hands to ward off the blows from an enraged crowd. The other is looking over his shoulder as he attempts to run. The camera has captured his bloody, bruised face and the despair and fear in his eyes with perfect clarity. Beneath the picture a caption reads: "Violence unleashed against non-English-speaking citizens after passage of Unification through Language Law."

I push away my bowl and keep flipping the pages. I'm not sure how much time passes as I read about the National Guard being deployed to cities that had a history of violent crime. Environmental laws being passed to curtail paper usage. Foreign aid suspended, leading to a rise of new dictatorships around the world as well as suffering and death to many who no longer had access to doctors, clean water, or food. And the temporary suspension of travel to and from other countries due to a fear of terrorist threats. Which clearly wasn't temporary because I can't imagine people in our country choosing to visit anyplace outside of our borders. We have everything anyone would ever want. And it isn't dangerous here.

Or is it? If people really are disappearing like Atlas says . . .
I want to shove the book away but force myself to keep reading.

While this new policy of shifting attention away from world issues has caused many to worry that other less dependable leaders will fill the void left by the United States' withdrawal, others applaud the desire to dedicate all tax dollars to efforts inside America's boundaries. Germany, the United Kingdom, and China have all pledged resources to those countries that no longer receive American financial and military assistance. American politicians have lauded other countries for stepping forward so the United States can finally dedicate its focus to the citizens they feel have been neglected at home.

The last paragraphs talk about widespread protests against the new doctrine. One large protest in Los Angeles got out of hand. Protesters and police officers were killed. Many leaders, including the president, were certain the instigators of the violence were spurred to action by journalists who wished to cause trouble. Which I can't imagine, since the anchors on both news channels are almost always upbeat as they cover the weather, City Pride Projects, entertainment news, and sports. Nothing that I can imagine ever causing upset. A news report shouldn't cause that kind of reaction, and if it did, people should never allow that kind of reporting to continue.

But even as I am glad our government was smart enough to put an end to that kind of thing, I hear Atlas's voice in the back of my mind asking if it really was positive. Is taking away the voices of disagreement on the news similar to removing the words? Does someone choosing what gets reported by the news and what doesn't limit our freedom?

I don't know.

Things are peaceful. That's what's important. Nothing else should matter.

But maybe it does.

Maybe if the news reported on different stories, I'd know if what Atlas is saying about people disappearing is true. Maybe . . .

I take a deep breath, turn to the beginning of the book, and flip through the pages. There are wars with different names from the ones I was taught. Dozens and dozens of words I have to look up, like "revolution" and "uprising." And when I find the chapter on World War II that Atlas told me to pay attention to, my heart goes cold.

Some of what we learned was the same, but so much was missing. First, the pictures of people being rounded up into a specific section of the city. Then the trains. The death camps. The bins of shoes left behind by those murdered by their own government. And the people inside Germany and Poland who tried to fight—to get news out about what was happening to those who could help— who hid people who were in danger, wrote papers and painted slogans to change minds. Group by group they were hunted down and killed by those they defied.

They were outnumbered—just like the Stewards.

I pull out my tablet and scroll through my school text just to make sure I am not mistaken about the differences. I'm not. The chapter on World War II is less than half the length of the one in the paper textbook. In fact, it appears that the entire on-screen textbook is half as long, even though it covers an additional eighty years of history. And the final page . . .

I read the words I read only a month or so ago for my history class. Then, I agreed with them. Now . . .

The consolidation of the media and reduction of internet pro-
viders combined with the restoration projects of City Pride has
cemented the country's positive return to a shared sense of com-
munity and culture. That sense of sameness has helped bridge
many cultural and religious divides that have long plagued the
country. It is clear from the success of these new laws and pro-
grams that government leaders will work to continue this trend.

I shove away from the table and walk down the hallway to my
mother's studio as words swirl in my head.

Limiting what people see on the screen so everyone sees one
thing—believes the same ideas—feels wrong. Rose and I have been
friends forever. We agree on a lot of things, but we have disagree-
ments. I hate when we fight, but I've learned things from our
arguments—often things about myself. My mother always told me
actively looking and listening were the best ways to learn. I look
at the stool I had been sitting on when she demonstrated what she
meant.

"What is this?" she asked, showing me a picture on her tablet.

"You took that long to draw a purple square?"

"Is that all it is? Are you actively looking?"

"It's a square. It's dark purple. It's . . ."

She flicked the screen and it rotated just a hair—enough for
me to see that there was a whole picture beyond the one she first
showed me and the purple square was just one part of the image that
lay beyond.

"A good artist always looks at all the angles if she wants to really
understand what she sees."

I heard her words. I understood them, but I never applied them to more than art. If I did, then one type of news meant my view of the square was preventing me from seeing the entire picture. If words have been altered, then I can no longer be sure if all I'm seeing is the purple square.

I think about the new version of the dream that haunted me last night.

The car's lights barreling through the fog.

The pill my mother placed on her lips. The deadman's switch Atlas described to me as the men from the car lunged toward her.

Everything inside me screams that her death was a terrible accident, but I can't ignore the missing or changed words in the electronic version of the history book in front of me or forget my mother's mural on the wall of the train station.

The truth is found when men are free to pursue it.

My mother chose those words. Her hands drew each line and curve. They were the first ones my eyes focused on when I looked at her mural, and I cannot stop thinking of them now.

Atlas told me words were missing from the books I have read. That history is different from what I have always believed. And he insinuated that my mother's death might not have been an accident.

Trust, but verify.

Those words that I hadn't known before meeting the Stewards ring like a chorus of brass bells in my head, as if they are instructions that my mother insists I follow. There has to be a way for me to find out the truth.

I go back to the kitchen, dump my dishes in the sink, then grab the books and my tablet and head upstairs. My tablet has barely any charge left. I check my phone, still in my bag at the foot of the bed, and find that it is dead. I plug both in, and as I am pulling up a search window on the tablet screen, the phone buzzes to tell me I have a message. Rose saying she has to work at *Gloss* today, but she hopes to hear from me soon.

Rose, a friend I've trusted all my life. The one I always can count on even when I shove her away. If anyone would understand my confusion and want to help me get to the truth about my mother, it would be Rose. But as much as I want to ask her opinion, the truth is something I have to figure out for myself.

Setting the phone to the side, I try to decide how best to go about learning whether my mother's accident was real. Atlas suggested that like the words being taken away, hundreds, quite possibly thousands, of people have been removed from the city by those who work for the government. Well, accidents are reported in the news, right? My mother's accident was, of that I'm certain. Maybe there is a detail in that article that I missed before, one that can help me now.

I grab my tablet, type my mom's name into the search field, and hit Enter.

Links appear for dozens of articles discussing the accomplishments of the City Pride Program—most I've never thought to look for, much less read, before today. My heart squeezes as I click through the various articles that praise the parks and murals and buildings in sections of the city that once were plagued by gangs, violence, crumbling buildings, and homelessness. Atlas's voice whispers in the back of my head that not a single article mentions what happened to the gang members, criminals, or homeless who had been there before. Only that the revitalized areas sparked a renewed interest and pride in community, which led to lower crime rates and better living. Something I believed with my whole heart to be true. And now? Now part of me wants to shut off the device and ignore it all. But I can't, because I need to know if my mother died in an accident or if she was deliberately killed.

Taking a deep breath, I do another search for the article I read the day before my father and I stood in the cemetery and watched my mother's coffin being lowered into the ground. The article was about the accident. It referenced the unseasonable snow and the driver losing control on the black ice—all facts the police officers shared with me on the night it happened. Only, the online column that I once read through tears doesn't appear. I search again and get the same results.

I must be doing something wrong.

I move to my desk and turn on my computer to find the bookmark that I created for that column. I click the link and get an error message telling me the page I am looking for no longer exists.

My phone signals I have a message from an unknown number. WILL BE AT YOUR HOUSE THIS AFTERNOON. BE READY AND DON'T DO ANYTHING STUPID BEFORE I GET THERE. —A

Atlas.

Part of me wants to call him and ask what he knows about my mother's accident. The other part knows I won't be able to trust anything he tells me. Not without learning it for myself.

Frustration simmers as I shove the phone aside and try several more searches using different key words. Finally one link does appear—Mom's obituary. It cites a car accident as the reason she died. But that's the only reference to the accident that I can find. The rest has vanished, which only strengthens my need to know the truth.

The computer won't help me. My father can't. But there is one person I can think of who can help me understand. She might not have wanted to talk to me before, but I'm not going to give her the option of turning her back on me again.

ELEVEN

I hurry upstairs and do a search for the address of Kacee Anderson—my mother's friend from work—the one I spotted when I was there the other day. She hugged me at my mother's funeral. She promised she would be there if we needed her, and yet she pretended not to see me when I was at the City Pride Department this week. It's time to find out why.

I hide the Stewards' books, leave my father a message on the kitchen tablet letting him know I'll be out for the day in case he gets home before I do, and quietly slip out the back door so the men in the car out front won't see me.

The trip to Kacee's condominium building, which has a view of the sun-kissed, sparkling sapphire lake takes twice as long as I zigzag up and down alleys and side streets to make sure no one is following behind. I'm drenched with sweat and quivering as I climb off my bicycle and awkwardly navigate wheeling it into the building's oak-paneled entryway. I punch the apartment number into the keypad and wait as the intercom signals Kacee upstairs.

"Hello?" a young girl's voice chirps.

"Hi . . . April," I say, digging up the foggy memory of the little girl I'd seen smiling from Kacee Anderson's personal screen. "Is your mom around?"

The girl babbles something incomprehensible before yelling, "Mommy!"

The intercom crackles, and a few seconds later I hear a warm, familiar voice ask, "Who is it?"

"It's Meri Beckley, Mrs. Anderson. I need to talk to you."

A woman with a cotton-candy-pink double-wide stroller rolls down the sidewalk. Somewhere cars protest something with offended honks. Finally, the door-lock buzzer sounds and Mrs. Anderson instructs me to come up.

I leave my bike in the lobby and press the elevator panel for the twelfth floor. A short, sandy-haired man and a skipping girl in a yellow dress with matching hair bows are coming out of a door just down the hall as I step off the elevator.

"You guys play on the swings," Kacee calls to them from the open doorway. "I'll be right behind you with the picnic." Her eyes meet mine. "Ten minutes. Tops."

"Don't worry about us, right, Munchkin?" The man tousles the girl's hair and gives me a smile dripping with the pity that I despise. "Maybe there will be some ducks for us to feed."

"Duck, Daddy. Duck," the girl babbles. Kacee waves and smiles as they get on the elevator. When her family disappears, both her hand and smile drop. "Come inside," she says. She then turns her back and heads into the apartment.

"You don't seem surprised I'm here," I say, following her inside. The Andersons' living room is colorful, with a pink dollhouse and at least a dozen dolls of varying colors, sizes, and hairstyles sitting in the middle of the floor.

"I was hoping you would have found a way to move on, but after the other day I knew you'd find your way here." Mrs. Anderson pulls the tie out of her hair and shakes out her long curls. She then paces the toy-laden floor and stares out the window at the glistening lake beyond the glass. Quietly she says, "You're too much like your mother, Meri. If you're not careful, it's going to get you in trouble."

"The other day you pretended not to see me."

"I had to, for my family's sake. For both our families' sakes."

"Was my mother in trouble when she died?" I ask, taking a step toward her. "Was her death really an accident?"

"Your mother used to love the job we did," she says with her back to me. "She believed in it, just like I did . . . do. But something changed. She asked questions that were unusual about the project sites."

"What kind of questions?"

"About the history of the sites. About people who she seemed to think had once lived there. She claimed she was looking for inspiration for her designs. I would have believed her, but . . ."

"But what?"

Mrs. Anderson takes a deep breath. "I was tired. April wasn't sleeping because her molars were coming in. When I put her down and couldn't get back to sleep I decided to just go into the office to try to catch up on work. I saw your mom getting onto the elevator, but she wasn't on our floor when I arrived. And when I asked her about it the next day . . ." Mrs. Anderson takes a deep breath and turns toward me. Fear shines bright in her eyes. "She said she was in the archives. She found some kind of information about a future project site that couldn't possibly be true. When I told her she was crazy for wanting to look into it she told me about other things. She said she was working with people who were going to share everything they knew with the city. They had a plan and . . ." She shakes her head as if to clear the memory, but I still see it shining bright in her eyes.

"Plan?" I ask. "What plan?" Mrs. Anderson shifts her weight from foot to foot. "Did my mom tell you about the meaning of 'verify'?"

"I don't know what that is," she insists, but the way her eyes dart to the side tells me she is lying. "I don't want to know what that means or what she thinks she saw in the archives. It's not supposed to be my concern."

She picks up a stuffed elephant from the floor and clutches it to her chest. "Look, I like my job. I love my family, and I don't want anything to change. I'm happy." She crosses the room and drops the elephant on the top of an overflowing toy bin. "Everyone I know and care about is happy. Your mother didn't understand that when I told her I wasn't interested in whatever she had to say, but it's true and I have nothing more I can tell you."

"Did they kill my mother?" I ask quietly.

Her eyes shimmer with emotion. "Your mother died in an accident." She fiddles with a prism hanging from a chain around her neck. "They said it was an accident, Meri."

"They can *say* a lot of things," I press. "Just because they say it doesn't make it real. I never knew that before. I do now. Please. I deserve to know what actually happened. She was my mother, and your friend."

Mrs. Anderson goes completely still—like a deer in headlights trying to decide which way to flee in order to avoid the collision. Then she blinks as if breaking free from a dream and reaches for the doorknob. "They say it was an accident. That's all I know for certain. Now I have to get to the park. I only have so much time to spend with my family. Work has been so busy. Most of the team your mother and I were a part of has been transferred to other cities. Now Mr. Beschloss and the other government administrators are evaluating my work to make sure I'm still a good fit for City Pride. Just after your mother's funeral, Mr. Beschloss came to find me. He was curious as to whether I would follow in your mother's footsteps. He wanted to know if I had her interest in spearheading unique projects. If I did he planned to reward me as he had rewarded her." She lifts her eyes to meet mine. Fear shines bright. "Do you understand what I'm saying, Meri?" she asks carefully.

I nod as the truth slams home. Mrs. Anderson suspects they killed my mother and they are threatening her with the same fate.

"So you're just going to pretend you don't know what you know?" Bile churns as I look at a woman my mother called her friend. "How can you do that?"

"I don't *know* anything. Neither do you, and I can't tell you anything more. A good mother wants her child to be safe." She looks back at the view of the lake. "I miss your mom. I wish she was here, and I sometimes can't help but think about the things she said. If she was correct about . . ." Mrs. Anderson shakes her head. "What happened in the past is in the past. No one can change it, no matter what your mother might have thought. All I can do is make things better now. When I look at the city I realize how far it has come. . . . I don't think any of us would be happier or safer if we went back to the way things used to be. Do you?"

"You're working for the people you think might have killed my mother." My voice cracks. "How can you put that in the past?"

Her lip trembles. "I loved and admired your mother, but I can't live the way she did. The things she wanted people to know would only lead to unhappiness. I very much hope you won't make her mistakes."

She opens the door and shifts to the side for me to pass. "I'm sorry. But please don't contact me or my family again."

"The truth should matter," I insist.

"Maybe." Kacee Anderson shrugs. "But if everyone believes in something, isn't that just another kind of truth? Who's to say your version is better?"

Mrs. Anderson shuts the door on me and the truth I represent. I know she won't open it again. But now I have confirmed that she's scared of the government she works for and worried that they might do to her what they did to my mother.

The weight of that snaps the last thread tethering me to the lie I was living.

My mother was murdered.

The words whisper in my head as I retrieve my bike. They grow louder as I roll it down the sidewalk, past people walking their dogs, laughing in the sunshine, or going about their day. Every couple of blocks a weatherproof public screen chirps out the news, even though almost no one is paying attention. I never did until yesterday. But the screens were always there. The stories were constantly on the edge of my awareness. Part of my life. I trusted the anchors on those screens to tell me if there was something I needed to hear. I never questioned that. Now I wonder if any of them know they aren't giving me the truth. If they made that choice or if those choices were taken away from them, too.

Like the words were taken. Like my mother was.

Anger churns. I climb on my bike and start to pedal. Only, I know I can't go home. I can't just pretend everything is okay, and it's not like I can tell Dad what I've learned. Not without more proof than an old textbook and a battered dictionary.

According to Mrs. Anderson, Mom found information in the archives she wasn't supposed to have and planned to share it with the public. I saw the sign for the archives when I interviewed with Mr. Beschloss. It had the same security keypad as the elevator did in order to reach that floor. Maybe it's reckless, but I'm determined to get into the archives myself to see if I can find what she found. And I have an idea of how to do just that.

I pedal hard along the city streets, looking behind me every few blocks, just in case anyone is following. When I pull up in front of Rose's condo, I watch the street for several minutes as I catch my breath. No cars appear. When I'm as certain as I can be that no one is watching, I head inside. I punch the code that lets me into the building and replay what I'm going to say in my mind as the door to Rose's condo opens.

"Hey, Meri." Isaac's eyes go flat when he spots me. He's dripping with sweat and wipes the back of his neck with a towel as he snaps, "Rose isn't home and I was just about to get in the shower."

I'd forgotten Rose wasn't home. I was hoping she would distract her brother while I got his badge. But Isaac's rude welcome gives me another idea. I offer what I hope is an embarrassed smile and say, "I've been trying to send her a message, but my phone has been acting strange so I figured I'd stop by. If nothing else, it gave me a chance to apologize again. For making you late."

"It wasn't that big a deal," he mutters.

"I'd still like to make it up to you," I say. "I was thinking maybe

I could do a portrait of you in your security uniform? Your mom's birthday is coming up."

Playing to his vanity does the trick. "That would be really great." He smiles and steps back, letting me into the condo. "You really don't have to go to the trouble, but Mom would love the portrait. And it would save me from having to come up with a gift."

"It's no problem. Really. And since I have pictures of you to use as a reference, I just need to see your uniform and badge." When he brings everything out to the living room, I add, "If you need to take a shower now, I can put it all back in your room when I'm done."

"Wow. Thanks, Meri." He grins. "Man! Mom's going to flip. I'll tell Rose your phone is on the blink." And with that he's gone.

When I hear the shower running, I pocket the identification badge, take several pictures of his uniform (since I'll eventually have to draw the portrait I promised), then return the clothes and head out. Now I just have to use the card and get it back to Isaac before he realizes it's missing.

By the time I bike from Rose's house to Liberty Tower, I am feeling less confident about my plan than I was when I started. But it takes only a thought of my mother and how she died to shove my doubt aside.

I stash my bike in a rack and glance through the window at the security guard sitting half-asleep at his desk. The building is always open on weekends, since the architecture makes it a popular tour stop and wedding reception location. Today, aside from the drowsy guard the reception foyer is empty. There's no way to get to the elevators without him seeing me.

Unless . . .

I spot a frazzled woman outside, herding a group of children.

Their behavior ranges from out of control to loudly petulant. She's turning a tablet around in her hands, a map displayed on the screen.

"Excuse me," I say. "If you're lost, I'm sure the guard in there will be happy to give you directions."

The lady blinks up from the screen. "Are you sure?" she asks with desperate hope. "We've been going around in circles and they're getting tired."

"I'm positive."

She gives me a grateful smile, then makes a beeline to the security guard. The kids follow, chasing each other at high volume.

Holding my breath, I ease into the lobby, hurry past the woman and her hyped-up charges and into a waiting elevator.

Please don't let all this be for nothing, I think as I wave Isaac's security ID in front of the scanner and hit the button for the eighth floor. The doors close. After what seems like an eternity, the elevator starts to rise.

The eighth floor is as still as a tomb as I step off the elevator and hurry to the door marked "ARCHIVES." Isaac's badge works its magic on the door lock there, too. A small red light next to the scanner turns from red to green. As I open the door, I can't help but wonder—does the security guard downstairs get an alert when this door is opened? If so, I have to move fast.

After setting the alarm on my phone for five—no, ten minutes to search, I hit the light switch and step inside.

The room is filled with large metal cabinets that all appear to be marked with the status of City Pride Department Projects: "Current," "Future," "Completed," and "Unexplored." I pull open the drawer closest to me, one marked "Completed," and find . . . paper.

Lots and lots of paper.

All grouped in individual folders marked by the project's address.

All my life, I've heard that the government cares about the environment and that using paper was selfish—unpatriotic—bordering on treasonous. The government claimed to have electronically stored all records before recycling every scrap of paper in their possession. And yet, here this is.

Renu said paper records are impossible to hack. Looking at this room, I have to think that is the reason the city government has these documents stored here. To keep their secrets from people like the Stewards and now me.

I count the dozens of cabinets in this room, then throw open drawer after drawer. Every single one of them is crammed full. My mother came in here to search for something. I could search for hours and still not find it.

Feeling the seconds I've allowed myself ticking away, I slide out the first file in the front of the drawer and flip it open to examine the papers inside.

Blueprints for an apartment building. Color schemes and design concepts. Budgets and itemized lists of supplies and costs. None of it seems important until I get to a page with the names of the people who lived in the building being worked on. Next to most of the names was the word "returned." A few were marked as "resettled." But there was one followed by the word "transitioned."

Transitioned? What did that mean?

I locate another apartment building project in the drawer and find four names with the "transitioned" distinction. And another with three. None explain what the term means, but a sick feeling grows as I pull out a file with blueprints for an abandoned building that was, according to surveys, too hard to repair. The site was turned into a park. I am about to put the folder back, since an abandoned building wouldn't have a resident list, when I see a note at the bottom of the final page.

Twenty-two trespassers now at holding facility waiting transport for transition resettlement.

I think of what Atlas told me—about the people who just go missing. Were they designated for "transition resettlement" as well?

My phone beeps. Ten minutes have passed. I need to go. Every minute I spend in here gives them more time to catch me. I take pictures of the files I looked at and shove them back in their drawer. But I don't leave yet because I realize there is one last thing I need to do.

I know the address by heart. A week after my mother's funeral, I took the L and stood on the sidewalk where she had died, angry that there was no sign that she had ever been there. No skid marks, no blood.

Mrs. Anderson said my mother talked about a future project, so I move to the lone cabinet marked "Long-Term Project Research" and flip through the files.

"Ow!"

A thin red line bisects the pad of my index finger. I actually got a cut from paper?

I stick the cut in my mouth and keep searching with my other hand.

I don't see the file I'm looking for in the top drawer or in the two middle ones. My heart ticks off the passing seconds as I rummage through the bottom drawer.

There. I grab the folder and push the drawer shut. I want to open it, but that will have to wait. I need to get out of here before I get caught. So I shove the folder into my waistband as far as it can go and tug my shirt over the rest. Whatever the folder contains, it is labeled with the exact address where my mother died. I'm not leaving it here for them.

I flick off the light and put my ear to the door. There is only silence, so I head out into the hall. Instead of the elevator, I head for the stairwell. I barge my way through the door and race down the distinctive corkscrew steps. The muted sounds of voices hit me halfway down. The voices grow louder as the spiral stairs end on the second floor and I head down another set of stairs into the atrium.

The source of the voices becomes clear. An architecture tour group has arrived.

I press one of my arms against my midsection to keep the folder in place as I walk down the white-marble-and-wrought-iron staircase that is a focal point of the room. When I reach the bottom, I spot several security officers in a heated conversation near the elevators and veer toward an older couple admiring the impressive light fixtures suspended from the glass ceiling.

The security officers move closer to the bank of elevators. One of them peers into the atrium and I nod my head as if I'm part of the conversation the couple is having, even though I can't hear anything over the pounding of my heart. Finally, the guards are gone. I want to run, but I wait for the tour guide to direct everyone to follow her, and I walk with the crowd down the hall, through the revolving door, and out onto the street.

Then I get the hell out of there. I retrieve my bike and pedal as fast as I can without dislodging the folder still tucked under my clothing. When I'm finally out of the Loop, I spot a mostly empty park and stop. A woman walking her dog smiles at me, and I smile back as I head for a large play area with swings and an enclosed fort at the top of a slide. I climb the ladder, and when I'm safely hidden from view, I peel the folder from my sweaty skin and open it on my lap.

Like all the other files, it contains blueprints. Only this one has two sets. One from 1992 when the condominium building was constructed, and another from fifty years later when the structure was overhauled by the City Pride Department. I spread the second set of blueprints for something called a Unity Center in front of me and understand why my mother thought this was important.

In this version of the plans, the shimmering black-and-silver building my mother died next to has been transformed into what can only be described as a jail.

TWELVE

Unity Center.

The name evokes people coming together. But this . . .

All windows are tinted so no one can see in. The building has been soundproofed so that none of the people held in the eight-foot-by-six-foot cells on the upper floors, or in the large barred-in spaces in the lower levels marked as "transfer area," would be heard by anyone on the outside. There is also an underground garage. The plans call for a restructuring of the entrance to accommodate the "transition transportation" vehicles.

A hollow ache grows inside me.

There are still prisons in Chicago. Crime hasn't vanished completely. That would be impossible. But the news continuously reports on the historically low number of residents in those jails. So there should be no reason for something like this unless everything Atlas told me about people being taken by the Marshals and not being seen again is real.

Is this what my mother was looking for in the archives? Could this be what she wanted people to know about and why she was on that sidewalk the night she died? The folder was in the future projects drawer. If the building still exists . . .

I pull out my phone and dial Atlas.

"Has anyone heard anything about your father yet?"

"Meri? I told you I'd come find you later—"

"If the Marshals took your father, I think I might know where he's being held."

There's a beat before he asks, "What are you talking about?"

"There's a place my mother learned about. I have the archives file and I think it might be why they killed her. I don't know exactly what the building is used for, but I can go and—"

"Stay right where you are," Atlas says. "I can be at your place in twenty minutes."

"I'm not at my house," I admit.

"I told you to . . ." He takes a loud breath, then quietly asks, "Where are you?"

"A park." I scramble up to my knees and peer out over the slide. "Freedom Fields Park."

"I'll find it. Don't move until I get there." The phone goes dead before I can reply.

So I sit and wait, staring at the plans in front of me with my legs pulled tight against my chest, unable to stop myself from imagining all the things my mother must have thought when she found this file. How horrified she must have felt when she realized the job she loved was a lie, and how scared she must have been.

She had to have known there was a chance the government would learn about the things she was looking into and that if they found out they would be watching Dad and me to see if she shared what she suspected with us.

If she had only left things alone, she would be alive. She would be like Mrs. Anderson—home with her family. With me.

Anger burns hot and bright, then flickers and dies, because I understand why she couldn't live her life pretending not to know what she had learned. And maybe she loved me enough to not want me to have to live that life, either.

Was that why she created the paintings?

So I would follow them, find the Lyceum, and reveal the truth? So I could finish the work she had begun?

A childish laugh rings like a bell, reminding me where I am. My hands shake as I fold up the blueprints, shove the papers into the folder, and tuck it back under my shirt. Then I swipe away the tears that fell without my being aware of them and wait.

Finally, my phone dings.

I'M HERE. WHERE ARE YOU?

IN THE FORT.

I start to climb down but my phone dings again.

BE RIGHT THERE.

Atlas's face appears. He looks pissed and sweaty as he pulls himself into the fort, which suddenly feels really cramped. He shrugs off the backpack he's carrying, sets it to the side, and glares. "I told you to stay inside your house until you saw me again."

"Well, I didn't listen and I'm not sorry. That's how I found this." I pull the file out from under my shirt.

Quickly, I tell him about my trip to visit Mrs. Anderson and how I followed my mom's footsteps and snuck into the City Pride Department archives. A small spot on Atlas's temple starts to pulse as I talk, but he doesn't flip out, which I take as a positive sign. I slide the blueprints out of the folder and hand them to him. "Your dad could be there, right now."

Atlas frowns as he studies the page, then looks up at me. "You should have called instead of taking so many unnecessary risks. If you'd been caught at Liberty Tower—"

"But I wasn't."

"You got lucky, but . . ." He slowly reaches out and takes my hand in his. "If it helps me find my dad, I will never be able to thank you."

His strong fingers curl around mine and hold tight. Warmth floods through me. I squeeze his hand back and find that I don't want to let go.

"We'll see if that changes after I check out the building," he says. "I'll let you know what I find."

I drop Atlas's hand as the meaning of what he said hits me. "Wait," I say, scrambling to grab the folder from him. "What do you mean you'll let me know? I'm going with you."

"No," he says, yanking the folder away and shoving it into his bag. "You've taken more than enough risks, and if my dad is being held there, just hanging around on that block could be dangerous." He crouches in the tight space and heads for the ladder. "I've got this."

That's what he thinks.

He starts down the ladder and I head for the slide. When he climbs out of the fort, I'm standing at the bottom waiting for him. "I can go with you, or I can meet you there," I say firmly. "Take your pick."

He shoves his hands into his pockets and sighs. "Have you always been a pain in the ass?"

"Yes." My matter-of-fact response seems to take him off guard. "Look," I say. "I get that this is about your father, but my mother died looking for this information. You said the two of them were working together. I'd say whether you like it or not we're going to have to do the same."

He shakes his head, paces away from me, then turns back. "Okay, here's the deal. You agree to do what I tell you." He cuts me off when I start to object. "Meri, you're smart and more than capable, but you're also new to this. I've lived with it my entire life. If I tell you to do something, you have to do it. There won't be time to play twenty questions. Okay?"

"I'll try." It's not exactly what he asked for, but it's honest. "That's the best I can do."

Atlas shakes his head, but I see a hint of a smile tugging at the corners of his lips as he agrees, "Fine. We have to get moving. Just remember that you wanted to do this. Do you like to run?"

"I hate it."

Atlas turns and gives me a wide, toothy smile. "That's the best thing I've heard all day. Lock up your bike and we'll go find my dad."

My throat and side ache by the time we go three blocks and stop to wait for the light to change. Atlas, however, has barely broken a sweat. The light turns, and Atlas jogs across the crosswalk with me scrambling to catch up.

"Do you plan on us running all the way?" I gasp. Because the building is across town and maybe Atlas can make it on foot, but there is no way I'll be able to walk by then. Maybe that's his plan to ditch me?

"Just to the next block." He glances at his watch and picks up the pace. "Come on, we have to hurry."

Atlas mercifully slows down after we cross the next street. He reaches into his bag and pulls out a red-and-orange-colored Chicago Transit Card. "You're going to need this."

"I have my own," I say, digging into my back pocket for one of the few things I always have with me. I mean, I live in Chicago.

"Personal cards are never to be used for Steward business. Not unless you want them to track all your movements back to you."

I stare at the piece of plastic in my hand. I hadn't considered that anyone could use it to monitor me. "They couldn't possibly care where I take the bus or the L. I'm just a normal high school student."

"You are definitely not normal. And they'll care when you're suddenly going to locations you've never visited before. They've designed programs to flag that kind of thing. Someone is always watching. Someone is always looking for you. You're on the train, Meri, and there's no turning back." His eyes are fierce. They shift from side to side, scanning everyone as we duck through the wide silver archway doors that I've passed through hundreds of times before and enter the L station. "Always be on your guard. You have to remember that you are seeing a world they don't want you to see. That makes you dangerous."

The idea that I could be dangerous is laughable. Only, Atlas isn't laughing as he runs his card through the gateway. The red light darkens and the one beside it shines green. He passes through the turnstile, then waits for me before heading toward the stairs that lead up to the tracks. "The Marshals are out there to protect the government's version of the world—crafted by their words and their truths. They'll destroy anything that contradicts their version. That's why they went after your mom and my dad. If they realize you're questioning them, they'll be after you. So you can't take any more risks. If they recognize you, you'll never be safe again and nei-ther will your dad."

My head whips around to stare at Atlas. "My father doesn't know anything."

"They'll never believe he didn't know what his wife and daugh-ter were doing. They'll take him. Just like they took my father."

My mind clouds gray. I'm here because I wanted answers. I never intended to put my father in danger.

"You just need to be careful and he'll be fine." Atlas gently places his hand on my shoulder. I focus on its steadiness and warmth to help push away the budding panic.

"How do you live with it?" I ask, and look up into his dark, clear eyes. "Knowing what could happen if you do something wrong?"

"I've lived in the Lyceum my whole life. My friends and family are all used to being hunted. It doesn't make me any less scared, but in some ways it makes it easier. At least, I thought it did until this week."

The L approaches. The line of shiny silver train cars screeches to a stop. I stay close to Atlas's side as we snake through the exiting passengers and shove our way through the connected doors into the last car.

Atlas wedges himself between a guy in a blue-and-white-striped jersey and another in a T-shirt, who are busy chatting with their friends.

The doors swish closed. We lurch forward, and I grab the back of one of the seats as the train picks up speed. I glance at Atlas, who is slowly looking around the car—no longer interested in talking. He's surrounded by people, but to anyone who looked closely, it would seem that he's alone.

His jaw is clenched. His weight is balanced on the front of his feet, making him ready to bolt at any moment. And his eyes—they are dark and intense and searching as they shift from person to person until they finally fall on me. "Next stop."

I follow him onto the platform and onto the next train. This one isn't as crowded, but Atlas stops me when I start to slide into one of the orange plastic train seats.

I stay standing and grab one of the silver poles as Atlas leans toward me and quietly says, "When you sit, you relax. When you relax, you let down your guard. Keep standing. Keep watching. Be prepared to take action."

"Watching for what?" I ask, looking around the train at the people riding with us.

"People watching you." He points to one of the advertising posters that run along the top of both sides of the car, then nods to a man at the end of the train who, every couple of seconds, looks up from his phone and studies the remaining passengers.

SEE SOMETHING UNUSUAL? WE WANT TO HEAR ABOUT IT. HELP KEEP CHICAGO STRONG AND SAFE.

"When we get off at the next stop, follow my lead. We're going to look for anything that will confirm what's in that file. If we do, we'll figure out our next steps from there."

Atlas reaches for my hand, and I take his in mine as we exit the train and walk slowly toward the block that I see every night in my dreams. I try to move faster, but Atlas tugs me back. "People see what they want to see as long as you don't give them any reason to think different. If we look like we're out on a date, people will assume that's the case. No one will think we're searching for things that we're not supposed to know about."

I force myself to smile and give one-word answers to the inane questions Atlas asks to make it look like we're a couple. He isn't buying my acting skills. "If this is how you think a date is supposed to go, Meri, I can see why you're on your own."

"Some of us have more important things to think about," I shoot back. "You should understand that."

"I do, but that doesn't mean I don't date." I can feel his eyes on me, so I force myself to keep looking toward the intersection ahead. "Should I take your silence to mean you're jealous?"

"You wish."

"You could be right," he says so quietly I can hardly make out the words. "It's hard to tell."

"What's that supposed to mean?" I ask.

"That's a conversation for another time," he says, grabbing my hand as we approach the building from the file. "Right now we're going to pretend to fight. That should come easy for you."

He grins and I stifle the urge to stick out my tongue.

"We're almost there. I promise the walk will be totally worth it." Atlas's voice is raised loud enough for anyone nearby to hear. "Best tacos in Chicago."

We wait for the light to turn, cross the intersection, and step onto the sidewalk where my mother lost her life. The dream replays in my head. The headlights. Her scream. Blood running on the concrete beneath my feet.

"Meri," Atlas whispers in my ear. "You okay?"

I shake off the dream and focus on why we're here. "I don't see your taco place."

He looks around. "I know this is the street."

I roll my eyes. "You always do this. Why is it you never know where we're going?" I demand.

"Just help me look, okay?" He lowers his voice again. "You take that side. I'll check this one. If you find any evidence of this being what the plans say, come find me." He walks up and down the sidewalk, looking at the black-and-silver building. I take the other side, searching for any signs of the terrible things we suspect are happening inside. The front door is locked. The small bronze plaque that reads "Unity Center West" is smudged with dirt and doesn't appear to have been cleaned in a while. The tinted windows make it impossible to see inside.

I head down the sidewalk to the end of the building and follow the alley to the entrance for the underground garage. It, too, is locked tight. If this is Unity Center West, could there be an East? Or maybe more? If so . . .

"Need help, miss?"

I stop cold and force myself to smile at the woman who steps into the alley. She has a bag of groceries in her hand and an earnest expression on her brightly made-up face.

"I'm trying to help my friend find someone," I say. She clearly lives nearby. Maybe she knows something that can help, since nothing about the building appears useful. "He used to work in this building. I was hoping someone he worked with might know where he went."

The woman's smile fades. "Oh, I'm sorry, dear. I haven't seen anyone go into this building in over a month. They must have moved to a new location. Thank goodness. They always had delivery trucks coming and going in the middle of the night. The trucks woke my husband, and he got me up to complain that they weren't obeying the curfew." She laughs.

Disappointment cuts deep. The trucks coming and going during the curfew time—when no one else would be driving on the streets—reinforce what the plans made us think this place was used for. But if the trucks are gone, chances are the building is no longer being used for that purpose, if at all. "Did you know anyone who worked here who might know where this company moved to?"

She blinks. "Not really. There were always men with badges coming and going. I figured that's why they were allowed to break curfew without getting in trouble. Maybe if you asked at the police station?" She shrugs and gives me a little wave. "I have to get my ice cream in the freezer. Tell your friend I hope he finds whoever he's looking for." With that she shuffles to a gate next to an apartment complex and disappears inside.

I check the entrance to the parking garage anyway, but it's locked up tight.

"It's empty," I tell Atlas when I meet him back by the front entrance.

"I know." There's a stark hollowness in his eyes that steals my breath. "The guy in the coffee shop said his business dropped off weeks ago. No one has been around since."

Laughter from the patio of the coffee shop makes the stab of defeat dig deeper. Others are happy, carefree, and oblivious—while Atlas is crushed by loss and all that he knows.

"I'm sorry," I say. "But there could be other places like this. And now that we know what the government is calling them, maybe—"

"Walk."

"But, Atlas. I think that we—"

"There's a Marshal coming toward us. We have to start walking. Now." He puts his arm around my shoulder and leads me out of the doorway. "Don't look."

Too late. I've already glanced down the sidewalk. There's a girl in a blue cap, a couple of twentysomething guys in matching green sports shirts, and one lone guy in khaki pants and a blue button-down shirt striding purposefully behind them. He has dark straight hair and thick eyebrows that arch above narrow-framed sunglasses, which suddenly seem to be looking right at me.

"This way."

We move toward the crosswalk and stop at the curb to wait as cars zoom past. Every second that passes, the guy in the sunglasses is getting closer. The guys in the matching shirts join us on the curb, and Atlas leans over to whisper in my ear, "Don't move when the light changes." He shifts his own backpack so that it is hanging from one arm, unzips it, and murmurs, "But be ready to run."

The back of my neck prickles as the light turns and the pedestrian Walk sign appears.

"Hey, I think we might be on the wrong block," Atlas says in a loud voice. He pulls me to the side and takes out his phone to make it seem like he's looking up directions. I shift the weight on my feet as the lanky girl in jeans and a blue ball cap hurries past us. The sign changes to Don't Walk as the guy with the narrow sunglasses reaches the curb.

I hold my breath. My muscles clench as I wait for Atlas's signal to bolt—for the person Atlas marked as a Marshal to charge at us. Instead, the man ignores the electronic sign by stepping onto the crosswalk and hurrying to the other side.

"We're good," Atlas says quietly. "He's after someone else."

"How are you so sure he's a Marshal instead of just some guy?" I ask.

"The way he's moving and the shoes."

"The shoes?" Now that I'm paying attention, I can see the smooth steps of the man are getting faster. He passes a couple pushing a stroller and is veering around the guys with the green shirts. "If he really is a Marshal, then who is he following?"

"He is a Marshal, and I'm pretty sure he's following that girl—there." He points to the lanky girl in the blue baseball hat, who has stepped off the sidewalk and is currently weaving between moving cars as she crosses outside the crosswalk to the opposite side of the street.

Sure enough. The guy with the sunglasses leaves the sidewalk and with even, measured steps follows the same route as the woman, who is moving north down the sidewalk, never pausing to look behind her.

"So what do we do?" I ask.

"What do you mean what do we do? We're going to go back to the park, retrieve your bike, and get you home."

"But what about her?" The girl in the blue hat disappears around the corner. The minute she's out of sight the Marshal pulls out his phone. He punches something on the screen, slides it back into his pocket, and quickens to a jog. "You're not going to just let him catch her, are you?"

"She's not a Steward."

"So what? That means it's fine for her to just . . . disappear?" To end up like his dad or my mom? To have her family told a lie about how she vanished or why she died? "You want me to live with knowing that I saw something bad about to happen and I did nothing to stop it?"

Yeah, I don't think so.

"Look, Meri, we have to—"

I don't wait to hear whatever Atlas thinks we have to do. Instead, I look both ways at the cars coming down the road and bolt across the street.

THIRTEEN

Cars honk.

Tires squeal.

"Meri! What the hell?" I reach the other side and ignore the blinking Don't Walk sign as I race across the next intersection. I'm not sure if I will be fast enough to find the girl, but I'm determined to try.

I dart around a couple stopping to admire something in a window display and stumble as Atlas appears, breathing hard beside me.

"What do you think you're doing?" he pants. "Are you trying to get caught?"

"No," I yell, jogging around a man shoving his chair back from an outdoor café table. "I'm trying to stop anyone else from feeling like we do."

"What are you going to do if you catch up to them? Ask the guy to dance? If you interfere with whatever it is he's doing, he's going to see you as a threat."

"I don't know what I'm going to do." I haven't really thought that far ahead. I have to find the girl first.

I keep my eyes forward and just keep jogging.

"Great," Atlas snaps. "But if you really mean to do this we're going to have to go a hell of a lot faster."

When Atlas says faster, he means faster.

A guy walking a German shepherd shoots us dirty looks as Atlas streaks by the dog and down the concrete sidewalk, past the boutiques and ice-cream shop and the weekend window-shoppers. He rounds the corner, and it's all I can do to keep up with his long strides as he cruises down the mostly residential block.

"I don't see them," I shout, squinting into the distance. "Do you?"

"Our scary friend just turned north at the far end of this block." He darts to the other side of the street and I jump off the curb and follow. "We'll take the alley and do our best to catch up. Let's just hope she's quicker than you."

Okay, the insult did the trick.

I ignore the fire building in my chest, dodge a skateboarding kid, and keep pace right behind Atlas. If Atlas is right about the Marshal and the girl, what we do next could save someone like me from losing a person they love.

Our footsteps slap against pavement.

Atlas shifts the bag on his shoulder before it can slide off and somehow manages to not slow down.

My chest is about to burst. My legs burn.

Atlas glances back, his forehead glazed with sweat, and gives me an approving half grin for mostly keeping up. That smile fuels me to keep going until the alley dumps us out onto the next sidewalk.

"At the end of the block." Atlas points. "See her?"

She's easy to spot because other than Atlas and me, there's no one on this street filled with three-story town houses or apartment buildings.

A dog barks somewhere nearby. The girl glances at us, then heads in the opposite direction from where we stand. Her back is to us, so there is no chance to signal to her that something is wrong.

"Where's the guy?" I say between pants, but see the answer to my own question come into view at the corner about twenty steps behind the girl. The guy with the sunglasses pauses and looks down at the phone in his hand.

"They'll make their move soon."

"They?"

Atlas nods. "This block is quiet. Almost no one's around. Perfect time for a grab. If we're going to stop them, it has to be now. You ready?"

No. But I started this. So I guess I have to be.

Atlas pulls his backpack off his shoulder, lofts it in the air, and yells, "Well, if you want this bag back, you're going to have to catch me."

And off he goes. He barrels down the sidewalk while letting out another shout. I urge my legs to get moving again as sunglasses guy turns to look in our direction. He steps to the side to let Atlas pass. When he does, I glance down at the Marshal's shoes. They are black—not boots, but not quite high-tops, with thick soles and buckled straps. A cross between a running shoe and something worn in military movies.

"Come on," Atlas shouts as he increases the distance between himself and the man. "You can do better than that!"

I'm trying, but I'm not sure I can. Every part of my body is quivering with fatigue. But this isn't the time to give up. I pump my arms and legs and am just closing in on the Marshal when a sedan zooms around the corner behind me and zips down the street. The man in front of me starts to run as the shiny black-and-silver car screeches to a halt just in front of where the girl in the blue hat is walking. The back passenger door of the car swings open and the girl spins.

Even from a distance I can see the fear on her face as a big man in a gray suit jumps out of the car and starts toward her. The Marshal in sunglasses is closing in as Atlas reaches into his bag, pulls out a handful of papers, and sends them flying in the man's face.

Sunglasses Marshal grabs at the papers, as if trying to pluck as many of them out of the air as he can. The gray-suit dude turns to reach for one of the pages sailing past his face and never sees Atlas spin and kick the man square in the chest.

The man in gray flies back into the open car door. He hits metal and crashes to the ground. Papers flutter in the air around him. The gray-suited Marshal grabs one that floats against his face, crumples it, and immediately climbs to his feet—feet encased in the exact same military-style running boots as the man who had been following the girl.

Sunglasses Guy slows and reaches behind him, under his shirt. When he pulls his hand back out, I see the sunlight glinting off the dark metal of what can only be a gun.

"Watch out!" The warning I choke out is barely more than a gasp of air.

A third man jumps out of the driver's side of the car and races toward the blue-baseball-cap girl, who is running toward the end of the street. Atlas kicks and blocks as he fights with the man in the suit. He ducks under a fist and isn't paying attention to the Marshal with the sunglasses. But I am, and that one is lifting the gun and taking aim.

I push myself to run faster, even though I know I will never reach the man in time. I'm still half a block away.

Too far back.

Too slow.

I yell out another warning, still not strong, but loud enough for the Marshal with the gun to hear and glance in my direction for just a fraction of a second. Thankfully, that's all Atlas needs. Atlas grabs the guy in the suit, locks his arm tight around the suit man's neck, and spins so that he is now standing behind the Marshal in the suit when the shot cracks across the air.

The world stops.

No one moves.

I can't breathe.

Then it feels as if everything speeds up. Atlas lets go of the Marshal in the suit. The man takes two staggering steps forward. His eyes go wide. The gray suit jacket flaps open. Blood blooms bright like a rose against the white of the shirt beneath and grows larger with every beat of my heart, and suddenly all of this is far too real.

The words.

The Stewards.

The Marshals.

The world hidden in plain view that I have known nothing about but which has surrounded me all along.

In my head I knew my mother had been killed, but I didn't really understand.

I knew running after the girl could be dangerous, but the reality of the danger was just verified by that single shot.

The injured Marshal falls to his knees, then slowly pitches face-first onto the pavement. The man in sunglasses glances down at the one he shot, then points the weapon at Atlas, who no longer has a living shield. The Marshal smirks. His arm straightens as I cross the last of the distance between us and half leap, half stumble into the man's side, sending him pitching over with me right on top of him.

"Get off!" The Marshal pushes up from the ground, and I am sent rolling to the side. My knee cracks against concrete. My elbow skids over the hard, rough ground. Pain sings down my leg and up my arm and I grit my teeth and ignore it all as I shove myself to my feet.

Something cracks and snaps beneath my shoe—the man's sunglasses are toast.

"Watch out!"

I turn to see the Marshal I just tackled now on his knees, pointing the gun directly at me.

A scream builds in my throat as Atlas's foot connects with the man's hand. I flinch when the gunshot cracks like thunder and the weapon goes flying.

I could have died.

Atlas saved me.

Our eyes meet for a split second.

Then the girl screams. The sound of her voice scraping the air acts like a sharp slap of a hand against my face—snapping me out of the shock and back into the moment. The girl bucks against the driver. He has her gripped tight in his arms as he drags her toward the open back-seat door of the car.

"Here!" Atlas tosses me a thick black book. I fumble but catch it, then dart forward. I skid on the loose pages scattered over the pavement and kick the large man as hard as I can in the shin. It's not the balanced, powerful kick Atlas used to save me, but it distracts him long enough for me to swing the book and crack it against the side of the man's face. The Marshal yelps, and his grip loosens enough for the girl to wriggle free. She stumbles forward, and I grab her arms to help her keep her balance. Someone from above yells, "What the hell is going on down there? I've called the cops."

Any cops that show up would be on the Marshals' side.

"Both of you, get out of here!" Atlas shouts. He ducks, throws his backpack into the face of the man with the gun. The Marshal stumbles. Atlas spins and rams his foot into the man's gut, sending him flying backward into the street as another black-and-silver car comes roaring toward us.

The Marshal who held the girl lunges toward me. I swing with the book again and connect with his shoulder as the girl lands a kick to his pelvis.

"Go! Now!" Atlas yells.

The new car screeches to a stop behind the first.

"I'm right behind you." He kicks the Marshal staggering to regain his footing and sends him back against the rear tire of the first car. Atlas then ducks under the fist of the Marshal I kicked, who has started to shout for someone to call for more assistance. "Go!"

The doors of the second car fly open and four new men in suits climb out. I don't want to leave Atlas. I got him into this, but there is very little I can do to help. I don't know how to fight—not against men who have guns and are willing to kill. And there's the girl to think about. She's the reason I insisted we come here. Now I have to get her to safety. If Atlas says he is going to follow, I have to believe he will.

I grab the girl's hand and pull her along with me as I run. Her footsteps echo in unison with mine. She asks me where we're going, but I don't answer. I just keep moving.

Fear propels me. Fear for the girl. Fear of the Marshals and what they might be doing to Atlas. We round the corner of the sidewalk and race down the block, the book I used to defend myself heavy in my hand. Shouted voices call for someone to follow and the sound of footfalls behind me urge my feet to move faster.

"Cross here!" Atlas barks from somewhere behind me and the girl, and my legs almost buckle with relief. But I keep moving, not looking back, and follow his orders.

The girl changes course with me. We bolt across the residential street and down the sidewalk past a father helping his son navigate their front walk on his training-wheeled red bike. Then by a woman with two fluffy black-and-white dogs and the people standing on their front porches watching us with curious eyes. At least some of them must have heard the shots and the squealing tires. If the Marshals ask, these people will certainly tell them which direction we ran in. They wouldn't have any reason to keep that information to themselves. After all, we're the ones causing a disturbance. As far as they can tell, we're the bad guys.

"One of them is coming," Atlas yells. He's closer now. I can hear him panting. His footsteps keep time on the cement sidewalk with ours. "Cut across the yard. Go around the next corner and head to the end of the block."

My sides ache. Sweat drips down my nose and my back. I grip the book harder as the girl and I cut across the last lawn and head for the next sidewalk. Atlas's footsteps crunch the grass behind me. Then suddenly the sound is gone. Fear spikes. I glance over my shoulder and spot Atlas with his back against the white three-story building we just ran past. I start to slow, then let out a yelp when a blond-haired Marshal rounds the corner. He smiles when he spots me. The smile is predatory as he reaches into his pocket. I hold the book up like a shield and that's when Atlas leaps forward. His hand knifes into the Marshal's throat. It is followed by his foot sweeping the Marshal's legs out from under him. Atlas waves for me to keep going as the Marshal hits the ground with a thud. I turn as Atlas's foot connects with the Marshal again.

"Where are we going?" the girl pants next to me as we dodge a group of boys on scooters. "Do you know?"

No, and I'm not going to be able to run like this much longer. So I give the only answer I can. "We're going wherever they aren't."

"Sounds right to me," the girl answers. I can tell by the way she is breathing that she's struggling, too. We have to hide. But there are too many people who have seen us—all will tell the Marshals what direction we went.

"Toss me the book!" Atlas's voice calls over my shoulder.

I slow a step as I turn and pitch it to him. My throw sucks, but Atlas manages to grab it without losing speed. "Turn right down the next street. Go through the third door on that side," he calls, reaching for his bag. "Red sign. Yellow flower. A Conductor owns the store. We have to move fast before the rest of them turn up. They can't be that far back."

The idea that we have somewhere safe to hide pushes me to keep moving. We round the corner and this time emerge on a street filled with coffee shops and boutiques and other businesses. The sidewalks are filled with people looking to enjoy the warm weekend evening, and I understand why Atlas told me to pass him the book.

I'd stand out like a neon sign carrying it around. I skirt by couples and kids, counting the doors I pass. Finally, I get to door number three and spot the rust-colored sign for a place called Sunny Side Up. It has a large sunflower painted on the wall next to the entrance.

The door dings as I yank it open. Arctic air blasts toward me as I step into a colorful boutique filled with a half dozen or so people admiring hand-painted bags, scarves, funky T-shirts and hats. Atlas and the girl slip in behind me, making the bell ding several times more before the door closes. Two women admiring purses glance over, and I realize what we must look like. Sweaty and nervous and in my case covered in scrapes and bruises. I glance back at the door, waiting for the Marshals to burst through, while Atlas makes a bee-line for the counter.

"Sorry I'm late." He rolls up one sleeve and shifts so that the severe, black-haired woman managing the cash register can see his tattoo.

Her eyes dart to the door and she gives an almost imperceptible nod before she curls her lips into a frown. "Boxes are in the back. The three of you had better work fast or I'll dock your pay."

Atlas jerks his head toward the other end of the store. The girl with the hat and I follow him around several display tables filled with a treasure trove of brightly colored materials and shining jewelry to the back, where he pulls open a narrow door marked "Employees Only." The three of us duck through, and when the door clicks behind us, I feel a small kernel of relief.

"Now what? Do we wait here for the Marshals to give up?"

"No," Atlas says, crossing to the back of the room. "After what just happened, I doubt the Marshals will leave the area anytime soon. The best option is for us to get out of this neighborhood."

I look around the cramped storage area, then back at him. "And I guess you know a way we can do that?"

He gives me the cocky grin I've come to count on. "Of course I do." He points to a black, circular staircase that spirals up through the floor above and says, "It's time to climb."

My legs are like rubber. Each footstep on the iron stairs rings loud no matter how hard I try to stay quiet. I make my way up to the next story—into a small living room filled with comfortably worn furniture and a vase of flowers that look so perfect in color and bloom I'm guessing they aren't real. The girl with the hat appears on the steps behind me and leans on the back of a deep green armchair, looking as if she is about to collapse.

But Atlas isn't going to let that happen yet. He makes a beeline for the window, throws it open, climbs out, and after several long seconds pops his head back in. "Let's go. Keep low when you reach the roof. Move."

I crawl through the window into the warmth of the early-summer air and keep moving upward. There's no way I'm letting the Marshals win today. They aren't getting anyone else. Not if I can help it.

There are a bunch of chairs and empty bottles on the roof, which tells me we aren't the only ones who have come up here. But we're the only ones who have been up here recently because ours are the only footprints I can see.

"Stay down and go over the rooftops to the one on the end. Most of them you can step between. For the last one we'll have to jump."

Jump?

I trip more than once as we move from rooftop to rooftop, most separated by only a foot or two. The last is several feet lower and four or so feet away from the building we are standing on now.

I glance over the edge and my stomach tilts.

The sound of sirens floats on the breeze and is getting closer.

"You can do this," Atlas says with conviction.

Not long ago he was telling me to stay in my house and not to go anywhere. Now he believes I can leap tall buildings with a single bound.

"I know," I tell him as I move several steps back and take a deep breath. "Let's do this."

Before doubt can take hold, I start to run. Atlas matches my steps on one side. The girl with the blue hat is a step behind on the other. Two steps from the edge of the building, I launch myself into the air. My heart stops. Inside my head, I am screaming at the nothingness of several stories beneath me. Then my feet hit the next roof with room to spare. The other two land right beside me.

I did it.

The Marshals were chasing us. I saw someone die. We could still be found, but that doesn't stop the pride I feel at getting this far.

"You're going to take that fire escape to the alley," Atlas says, leading us to the back corner of the structure we're standing on. "There's a dumpster you can hide behind until I get there."

"What are you going to do?" I ask.

"I'm going to erase any sign that we've been here."

"Do all Stewards know about that place? The one with the sunflower?" I ask as the girl in the blue hat starts down the iron fire escape steps. "Did my mom?"

"Each member is given information on the escape routes closest to their area of operation. We call them switching stations," he answers. "They were created for just this reason, and people with my job—we're drilled until we know them all. We have to move." He turns, and I head down the steps.

When I reach the landing next to the girl, I release the ladder and cringe as it whines and scrapes before it comes to a stop. Hand over hand, foot over foot, I climb down the ladder and drop the last few feet to the pavement behind a dumpster, that by the smell of rotting food, needs to be emptied. I crouch down and wait for the blue hat girl to join me. My knee throbs and my elbow . . . I gingerly touch the scrape and wince.

"I guess I should say thanks," the girl whispers, coming to kneel on the concrete next to me. She removes her hat, shakes out her long hair, then swipes at a line of blood at the corner of her mouth with a frown. "I'm not sure what all that was about or what those men want, but it can't be good."

"You don't have any idea why you were being followed or why the Marshals were after you?" I ask, willing Atlas to get down here so we can clear out.

The girl shoves her dark hair back under the hat, then shakes her head and peers around the dumpster. "Those guys must have thought I was someone else. Just a case of mistaken identity."

The girl is probably only a year or two older than me, with wide-set eyes; sharp, tanned cheekbones; and golden highlights streaking through her brown hair. Add to that the fact she is almost six feet tall and the idea that she could be mistaken for someone else is laughable.

Except nothing about this is funny.

I listen for the sound of footsteps in the alley or from the rooftops above. When I don't hear any, I say, "At first we thought the Marshal with the gun and the sunglasses was coming after us, but he was following you. And I'm pretty sure you must know that or you would've asked who or what the Marshals are."

She slowly turns her darkly lined brown eyes toward me. "And who are you? How do you know who the Marshals are? Why did you think one might have been after you and your friend?"

"I'm no one," I say, stretching my legs as much as I can so I'm ready to run when Atlas gets down here.

"That's not true." She cocks her head to the side. "You guys are Stewards? Right?"

I go still. According to Atlas, the Stewards are a secret from everyone except the Marshals and the government officials who directed their forces to track them down. And yet this girl knows their name.

"The tattoo," she explains, snapping the stretch of silence. "The flame. The book. The guy you're with showed the tattoo to the woman behind the counter in the store. That's why she helped us, which means she's a Steward, too. My friends and I have heard rumors for years. We even tried to get word to them to see if they would want to join forces, but it was like trying to find a ghost. We finally gave up because there didn't seem to be a point. The Stewards have only been interested in standing on the sidelines instead of doing anything to help change things. I'm surprised the two of you aren't ducking and covering."

"I never said we were Stewards. . . ."

"No, you didn't. But we both know you are and that I'm not on my way to one of their holding pens because of you." She shifts her position behind the dumpster and says, "I owe you. The friends I work with owe you, too."

Metal rattles overhead. I look up as Atlas hops from the escape ladder to the ground. He shoves the ladder upward, and I flinch as it shrieks back into place. We stay silent for several long seconds as we listen to the sounds of the city around us. A car honks. Somewhere there is laughter.

Finally, Atlas says, "The Marshals seem to be focusing their search on the shops of the street where we disappeared. But that won't last much longer. I'm going to check the alley and then we'll move out."

Before either of us can ask any questions, Atlas squeezes around the dumpster and heads into the alley.

"Here." The girl takes off her hat and holds it out to me. When I hesitate she shoves it into my hands and lets out a frustrated huff. "Take it."

Since I'm not sure how to reject the gift, I close my fingers around the brim. "Thanks?"

She lets out a sharp laugh, touches the side of her mouth where blood is starting to bloom again, and grimaces. "If you ever need help, or want to do more than just hang around on the sidelines, look in the lining of the hat. Tell whoever you reach that Stef gave it to you. They'll understand. There aren't many of us left anymore, but we're doing what we can."

"We're good," Atlas whispers from the other side of the dumpster.

I slide between the dumpster and the brick wall. Stef follows.

"They're looking for three of us," Stef says matter-of-factly. "It'll be better if I go on my own from here." She turns back to me. "I hope we meet again sometime." And with that she starts running. In a second, Stef is gone from view.

I jam the hat on my head and start jogging on tired legs with Atlas to the edge of the alley, then walk to the park across the street and out of the neighborhood. We don't say anything when we get on the bus and head in the direction of my house. My right knee is stiff. My feet ache, and my heart is pounding like I'm still running for my life. Did my mother ever feel like this? If so, how could I have not seen?

I glance at Atlas several times, trying to figure out what he's thinking as we ride. He's answering messages on his phone, but I'm not at a good angle to see what they are about. From his expression, I'd guess they aren't anything good.

When the bus reaches our stop and we climb off and onto the curb, I finally say the words I've been thinking since we reached the back room of that store with the sunflower sign. "Thank you."

Atlas gives me a long stare and says nothing. He's not going to make it easy, so I try to say the rest as fast as I can. "I should have listened to you. I didn't know what I was getting us into by trying to help that girl. I knew it was dangerous, but I didn't understand. Not until I faced it myself."

I turn and look toward the Loop—at the buildings shining silver and rose and gold against the dimming sky. "I've always trusted that everything the government did was to make us happy and safe. When you showed me the truth, I didn't want it to be real. But it is. I know it is. And knowing what I know, I couldn't just stand by and let someone else get hurt. I'm glad Stef is safe, but I shouldn't have forced you into putting yourself in danger to help her." The crack of the Marshal's gun echoes in my mind and I shiver. "That wasn't my choice to make."

Atlas sighs. "You didn't force me into anything."

"You don't have to try and make me feel better. You said—"

"I know what I said." He shifts his backpack on his shoulder and starts walking. I fall in step next to him. "And I meant it. I would have walked away from her and the Marshal had you not insisted on going off on your crusade. But I'm glad we did it."

"Why?"

"Because now I don't have to wonder whether that girl is dead

216

and whether I could have saved her."

Shades of regret and smudges of frustration shadow Atlas's face. It makes me wonder how many others Atlas has watched walk away oblivious to the Marshals he knew were on their heels.

"You could have been killed." My heart goes still at the thought. "They had guns."

"Did you think they'd be carrying knitting needles?"

"No. I've just never seen one, except in movies." No one I know of has, either.

There used to be a time when gun deaths in the country totaled in the tens of thousands every year. People didn't know how to make it stop. After years of debate, Congress changed the laws that governed firearm ammunition. Every bullet from a manufacturer had to be stamped with a unique identification number and registered each time it changed hands. Bullets used in a crime could then be tracked back to the person who last registered them and that person charged as an accessory.

After a few years of arrests, most people were no longer interested in the risks associated with owning a gun. And those who kept their firearms took more care with how they used their guns and stored their ammunition. Between the Ammunition Registration Act and the City Pride Program, crime plummeted in Chicago. Now the city was one of the least likely places to hear a gunshot. Any gun-related death was a huge story.

At least, that's what I'd been told to believe. Now I have to wonder if that is true or if there is another explanation for why Marshals and police officers have guns and few others do.

As we walk down the block, Atlas explains, "The Marshals can get away with firing their weapons as long as they do it in places where few people see. It's why the Stewards try to stick to busy streets and methods of transportation where we're rarely alone. The more witnesses, the less chance the Marshals or the government has of covering up a shooting. Panic is something they want to avoid."

I picture the Marshal swinging the gun toward Atlas and the way Atlas fought him. He moved so fast. "How did you learn to fight like that? I thought the Stewards were all about books."

"Just because people like to read doesn't mean we can't fight. All Stewards who spend time on the street are trained to handle themselves," Atlas explains. "More than a few of us are hoping someday our training will be good for more than running from the Marshals. I can teach you what I know after the lockdown. The way you clocked that Marshal tells me you'll be . . . What's wrong?" he asks as he realizes I have stopped walking.

"What?" he repeats as I stare at him.

"What do you mean, 'after the lockdown'?"

"Well, I can't teach you while I'm in the Lyceum and you're up here."

"You're going to go through with the lockdown after everything we learned about the Unity Centers? What about your dad?"

"My dad would want me to do what's necessary for the Stewards—"

"Your dad would want you to do what you think is right."

"And you think you know what that is?" Atlas shakes his head and turns into the alley that leads to my house. I have to race to keep up with his long strides. "You've been a part of this world for a handful of days. I've been living it my entire life. The Stewards have lasted longer than anyone else who knows the truth. There's a reason for that. If you bothered to read the section on World War Two you'd know that."

"I did read it," I shoot back. "I know all the groups that tried to get people out of Germany or were actively pushing back against the government were hunted down."

"I rest my case," Atlas says as we reach the gate that leads to my backyard. "Look, I appreciate everything you did today. For me and for my dad." He reaches out and brushes a lock of hair off my face. "You're not what I thought you were going to be when I sent you your ticket."

"What did you think I was going to be?"

"Uncomplicated." He looks down at me with an expression that is impossible to read.

"I'll take that as a compliment?" My throat is dry, so the words sound low and uncertain.

"I meant it as one. You're unexpected, Meri." Atlas gives me a smile that spreads slowly from his lips up to his eyes, and my stomach flips.

Rose's ringtone sings in the air, killing the moment.

"Sorry," I say, pulling my phone out of my pocket. "I have to answer this." If I don't, Rose will just keep calling until I do.

Giving Atlas an apologetic smile, I put the phone to my ear and barely have the chance to say hello before I hear Rose say, "Meri! It's Isaac. He's gone."

FOURTEEN

Gone? "What do you mean Isaac is gone?"

"He answered a call just after Mom and I got home and said he had to meet a friend for just a few minutes. He was late. Mom wasn't worried because you know how Isaac is, but then . . ."

"What?"

"One of our neighbors brought us his phone. She found it under a bush at the corner. Mom and Dad are at the police station now, and I'm here in case he comes back or someone calls, but I feel like I should be doing something and I don't know what to do." In all the years I've known Rose, she's never sounded panicked. She does now.

"I'll be right there." My hands are cold and shaking as I shove the phone into my pocket and look at Atlas. "My friend's brother is missing. I have to go."

Atlas assures me he'll have my bike retrieved from the park so I don't have to worry about it, but my bicycle is the last thing on my mind as I hurry through my backyard to the house.

A baseball game is playing on the living room television. Dad is sleeping on the couch. I lean forward to shake him awake when I spot the empty glass on the coffee table next to him. One sniff of the dregs inside the cup tells me what I need to know—there's no point in trying to talk to my father tonight or asking him to help look for Isaac. Even if I could wake him up, he shouldn't be driving.

I want to scream that I need him. That Mom needed both of us and we failed her and now I may have failed Isaac. Instead, I leave a note on the message tablet about sleeping over at Rose's house and head upstairs to get my things.

I wash off the dirt and sweat and bandage the scrapes I got facing the Marshals. Then I pull the bag of books out from under the bed and cram a change of clothes, my tablet, and stuff to stay overnight inside. With one last look at my father's flushed face, I shrug the heavy bag onto my shoulder and go out the back door.

Every snap of a twig makes me jump. The shadows on the sidewalk have me looking over my shoulder to make sure no one is following as I hurry down the familiar streets. Once, I swear someone is there, but when I pause I see and hear no one. So I keep walking.

I pass the sidewalk where Rose and I learned to ride our bikes while Isaac teased us by zooming circles around us on his own. I can see Isaac grinning from deep in the branches of the oak tree after scaring us when we walked by. Panic builds with each step even as I think about the security ID and the archives room I accessed with that card. As I walk, I pray that Isaac will be at his house when I get there.

Please don't let this be because of me.

Please don't let this be because of me.

This can't be because of me.

When Rose opens the door, the hope that this will all be over is shattered. The pain in her eyes punches into my chest and steals my breath. I do the only thing I can. I throw my arms around her and hold tight.

Her tears shatter me. Each shudder. Each strangled attempt to rein in the fear. I want to cry with her, but I can't. The weight of the ID I stole from Isaac is heavy in my pocket and my heart.

"Sorry," Rose says, pulling away. She closes the condo door, swipes the tears from her face, and takes several deep breaths. When she turns to face me again, she has regained a large measure of her trademark steely control. "I promised myself I wouldn't lose it. We don't actually know anything. Isaac could be at a friend's house. He could have just dropped his phone and didn't notice. It's just . . ."

"You're scared."

She nods and paces across the snowy-white living room carpet. "It's stupid, right? It's not like Isaac is the most responsible person around. He used to go off on his own all the time."

Before the divorce no one ever knew where Isaac was. Since his dad moved out, he's been better.

"But he has work tomorrow and he wouldn't put that in jeopardy," Rose continues. "The police say he hasn't been gone long enough to consider him missing and that we shouldn't worry."

"Did he say anything before he left?" I ask. "Anything that might give you an idea of where he went?"

"I wasn't paying attention. I didn't think I had to. And now he's gone. Even Dad is worried. Dad never worries. He gets angry. But he's not angry this time and that's scarier than—" Her phone rings and she puts her hand on her stomach as she looks at the screen. "It's Mom."

She walks toward the kitchen, and I put my hand on my pocket and feel the outline of the Isaac's security ID.

Then she returns. Her arms are wrapped tight around her chest and her jaw is clenched. "It's that gang."

"What?"

"The one that Dad told us about yesterday. The one that made you set off the alarm. The police say they've been targeting the families of government officials. Dad says a lot of them have been ransomed back, so he's going to do what he can to—"

"He's wrong," I say so quietly Rose doesn't hear. I swallow hard as my mind wars with my heart. Do I let her believe the lie or possibly put her in danger by telling her the truth?

The crack of the Marshal's gun rings in my memory.

I don't have to tell her what I have learned. I can keep quiet and wait and see what happens. The less she knows the safer she should be.

But as much as I want to believe that, I know it isn't true. No one is safe in a world where asking the wrong question can get you taken and possibly killed. Rose is going to ask questions. The only way to protect her is to set the truth free and hope she can forgive me for what I have done.

"Mom's going to work. She's going to put Isaac's picture up on the front of the *Gloss* website with a number for people to call if they have seen him. Dad's going to get the mayor to try and contact the gang. He thinks—"

"There is no gang," I say, raising my voice. "The gang your father described isn't real." My stomach clenches as my best friend looks square at me.

"What do you mean? You got the paper. You set off the alarm. You were there when my dad said—"

"He lied." The words crackle. Rose jerks back, and I force myself to keep going. "There's no gang of criminals terrorizing the city and kidnapping government officials' kids. Your brother wasn't taken because your dad works with the mayor." I pull out the card I took from Isaac earlier today and hold it out to Rose. "He was taken because of me."

"How did you get this?" she asks quietly.

"I took it from him when I was here earlier today. I needed it to get answers about my mom. I never thought anything would happen to Isaac or I wouldn't have taken it."

"Meri, you aren't making any sense."

"If you sit down, I'll try to explain." For years, Rose has been my friend. I have trusted her more than any other. I have no choice but to trust her now.

I'm probably breaking every Stewards' rule in the book, but I don't care. I tell her about following the paintings and the meaning of the word "verify." About meeting people who are determined to save paper books and the truth they contain. I don't tell her about the Lyceum because I don't want to jeopardize anyone there.

Rose is silent as I pull the books from my bag and hand her the dictionary the Stewards gave me. She looks nervous taking it, as if the book itself might injure her. I wait for her to look up the word "verify." I see her eyes narrow as she reads the definition. Then I tell her the rest. My suspicion that my mother's accident wasn't an accident. The search for answers and finally my decision to find the information that I believe got my mother killed.

"I know how crazy it all sounds, but it's true." I hand her the heavy textbook I spent hours reading. "My mom was murdered because she was looking for proof that the government was kidnapping people who knew the truth."

"Did she find proof?" Rose asks. Her eyes lift from the textbook to me. "Did you?"

I take a deep breath and nod. "I used your brother's security identification to get into the archives at Liberty Tower."

"And you think Isaac was taken because they believe he was there." She runs her fingers along the picture on her brother's ID. "You're telling me that my dad knows about all of this? About the words and your mom's murder and why Isaac is really missing?"

I nod again. "I know it's hard to believe. I didn't either at first. If it hadn't been for my mom, I might have ignored it all. But now I know that if you tell your dad or anyone else about what I've told you, the Marshals will come. They'll take me away, and they'll come for you, too." My throat burns.

Silence wraps around the room and stretches so tight I can hardly breathe. I want her to yell at me. To get angry or to ask questions or to say something. But there's only silence as she turns the ID over and over and over in her hands.

"Rose, I—"

"Stop." Rose shakes her head as if trying to clear it. "I get that you want me to understand, but . . . I need time to think. Okay?"

I swallow hard and nod. "Do you want me to go?" I wouldn't blame her if she wanted me far, far away.

"No." Rose frowns. "I'm going to stay in Isaac's room for now. You can take mine."

As she heads down the hall with the books clutched tight in her hands, I say, "I'm going to make this right."

I don't know how, but I have to. Atlas's dad. Rose's brother. The Marshals took them. We have to do something to get them back, but the Marshals have guns and numbers on their side. What do I have?

Do I sleep? I must. One minute I am listening to the sound of Mrs. Webster coming home and the next my eyes snap open and I'm squinting at the sunlight streaming through the frothy curtains.

I scramble out of bed and peer into Isaac's room. Rose is curled on the bed wearing Isaac's school jacket—fast asleep.

Mrs. Webster is already gone when I finish showering and pull on jeans, a fitted black T-shirt, and Stef's blue hat. A note on the refrigerator tablet says there has been no news. That Mrs. Webster has gone to the police station again and Rose should call her when she gets up. I'm not sure when that will be, but I am determined to have something to tell her when she does.

I pull my phone out of my backpack, ignore the voice mail from my father, and text Atlas: SOMETHING HAS HAPPENED. NEED TO SEE YOU NOW, along with Rose's address. Because I can't just stay on the sidelines like the Stewards. When I think about Rose and her mother—Atlas and his father; my dad and the voice mail I finally listen to that is filled with apologies that he seems doomed to make again and again because of what the people in charge of our government did to my mother—I can't just wait for something to happen that will change things. I have to try to put things right no matter the danger.

Relief flickers across Atlas's face when I answer the door. "I was worried something happened to you," he says, stepping into the living room. "I'm supposed to be helping prepare for the lockdown. So I have to make this fast."

"My friend Rose, her brother was taken yesterday—because of me. I took his ID and used it to get into the archives. Now they think he's one of you, and I have to get him back."

Atlas shakes his head. "If you try you'll get taken, too."

"I don't care."

"I get why you say that." He takes a step forward. "But you don't mean it."

"Yes," I say firmly. "I do. I can't unsee what you've shown me. I can't pretend not to know what I know. How can you?"

"I'm not pretending anything, Meri, and you don't understand."

"You're right," I admit. "I don't understand how you can plan to lock yourself underground when your father needs your help."

His jaw tightens. Hurt colors his eyes and I realize I've gone too far.

"Atlas, I know you want to help your father." I place a hand on his arm. "We can still do that. We can help him and Isaac and all the others they've taken who are still in the city."

"We don't know where he or your friend's brother are being held."

"No, but how long do you think the government can keep holding them if everyone in the city knows the truth?" I ask. "There has to be a way to get the word out to people about what's happening. The more people who know, the harder it will be for the government to take people away or to keep the Unity Centers secret." Atlas doesn't automatically shoot me down, which gives me hope I might be onto something. So I barrel ahead. "There have to be other Stewards who don't want to wait around to see how many more people are taken or die. Maybe if we all work together we can spread the truth to enough people to make a difference. We can convince them to speak out and—"

"Don't you think I want to?" Atlas runs a hand over his head. "People aren't ready, Meri. They won't believe just because you say they should."

"I did."

Atlas and I jump at the sound of Rose's voice. She's standing in the hallway in leggings and an oversize blue Chicago Cubs T-shirt, holding her brother's ID in her hand.

"Meri told me about it all. I didn't want to hear it, but Meri made me listen. And I believe."

"You told her?" Atlas turns toward me.

"I trust her. And I owed her the truth." I straighten my shoulders and say, "Everyone deserves the chance to hear the truth."

"And if we fail?" Atlas asks. "What happens to my dad and her brother then? What happens to you?"

"The same thing that would happen if we did nothing," I say, feeling Rose move to stand at my side. "But at least I'll know we didn't let that happen without a fight."

Atlas turns and paces to the window. He runs a hand over the back of his neck and looks out as if searching for answers. "I don't want to hide in the Lyceum. I don't want to keep waiting for the right time. But if we don't have a plan, we don't have a chance."

"Our parents had a plan," I tell him. "We just have to figure out what it was."

He turns. "We don't know what they were working on."

"My mother's friend—the one I visited—said my mother was working with people to reveal the truth to the entire city. You said your father and my mother weren't working alone. Atlas." I step toward him. "Do you believe that's true? That there were others?"

Slowly he nods. "There's at least one more. But . . ."

"Then we have to find them."

"How?" he asks.

"We go to the Lyceum and figure out who it is. We have to at least try."

It's not much of a plan, but it's better than nothing. Atlas paces the room, sighs, then turns backs to me. "Well, if we're going, we'd better do it now because the lockdown starts at midnight."

That doesn't give us much time to figure this out. But we have to make the attempt.

"I'll go get changed," Rose says, turning toward the hall. "It'll only take me a few minutes to get ready and to call my mom."

"No," Atlas snaps. "She can't come, Meri."

"The hell I can't." Rose spins around. "We're talking about saving my brother."

"We won't be talking about anything if you—"

"Stop," I shout. They both turn toward me. "Atlas," I say, forcing myself to sound calm. "Can you please give Rose and me a couple minutes alone? I'll meet you downstairs."

Atlas closes his eyes and exhales slowly. "Make it quick. We don't have a lot of time." He turns toward Rose. Sympathy storms into his eyes. "I really hope we find your brother," he says. Then he turns on his heel and heads for the door.

"I'm going," Rose says when the door closes. "You can't make me stay here because some guy named Atlas says so. What kind of name is that anyway?"

"All the Stewards have names that belong in a library. My mom was Folio. Rose, I'm not asking you to stay here because of Atlas. I'm asking because if you don't stay here your dad will wonder where you are. He'll start asking questions about what you are doing and what you know. He has to think you're still in the dark . . . that you're on his side. If he does, there could be a way for you to use that to figure out where they're holding Atlas's father and Isaac."

Rose tightens her grip on her brother's ID card. "You really think that my dad is . . . part of all of this? That he knows about Verify and about your mom's murder?"

"He has to."

"That means he's part of the reason Isaac is gone."

"No," I say. "That's on me."

"It's on them," she says, taking my hand and squeezing it. "They lied. You uncovered the truth. Together we'll fix it."

I hope so. "I'll let you know what the plan is as soon as we figure it out," I promise. "Can you stay here until then? Please?"

Tears sparkle in her eyes, then harden like diamonds. "I'm counting on you. And don't do anything stupid."

"Now you sound like Atlas."

Rose gives me a small smile. "Maybe he's not so bad after all."

Atlas is waiting in the shadow of a tree at the corner. "Is she going to be okay on her own?" he asks. "I know what it's like to feel helpless." The concern I see in his eyes tugs hard at my heart.

"Rose is the strongest person I know. You can trust her," I tell him. "She won't say anything that will jeopardize us or our chances of finding her brother."

"And how about you?" He steps toward me. "How are you holding up?"

I start to say I'm fine, but I can't choke out the words. And when Atlas opens his arms, I don't shrink back. I walk into them. He pulls me tight against him and I bury my face in his T-shirt while fear and anger and regret fight to burst free. I take several deep breaths to tamp down everything I'm feeling and concentrate on the sound of Atlas's heartbeat. Strong. Steady. Just like I need to be now.

As I slowly step away from Atlas, he gently says, "None of this is your fault, Meri. You know that, right?"

A reluctant smile tugs at my lips. "Rose said the same thing."

He shakes his head, but I can see the answering smile in his eyes when he says, "Maybe she isn't so bad after all."

"She said that, too." I take another steadying breath, shift the cap on my head, and say, "Are you ready?"

"Do you still have the CTA card I gave you?" When I pull it out of my pocket, he nods. "Then let's go."

My knee is stiff and aches as we head to the nearest L stop. The train is packed with people headed to work or for a day downtown. The sidewalks are just as full as Atlas leads me to a small brick building wedged in between taller ones constructed of glass and steel just a block or two away from the La Salle Street Bridge—where Atlas and I first met.

"This station will be the last one to close." Atlas steps into the building's doorway, then explains, "After the lockdown, any Steward who didn't make it to the Lyceum or is worried about exposure will come here to be routed to stations out of the city. The last relocation run will be a week after lockdown and this station will officially shut down then. If anything goes wrong—if we get separated or anything—this is the place you should come to get out of Chicago." He presses a square button twice on the occupant panel, which lists only one name—a business called Substantiate. He waits a beat. Then he presses it three more times.

The intercom crackles to life. "Who is it?"

"Atlas Steward."

"What do you need?"

"I was hoping to verify something with you."

There is a pause before a buzzer sounds. Atlas yanks the door open, looks up and down the sidewalk one last time, then enters. I follow him into the narrow but brightly lit foyer, around the corner to where an older woman with salt-and-pepper hair, a pink tank top, and a long, colorful patchwork skirt stands waiting in an open doorway.

"This is Index," Atlas introduces the woman. "She's the Master for Station One."

"At least until they shut me down." The woman nods. "The Engineers look like they're planning for this lockdown to last a good, long time."

"If you're in charge of shutting down the last station, doesn't that mean you'll be locked out of the Lyceum?" I ask.

Index smiles. "Don't worry about me. I'll be driving the last train of stragglers out of the city myself. I've been through enough lockdowns to know I'd rather be on the run than trapped." She turns to Atlas. "I'm sorry about Atticus."

Atlas nods and we head down a narrow hall and around the corner. He punches the code 1773 into an elevator with dented silver doors, and the doors slide open. He looks over at me and says, "That's the year of the Boston Tea Party—in case you read that part of the book."

"A protest event that ultimately led to the . . ." What did the book call it? "The Revolutionary War."

Atlas's eyes widen.

"I told you, I read the book."

"I keep underestimating you. I should probably stop doing that."

The metal doors slide open, revealing a long hallway covered completely—the floor, the ceiling, and the walls—with large squares of dingy white and yellow ceramic tile. Long tubes of fluorescent lights shine down from above. We follow the hallway as it slants downward and to the left.

"Where are we?" I ask. "This isn't anything like the entrance we went through before."

"It's an old pedestrian walkway. There are a bunch of them that connect buildings around the city. My grandfather and his friends removed some of the pedways from the city's maps and then created new walls to separate them from the ones they didn't take off the grid."

"And no one noticed?"

"The City Pride Program was making so many changes it was hard for everyone to keep them straight. If anyone asked them what they were doing, grandfather's friends created official-looking memos that said there were structural damages, which required certain pedways to be sealed. Then they swiped the paper files—like you did. People didn't know how to verify what they were told." He shrugged. "Sometimes, that's useful."

That's what we are going to change.

The wide, tiled path slants downward a bit more. There is a large concrete wall in the distance, probably one of the walls that Atlas was just referring to, but we turn right before we get that far.

"We used to have a longer path to get to the tunnels, but my father thought it took too long and created his own here."

A shadow passes over his eyes. Then he shakes his head and opens a door set back in an alcove. We slip inside to a concrete closet that has no light source. I kick a metal bucket and almost trip over an old mop as Atlas shoves a piece of plywood to the side, revealing a jagged hole in the concrete. When I duck my head I am able to fit through without any problem.

He grabs a lantern from the floor, turns it on, and heads right down the low, dirt-packed tunnel.

Since I've already been to the Lyceum, I assumed I knew what to expect. But when we step through a doorway built in the middle of a towering bookshelf, I find the place more magical than before. The lights from above are brighter. Or maybe it is the energy of the people—dozens of them hurrying with papers or boxes and some with suitcases or overnight bags—that makes it feel different.

Or maybe I am different, because when I step through the doorway I don't see only books of all sizes and scarred wood shelves and paper—I see the potential to change the world. We just have to figure out how to do it.

"Well, we're here," Atlas says as we start walking through the shelves. "Now what?"

Good question. I wish I had a good answer, and time is ticking away.

"Do you have any idea who your father and my mother might have been working with?"

"If I did, I wouldn't have made contact with you."

Fair point.

"Once, I overheard them talking. Dad said they should meet when your mom was painting the station. Your mom said something like 'He's going to hate that.' Before they said who *he* was, Dad noticed I was there. That was a month or so before your mom died."

"How long was my mother in the Stewards?" I ask.

"Eighteen months. She was eased into her ride, so it took a few months before she was brought here and officially made a Steward," he offers.

A year and a half or a little less sounds about right. That would coincide with the time Mom suddenly stopped wanting me to pursue my art and started spending more time alone.

"Did she have a lot of good friends down here?"

"She wasn't in the Lyceum all that often that I can remember," Atlas says. "She spent most of her time aboveground on the station design."

"So she wouldn't have gotten close to very many people," I reason. So far, I had met just a handful of Stewards. Only one of them said he liked my mom.

"This way," I say as I pull Atlas along through the rows of shelves.

"Where are we going?"

"To find him," I say. After a few twists and turns, I spot Dewey sitting at the same desk Atlas and I found him at before, his beaten-up brown hat pulled low on his head. Around him people are scurrying through the tall stacks with lists—yelling about books to pull or supplies to get, but he just turns pages of the volume in front of him as if nothing is happening. He stops reading to make a note and notices us standing in front of him.

"More people. It's like roaches. You deal with one, and more turn up. Lists for editions to pull and send to the vaults are back there." He waves his hand over his shoulder and hunches over his book. "Data will deal with you. Better hurry."

"We're not here to pack books," I say. "I'm trying to find people who were friends with my mom."

"There will be plenty of time to bother me about that after the lockdown starts." He pulls his hat farther down on his head.

"We're not going to be here when the lockdown starts," I say.

Dewey pauses turning his page and peers up at me. "Really?"

I nod.

"Well, two less people to worry about." He yawns, then blinks as if surprised to see that we are still standing in front of him. "If you're not here to help, at the very least you can let me get back to my work."

"Dewey," Atlas says, far more calmly than I feel, "we just need you to answer a few questions. We're trying to do what my father and Folio would have wanted."

Dewey lets out a high-pitched, mocking laugh and swivels in his chair. "My dear Atlas, any one of the people running around here will say that Atticus and Folio would want you to do what is best for the Stewards. Which from my point of view is to go somewhere else." He leans back, stretches so that his hands brush that shelf of red books next to his desk, and then pulls his hat back down over his eyes, dismissing us.

"Come on," Atlas says. "We can ask someone else."

I start to turn, then stop dead in my tracks. "Wait a second."

I take a step toward the shelf of books.

"I told you to go. Or I'll let Scarlett and Holden know—"

"I know those books," I cut him off, and start digging in my bag for my tablet. My hands fumble with the On switch as I look at the line of red books again. I saw them the last time I was here, but I didn't see them. Not really. But I see them now and they have gold lines and a small stamped symbol on each that makes my heart race.

Yes. I call up the image of my mother's work and my heart jumps. The squat lines of red rectangles depict only the middle section, making them look more like bricks than books. But the gold-winged tree symbol on each of those rectangles is unmistakable.

I turn the tablet to show Dewey the picture and smile because I am still on the path my mother left for me. She left me a trail to the truth. And now I am going to follow it all the way to the end.

FIFTEEN

Dewey squints at me. "Why are you still here? Do you need me to speak slower so you can understand? It is time for you to go."

I smile. He frowns.

"You said, if we asked anyone running around the Lyceum, they would say my mom and Atlas's dad would want us to do what is best for the Stewards."

"Well, there's nothing wrong with your hearing."

"But you aren't running around the Lyceum. What do *you* think they'd say to us?"

He leans back again and studies me. "Maybe you're more like your mom than you look. She was good with details."

"An artist has to see the little things." I say the words I recall from years ago. "Because that's what makes up the bigger things."

Just like her paintings captured a smaller piece of a larger picture.

Something an artist would notice. Something she trusted me to see.

"There's something my mother started that I plan on finishing.

And you can help me do it."

Dewey removes his hat, flips it onto the desk, and leans toward me. "And how do you suppose I can do that?"

"By showing me . . ." I ignore Atlas's confused look and punch up the image of my mother's final, incomplete painting. Then I turn the tablet to face Dewey. "Where to find this."

"That painting's not finished," he says.

"No. My mother never had the chance to complete it. That's what I intend to do."

Atlas shifts to study the image on the screen while Dewey stares at me. He clicks his tongue three times. Then he takes his hat off the desk, turns it over in his hand, and jams it on with a sigh. "It's too noisy for me to read with all these people underfoot." He jumps to his feet and disappears around the corner of the bookshelf next to his desk. A moment later, he appears again. "I'm assuming your feet work. Or did you plan on me carrying you?"

"I still have no idea what's happening," Atlas admits as we scurry after Dewey, who darts around Stewards preparing for lockdown and weaves through shelves. "Why didn't you tell me about your mother's paintings?"

"I'll explain everything later," I say as I rush to keep up. Finally, Dewey leads us into a small area in a dimly lit back corner of the Lyceum tucked away under scaffolding used to reach the upper bookshelves.

Dewey glances around the edge of shelves to make sure no one is nearby. Then he asks, "Do you recognize anything?"

I'm about to say no, when something catches my eye. A book shelved near the bottom, placed so that the image on the front is facing out. The cover is torn and faded, but even in the dim light

I recognize the red stars at the edge of a black background and the faded pale lines that point to an image in the center. An image my mother never got the chance to paint. Not a door, as I drew so many times while trying to re-create my mother's vision, but an eye—wide-open—determined to see.

"What are you waiting for?" Dewey asks. "Take it."

I lean down, pull the book off the shelf, and brush my hand over the front.

I found it, Mom, I think. *I know what you wanted me to see now. And I'm here.*

Dewey's voice pulls me back. "There's a switch. You might have to feel around a bit. No good having a secret room if anyone who pulls a book off a shelf can find it."

My fingers find a cool metal inset in the wood and I pull. Something clicks, and a section of the shelves shifts.

"Now stand back." Dewey helps haul me to my feet, and I scramble out of the way as he carefully pivots the shelf.

"Atlas's grandfather created this when he and his friends built the Lyceum." He waves us inside the darkness. I reach for Atlas's hand and step over the threshold. Dewey follows. "Atticus decided it should be used for this." Dewey hangs a battery-operated lantern on the wall and pulls the door shut behind us as I blink at the contents of the small, hidden space.

In a movie a room like this would contain treasure or some kind of alien device that could destroy the world. Instead, there are stacks of red books and neat piles of paper and dozens and dozens of bags on slightly rusted metal industrial shelves.

"Not what you expected?" Dewey asks as I take a page from the top of the stack.

Do you know this word?

VERIFY—*(v.) To ascertain or prove the truth or correctness of.*
You don't know it because the government does not want you to.
They took this word away from you. Do you wonder what else they
might have taken?

The paper goes on to list other words—many are ones Atlas made me look up when he told me about the Stewards. The final word, however, is one I discovered myself in the history book.

REVOLUTION—*(n.) An overthrow or repudiation and the*
replacement of an established government or political system by
the people governed.

"I'm not sure what I expected," I admit. Weapons, maybe? Or the names of soldiers in a secret army they had amassed?

Atlas picks up one of the red books. It's a copy of the Merriam-Webster collegiate dictionary. And there are stacks and stacks of them. "What did you plan to do with all of this?"

"What do you think we planned to do?" Dewey asks, leaning against the edge of the door.

"You were going to spread the truth," I say, unzipping one of the bags. Inside are more papers. More books. "But how? Are there others helping you?"

He dashes my hopes with the shake of his head. "It was just the three of us. The other Engineers made it clear they valued safety above the truth. So the three of us decided to create a method of spreading the truth on our own. I was in charge of siphoning off inventory and printing those sheets. Atticus and your mom were going to get the materials out onto the streets. We hoped to have more damning information to add as we waged our campaign."

Which is what my mother was attempting to do when she was killed.

Atlas shakes his head. "How did you plan to change anything when there were only three of you?"

Dewey adjusts his hat and straightens his shoulders. "Ovid and his industrious medieval collaborators gave us the idea that 'dripping water hollows out stone, not through force, but through persistence.' We decided to put that theory to the test."

"I don't understand," Atlas says.

Maybe he doesn't, but I do. Drip by drip. Little by little. A painting doesn't just happen. It comes to life stroke by stroke—seemingly without shape or purpose at first until suddenly it bursts into view. "You were going to do what the government did. Change things a little at a time. If a dozen people do searches on those words, they'll set off alarms. Then a dozen more. The more alarms that go off, the more people will notice and ask questions." Which will lead to more questions and demands for answers. "Every question they ask will teach them, by degrees, that the life they have been living is a lie. And once they know this, they won't be able to go back. They'll question everything and tell others to do the same."

Dewey nods. "Only now Atticus and Folio are gone and the Lyceum is going into lockdown for months . . . maybe years."

"Which means we have to put this plan into motion now," I say.

"How?" Atlas asks. "My father and Isaac will be long gone by the time Dewey's dripping truth has any chance of making a hole in the government's lies."

"There are faster ways of putting holes in a stone," I say. "We get all of this out, into the hands of people all at once. The government can't pull that many people off the street or out of their houses without everyone in the city taking notice." And the upheaval might just provide enough cover for Rose to search her father's offices for information about where they are holding Isaac and Atticus.

"Sounds great—but there are only two of us."

"Three," Dewey corrects. "I'd rather be working up there than stuck with all these people down here."

Atlas scoffs. "Fine. Three. The Marshals will figure out what we're doing before we have a chance to hand out a fraction of this stuff."

He's right. As soon as we start putting paper on the street, people will notice and someone will report it. The only way this will work is if we can deliver all of these books and papers into people's hands in a short period of time.

"There have to be other Stewards who would be willing to help," I say, picking up one of the red-and-white hard-covered dictionaries. "You said a lot of Stewards trained to defend themselves against the Marshals. Would any of them be willing to make a stand?"

"A lot would never think to go against the Engineers or the Stewards' preservation mission. But there are some who might."

Atlas turns to Dewey. "What do you think?"

Dewey adjusts his hat again and smiles. "Couldn't hurt to ask. But whatever you're going to do, you're going to have to do it now. The clock counting down to the lockdown is ticking."

"Our best shot is talking to the Stokers in the hopper."

When I give him a confused look, Atlas explains, "Stokers are what we call the Stewards on the streets who are trained to fight. There's a separate area in the Lyceum where we practice. A bunch of us call it the hopper."

"The coast is clear," Dewey says, peering through a small hole. "Atlas, take her to the hopper. I'll gather up whoever I think might be open to making a stand and meet the two of you there." He flips a latch, opens the door, and turns toward me. "I hope you're good with words, my dear. To convince that crowd to put their lives on the line for you—well, let's just say you're going to need all the words you can get."

The gravel on the floor of the hopper crunches under my feet. The cave-like space is lit by spotlights of white and pale blue positioned near the dirt-packed walls. In the center of the room are sections of wrought-iron and chain-link fences—many taller than me. At least three dozen people weave around the fences. Some carry boxes. Others have bags slung over their shoulders. An older woman with long brown hair and a diamond stud twinkling from her left eyebrow is perched at the top of a rusted section of fence, shouting orders about sleeping arrangements.

"That's Spine," Atlas says. "She's head trainer, one of the most fearless people I've ever met, and unofficial leader of the Stokers. If we can convince her, the majority of the others will follow."

"And if we don't?"

"Be glad you know how to run."

"Lockdown doesn't mean we slow down! And you don't need to talk to each other right now," Spine yells. "You'll have a whole lot of time down here to talk once the doors are closed."

Dewey appears behind us with the long-nailed Renu and a half dozen others in tow. He nods and Atlas whispers, "Let's do this."

The floor slants slightly downward as we walk deeper into the hopper toward the center, where Spine is shouting about final assignments for taking books to the vaults and people to out-of-town stations. While a lot of Stokers are paying atten-tion to her, a number have turned to watch Atlas and me striding across the gravel floor.

"Anyone who doesn't think they need to pay attention to what I'm saying will have to run extra drills when we resume our training sessions tomorrow. Do you hear me?" Spine yells to a group of Stok-ers to her right.

"We hear you, Spine." A bulky guy in a white T-shirt with a mop of brown hair with almost glowing white-blond streaks points toward us. "But I don't think those two are listening."

Spine looks down at us. "Atlas, I thought you told me you had to deal with something important before the lockdown."

"I am dealing with something important. That's why I'm here now. We have something we have to ask you." He turns and looks around the room. "To ask all of you."

"'We?'" Spine asks. "Whoever this is, she's not even old enough to be in the Stewards."

"I know you don't like the idea of a lockdown," Atlas says over the whispers from those looking on. "I know you hate the idea of hiding down here while my father needs our help. You train every day. You push yourself to be able to take on the Marshals, yet you are told to run from them even when you see someone who isn't a Steward in danger. And you wonder about those people and whether you could have made a difference if only you had broken the rules and tried."

Several Stokers nod their heads. I hold my breath.

"My father wanted to do more than just hide down here in the Lyceum. It's the reason he's not here with us now, and why I'm ask-ing for your help to tell the people in this city what we know."

"Yes, we train." Spine leaps off her perch on the fence, lands gracefully, and strides across the gravel toward us. "Yes, we prepare to fight. But our mission is to keep the truth alive until people are ready to listen. We have to wait until the time is right. I'm sorry about Atticus." She pats Atlas's shoulder then starts to walk away.

The rest in the room begin to go back to their business. Panic bubbles. That can't be it. They can't just leave.

"And when will that be?" The words burst out of me. "Do you really think there will be a magical day when people are ready to hear the truth?" I hold up the dictionary as Spine turns back toward me—anger hot in her eyes.

"There's a reason the Engineers don't want people your age to be part of this." She takes slow steps toward me. "Young is easy to influence. Young makes impulsive choices. And they speak about things they don't understand."

"I understand that hiding out waiting for the right moment to spread the truth hasn't worked all that well. People have forgotten the words that were taken. Every day that passes takes them farther away from the ideas those words would give them and makes it harder for them to believe. There will never be a good time to tell the truth. It is never going to be easy. We have a plan, but we need more people for it to have a chance of working, and if it is going to help Atticus, we need to do it now. If we wait . . ."

"'We?'" Spine barks a mocking laugh, and my stomach curls as she stares down at me. "You just got here. Now you're telling us we should abandon the mission we've been following for years?"

"No." My heart pounds hard and loud in my ears. "I want you to ask yourself what you're waiting for. I want you to stop hiding and fight for the truth you claim to believe in. I want the Steward mission to be fulfilled."

"And you think you're ready to lead that fight?" she asks quietly. When Atlas starts to speak, Spine cuts him off. "Not you. I know what you can do. If this child thinks she can lead people who have risked their lives for years, I want her to make me believe it."

The room goes still.

I look at Spine, who is tall and muscular and confident. She is what a leader is supposed to look like. But I've faced Marshals. I was scared, but I didn't freeze, and I survived. "Yes," I say in a clear voice. "I am."

"Then prove it," she says. Spine kicks her leg out and hooks mine. My feet slide out from underneath me and I land flat on my back on the gravel. The dictionary drops with a thud beside me as laughter echoes.

I gasp for breath as Spine looms above. Her lips spread into a thin, satisfied smile. "Do you *really* think we should follow your lead?"

"This isn't necessary," Atlas says, holding out his hand to help me up.

But I ignore his offer of help, and my eyes never leave Spine's as I pick up the dictionary and climb to my feet. "Yes," I say. "I do."

This time I'm ready when she launches at me. I dodge the punch she throws and swing the dictionary down on her arm with both hands. She stumbles. Pride flares for a split second before her leg once again sweeps mine out from under me. Breath kicks out of my lungs. My head cracks against the gravel. My heart thunders as I roll to my side, get to my knees, and shove slowly upright. The dictionary is still clutched in my hands when I set my feet under me and face Spine again.

She shakes her head and puts a hand on her hip. "We don't have time for this."

I straighten my shoulders and grip the book so that its edge is facing toward her.

She arches her eyebrow as if to ask, *Really?* And this time when she punches I step to the side and with as much force as possible slam the edge of the dictionary into her stomach. She gasps and turns. I block her kick with the book. The second one lands. Shock and pain bloom in my hip as Spine shoves me to the ground. The dictionary skitters over the gravel and Spine puts her boot on top of it and says, "Get out of here, kid."

Kid.

I stopped being a kid when my mother was killed, I think as I push myself up and look around the room. The lights scattered around the edges seem to make the dozen or so Stokers' eyes shimmer as they stare at me. Are they waiting for me to cry? To back down?

If so, they are going to be waiting a long time.

I climb to my feet, lift my eyes to meet Spine's, and say, "That book belongs to me."

Spine kicks the book across the gravel. As I reach to pick it up, she says, "I'm stronger than you are. I've trained for years. Why keep fighting if you are going to just end up on the ground?"

"Because I have to," I gasp. Pain and fear and anger war inside me, but that is the truth that I know. "They killed my mother for searching for the facts. They've taken Atlas's father and one of my friends. People deserve to hear the truth. If we aren't willing to risk everything to share it with them, I don't see how we are any better than the ones who took it away."

SIXTEEN

No one says a word.

My heart pounds loud as I set my feet and brace myself for another attack. Only, Spine doesn't charge. Instead, she places her hands on her hips and studies me.

There is the crunch of gravel as Atlas crosses to stand at my side. "I know the Stokers," he says. "I've trained with you—worked alongside you. I know you are never comfortable with the idea of retreating. You want to do something. Now we're giving you the chance to do it. Instead of locking up truth, we want to spread it."

Spine slowly turns and scans the faces of her Stokers. Then she shifts her attention to me. "You really think that we have enough of us to make a difference?"

"I do," I say, and I mean it. If we do this right, there are enough gathered here to bring the truth to the city. And hopefully, the spectacle we create will give Rose the opening she needs to find the location of Isaac and Atticus. "The history book I was given to read gave lots of examples of how small groups of people can create change by doing something hard. I guess we're asking you to be those people."

Dewey steps out of the shadows, his hat in his hands. "'Informed, concerned, and thoughtful citizens can change the world.'" He shrugs. "Reverend Espy—his quote seemed appropriate at this moment in time. Also appropriate is reminding you that our little gathering here will not go unnoticed by the Engineers much longer. Perhaps a decision needs to be made."

Spine glowers at Dewey, but there is a spark of excitement in her eyes when she lifts her chin and says, "I will not speak for anyone else, but I am not interested in hiding down here when there is a chance to fight for the truth up there."

A bunch of Stokers cheer. Atlas puts his arm around my shoulders, and Spine continues. "I will not judge anyone who wishes to stay here in the Lyceum during the lockdown. You must make the choice that is right for you. If you wish to leave, you can do so now. All I ask is that you not say anything to anyone else in the Lyceum until those of us who wish to take this step have gone up to the city."

Not one person moves, and a brilliant smile spreads across Spine's face as she turns toward me. "Well, you've managed to gain a small army. What do you need us to do?"

We give her a quick outline of how spreading the truth is going to work—or as much of it as we have come up with so far. Handing out the books and the pages and our hope that people will ask enough questions or cause enough confusion for us to be able to locate the Unity Center where Atticus and others like Isaac are being held so we can free them.

"The Engineers are never going to let us operate from here," Spine says.

"No," Dewey agrees. "They ordered the lockdown because

they're worried about losing more Stewards. Scarlett and Holden will do their best to cause problems for us if they realize how many are defying their wishes."

"So we move everything out of the Lyceum before they figure out what we're doing," I say. "Maybe the tunnels?"

"I'll talk to Index," Atlas offers. "The exit station is close, it has supplies, and there should be enough room for all of us to go over the mission and hide out once we're finished."

And Index wasn't wild about the lockdown, either.

"That's good." Dewey rubs his chin, then snaps his fingers. "And if Spine can lend me a number of her Stokers, I can make it appear as if they are running books to the vault, but instead they'll be moving our supplies."

"Once everything is relocated, we'll go over the rest of the plan." Which will give me time to figure out exactly what it is. "Sounds good."

"As soon as Atlas gets the green light from Index, we'll get to work. I'll send my Stokers to Dewey in groups of two or three, and you . . ." Spine frowns at me. "What do we call you? Have you even chosen a name?"

I hadn't thought about it, but when I look down at the book in my hands I realize what it should be. "You can call me Merriam." If nothing else, it's close enough to my own name that I will remember to answer to it.

Spine smiles and holds out her hand. "Well, Merriam, it sounds like we need to get to work."

I take her hand in my dirt-streaked one and hold fast. "Yes, we do."

"Lockdown is in just over thirteen hours." Spine turns, leaps up onto a wrought-iron fence, and starts shouting orders.

"Merriam," Atlas says, "what you just did was . . ." He searches for the right adjective.

"Unexpected?" I repeat the word he used last night before Rose called.

"Yeah." He gives me a slow smile. "Spine and the others would have heard me out, but you impressed them. That's not easy to do."

"I was impressed that you understood some of the book you were given." Dewey appears at my side. "We have people and, if Atlas is correct, a place to assemble. But we still don't have a logistical plan that will make this work."

"We will," I say. "I just have to figure out what it is."

"I'll get you the map your mother, Atticus, and I were using."

Dewey is back in no time with a worn city map as well as paper and a number of pencils. He then heads off to organize how to remove the supplies from the hidden room. Atlas goes to talk to Index, leaving me to figure out how best to get the truth into the hands of as many people as possible.

Since I don't want the Engineers to spot me, I find an out-of-the-way corner of the Lyceum to spread out the map. Worry snakes through me as I study the small red X's someone marked throughout the entire city. There are fifty of them in all. Some in the heart of the Loop. Others along L and bus routes farther out from the center of Chicago. We might have enough Stewards to hit every area my mother and Atticus identified. The Marshals will be alerted not long after we start. So we will have only a short window to operate. Spreading out seems like the obvious answer. The more areas in the city we share the truth in, the less chance the Marshals have of putting a complete stop to our work. It makes sense.

And yet I can't help thinking that there is something wrong with that plan. Maybe if we were doing the slow release of information my mother and her friends had planned, I would feel more comfortable with the choices they made. But tonight's operation is different and—

I jump as something brushes my arm and turn to see the shining green, unblinking eyes of a sleek gray cat staring at me. "What do you think, Margaret?" I ask quietly, wishing Atlas were here to give his opinion. "Should I just do it my mom's way?" After all, she and the others had been working on this plan for months. They were Stewards. They knew all this stuff better than I do.

The cat saunters onto the map, sits in the center of the pages, and promptly puts up her leg to wash. And I take that as a sign. While my mom and the others knew the city, they were Stewards. They had been looking at the map for places to dispense the truth without drawing too much attention to what they were doing. But tonight, we want to be noticed. We want to get the attention of people who don't know the truth. The grander the spectacle, the more curious people will be to find out what the papers and books say and the harder it will be for the government to deny. And the bigger the action we take, the better shot we have at distracting Rose's father. We need lights and activity and people—places where there will be lots and lots of people.

Margaret curls up next to me as I pull out the paper and pencils Dewey demonstrated for me so I knew how to use them. Then, I start creating a list of locations. The resistance of the dark-tipped pencil as it runs along the paper is strange, and I break several black tips off the pencils as I work.

The Magnificent Mile
Navy Pier

The America First Theater
Wrigley Field
Grant Park

The signal for my phone cuts in and out, and Margaret swipes at me when I move around looking for better reception. While I appreciate the Stewards' lack of internet connection, not having it makes it harder to search for street festivals, concerts, and sporting events located near the places I've already identified. In between bouts of no-signal messages, I also look up the addresses of the two television stations in the city and add those destinations to the ever-growing list.

When Atlas finds me, I'm surrounded by pages filled with cross-outs and additions and ideas. He hands me a bottle of water and a sandwich and tells me Dewey's bags are slowly being relocated to Index's station.

"So far Scarlett and Holden haven't noticed," he says. "Spine is having a few of the Stokers creating problems they have to solve in order to distract them. Dewey is hoping we'll be done in another two or three hours. Once they've finished, Dewey and I will come back to get you. Dewey said he gave you their plan for tonight."

"I think I have a better idea," I say. Quickly, I explain my hope of creating a fast and furious spectacle of information that will be impossible for anyone to ignore. When I'm done, I wait for his reaction as he studies the map his dad helped create. "What do you think?" I ask.

He purses his lips, and I recognize the flicker of loss and worry that flashes in his eyes before he turns to me and smiles. "I think Dewey is going to be impressed again. But we can't cover all these locations. Not with a few dozen people. If this is going to work we'll have to focus on five or six places and do our best to reach as many people in those zones as we can."

He's right.

I break the rules without guilt and feed bits of my sandwich to a purring Margaret as I circle the sites I think will have the most people in attendance tonight. Then I call Rose to give her an update. She listens to my ideas, and I can hear the hope in her voice as she helps me winnow down the list of locations even further. *Gloss* magazine dispatches photographers and reporters to events around the city all the time, and Rose is a well of information as to what types of events are the best draws and even has an idea for how we can use a different location to create an extra distraction—one that will hopefully give us more time to get the truth out to the city.

My phone cuts in and out as Rose gives me a quick update on what is happening aboveground. Her father claims to be in negotiations with the gang he's blaming for Isaac's kidnapping but says the police don't have any leads as to where Isaac is being held. Despite the terrible connection, her anger comes through loud and clear, and she is glad to play her own part in our plan. By the time Atlas returns to tell me it's time to go, I have settled on six specific areas in the city that will be the main focus of tonight's rebellion. I just hope I've chosen well, because time is ticking and there is no telling how long we have before Isaac and Atticus are either killed or shipped out of the city to who knows where.

"Dewey and Spine are waiting for us in the tunnels," Atlas says as I fold up Dewey's map and shove it and the list I've created into my bag. "Are you ready?" he asks, holding out a hand.

Margaret barely looks up from her nap as I pull my hat down low over my forehead, put my hand in Atlas's, and say, "Let's go."

The Lyceum is humming with low conversations and hurried activities as the time remaining until the lockdown dwindles. I spot two Stewards hugging each other before one hurries toward an exit. It must not only be Spine and her Stokers who aren't interested in giving up their freedom for safety.

Spine and Dewey are just inside the tunnel when we duck through the exit.

"Are all the Stokers out?" Atlas asks as Spine turns and we fall in step behind her.

"All but four," Dewey answers.

And Spine explains, "They wanted the chance to convince a few of their friends to join us. They promised to be at the exit station in thirty minutes for their assignments. We could use the extra help."

We turn the corner and slow as we come face-to-face with Scarlett and two Stewards I've never seen before.

Scarlett slows. "Spine, just the person I've been looking for. I'm concerned with reports that a number of Stokers have yet to return from their final runs. I assured Holden they would be back before the doors are locked at midnight, but he is worried . . ." Her voice trails off and her eyes narrow as she spots me standing in the shadows behind Spine. "What is Folio's daughter doing here? I thought I made it clear we didn't need any distractions right now."

"I'm leaving," I say. "You don't have to worry about me distracting anyone."

"That's good to hear, but it appears you have already caused a distraction. Dewey . . ." Scarlett steps forward, and the two Stewards accompanying her follow suit. "You don't often leave the Lyceum."

Dewey shrugs and says affably, "Just stretching my legs."

"Well, I'm certain there are things that could use your attention back in the Lyceum. Which is where we all belong. Atlas, make sure your rider doesn't get lost on her way out. Spine, if you could come with me. Holden and I have several items we need to go over before the lockdown starts." She and the other two Stewards sweep past us. When Scarlett realizes Dewey and Spine have not moved, she turns back. "Are you coming?"

"No," Spine says, folding her arms over her chest.

"No?" Scarlett lifts her chin. "What do you mean, no?"

Dewey smiles. "We have decided Hans Christian Andersen was correct. Just living is not enough. One must have sunshine, freedom, and a little flower." When Scarlett just gapes at him, Dewey lets out a sigh and says, "We are leaving the Lyceum, Scarlett. We aren't interested in the safety of the shadows."

"The Marshals are closing in," Scarlett says. "Look what happened to Atticus."

"Atticus wished for people to learn the truth," Dewey says. "You refused to listen."

"Because I understand how important it is to protect the truth at all costs," Scarlett snaps back.

"The truth can only be protected if it is not hidden," Atlas says. "We have to fight their lies with our facts. If we hide, they win."

Scarlett turns toward Spine. "The lockdown is essential."

"The lockdown will keep those inside the Lyceum safe," Spine says. "But what of everyone else? We are tired of hiding."

"'We?'" Scarlett's eyes widen. "The missing Stokers . . ." She whirls to face her two Stewards. "Get inside the Lyceum. Tell everyone Holden and I have ordered the rails to be changed to red. Set guards at the door and prepare to close them when I arrive. No one is allowed to leave the protection of the Lyceum as of now."

"You can't force people to stay who don't want to," I say as the two race off to do her bidding.

"I will do whatever I must to protect the Stewards. Even if it means protecting them from themselves."

"You're taking away their choices," I say. "Isn't that what you're supposed to be fighting against?"

"I don't need a child to tell me what I'm fighting against," she snarls.

Atlas steps forward. "My father believed it was time to—"

"Your father would have led the Marshals right to us if he had been given the chance. I stopped him from putting the Stewards in danger."

"It was you?" The words are barely a whisper as horror spreads through me. "You said you stopped Atticus. How did you stop him?"

"You called the Marshals?" Atlas demands. "What about you being worried that he would tell the Marshals what he knew and how he could reveal where the Lyceum is?"

"I didn't tell them he was a Steward. Just a person asking strange questions about words and paper. Your father lost his way, and I was certain he would use the deadman's switch before telling them anything about the Stewards, if for no other reason than to make sure they never found you." Scarlett takes several steps backward. "I will keep the Stewards safe. And when people are ready, the truth will be waiting for them." With that, Scarlett vanishes into the darkness.

"Wait!" Atlas lunges after her, but Spine cuts him off and when he tries to get around her she shoves him back. Hard.

"Move!" he yells, trying to go around her, only to have Spine shove him again.

"I get it. I do, but going after her won't help us find him. Keep it together," Spine barks as Atlas struggles to get free. "Scarlett said she's locking down the Lyceum early. That means we have to get out of here now."

As if on cue, a loud, grinding whine echoes in the tunnel.

"Let's go!" Spine releases Atlas and bolts down the tunnel, and we race after her. The creaking sound grows louder as our feet pound the ground and flecks of dirt begin to fall from the ceiling above.

We turn the corner. More dirt and shards of rock rain down as a loud thud echoes and the tunnel shudders.

"That's the first entrance being sealed," Dewey yells. "The others will be right behind."

We race down the tunnel. Dust and debris make it hard to see. Dewey keeps pace with Spine ahead of me. I'm amazed at his speed and grateful for the bouncing light he holds aloft for us to follow.

We turn a corner and another tremor shakes the ground. The echoing sound of something slamming into place rings loud, as does the grating creaks of the gears.

"That's the second door dropping into place!" Atlas shouts.

"The next two won't be far behind," Spine calls, and somehow manages to run faster as she calls back, "Hurry!

I try to shut out the grinding metal and concentrate on running. The ground slants upward. Atlas yells that we're getting closer. I try to remember how far it is to the entrance we came through, but it is impossible to get my bearings. The thick, chalky taste of clay fills my mouth. My heart strains against my chest.

"There's the opening!" Spine hollers.

I see a glow through the haze far down the tunnel to the left, clench my fists, and run as hard as I can.

My heart jumps as another crash rumbles through the tunnels. Dirt showers from above from the force of another entrance slamming shut. The third of four. The last one will be sealed in moments.

I stumble. A rock cracks against the back of my head and I crash into the uneven ground—hard.

Pain spins.

The gears grind louder.

I push to my knees. Something hot and wet trickles down my neck, and I blink to bring the world into focus. Spine climbs into the opening. Dewey and his light are right behind.

"Meri!" Atlas shouts and starts back toward me.

"Get out!" I yell as I climb to my feet, ignore the blood running down my back, shift the bag on my shoulder, and run.

My head throbs. The tunnel shudders. Dirt falls faster from above. Spine shouts that I'm almost there. Atlas waves from the entrance as if willing me closer. The grumbling of the gears swells as I reach out, take Atlas's hand, and am pulled inside.

I gasp for breath and put my hand against the back of my head as something swooshes behind me. The ground jumps under my feet, and I turn as a solid steel panel slams down, sealing off the entrance I just climbed through.

SEVENTEEN

"And here I thought it would be close," Spine jokes, brushing dirt off her shirt.

"You're hurt." Dewey lifts his lantern and digs out a handkerchief, which Atlas presses to my wound.

"I'll be fine." I wince. "But I could use a Band-Aid and some aspirin."

We follow Spine through the pedway to the exit station, Atlas holding the cloth against my cut as we climb into the elevator and head aboveground. When the doors open, the buzz of conversation washes over me.

"We were wondering what happened to you." Index comes around the corner. She takes one look at us and frowns. "What happened?"

"Scarlett initiated the lockdown early," Atlas explains. "If anyone else wants to go down, you'll have to tell them the Lyceum is closed."

"But why?" Index asks.

"That's a longer story than we have time for right now." Spine glances at Atlas. She clearly doesn't want to bring up Scarlett's betrayal of his father in front of him. "If we are going to be ready to spread the truth tonight, we need to get our plan together and give my Stokers time to prepare."

"Here." I pull my notes and the map out of my bag and explain the plan Atlas and Rose helped me come up with. "These locations should be filled with enough people to make this work," I say, showing them the five I have starred. "Scheduled events will be starting at those places in the next few hours."

"What's this one?" Dewey points to the sixth location I have circled on the page.

"Have you ever looked at an image you see every day and realized you never noticed parts of it before?" I ask. "A good artist knows how to force the eye to focus on the thing they want to be seen. This—" I point to the sixth location. "This is our attempt to change the focus."

Spine nods. "Atlas, see that Merriam gets patched up. Dewey and I will assign teams to hit each of these locations and brief them on the strategy." She glances at the clock on the wall opposite the elevator. "We have two hours to put together our game plans."

"Come on," Atlas says as Spine and Dewey follow Index to where the Stokers are waiting. "Let's get you cleaned up."

"I'm really fine," I protest as he nudges me toward an open door at the other end of the hall. When he flips on the light switch of the sterile beige bathroom, I catch a glimpse of myself in the mirror and let out a small shriek. My face has taken on a gray, dusty color, and there are smears of blood and dirt on my neck and ear.

Atlas digs a fluffy, turquoise-blue hand towel out from the sink cabinet and runs it under the water. "Take a seat and let me see how bad it is."

Wincing, I remove my hat, sit on the closed lid of the toilet, and shift my hair to the side to give him a better view.

"It could be worse," he says as he gently presses the wet cloth to the wound.

"I guess I'm lucky I have a hard head." His fingers brush back my hair as he works on cleaning away the blood and dirt, sending a cascade of jittery bubbles through my chest.

"Sorry if that hurt," Atlas says. "I'm trying to be careful."

"It didn't hurt."

His eyes lock with mine, and the warmth inside me spreads. He runs his thumb across my cheek, then shakes his head, breaking the moment. "I think there are bandages in the medicine cabinet."

I push to my feet and head to the sink to wash my face and arms as Atlas rummages through the small white cabinet and comes up with antiseptic spray, gauze, medical tape, and a bottle of aspirin. "Index keeps things stocked, just in case of emergency."

I stay standing. Atlas pushes my hair out of the way again. I wince at the sting of the antiseptic spray while attempting to ignore the whisper of Atlas's warm breath on my neck as he affixes the bandage.

"Better?" he asks, lifing my hair to cover his handiwork.

"I think so." I turn to face him. Now that there are no medical ministrations to be done, the room feels smaller. "How about you?" I ask as I look up into the face that in a handful of days has become so familiar. "Are you okay?"

"Truth?" Atlas takes a seat on the closed toilet lid. "I don't know." He drops his head into his hands and takes a deep breath.

"I've known Scarlett my entire life. She's like family. She worked with my dad for years. I never dreamed she'd turn on him or the Stewards. Or me."

"She doesn't think she did." I kneel next to him and try to put into words what I saw and feel. "She wants the truth to be protected and wasn't willing to see there might be another way."

His head comes up. "I want to believe he's still out there somewhere. That he's alive and he's doing whatever he can to stay that way."

I put my hands on his and hold them tight. "If he's anything like you, he won't give up. And we won't give up doing whatever we can to find him."

A ghost of a smile tugs at the corner of Atlas's mouth. "You know, when we stood on that bridge, I was certain giving you a ticket was the worst decision I'd ever made." He turns one of my hands over and presses his lips against the center of my palm. "It might be one of the best."

"Only one of?" I say lightly, even though I have never felt less like joking.

Atlas flashes a quick grin. "That's something we'll talk about later." He grabs the blue hat off the sink, brushes off the dust, and gently places it on my head. Then, with a playful tug of the brim, he adds, "For now, we have work to do."

Index escorts Atlas and me to the second floor. The smell of pizza and the hum of voices make it almost seem as if a party is happening, but there is nothing celebratory about the "war room" into which Index ushers us.

Dewey, Spine, and several other Stewards are huddled over

the map. My stomach tightens as I notice the papers that have been tacked on the wall with the names of the locations I chose to carry out my mom and Atticus's mission. Under those locations are lists of names.

"We lost six Stewards to the early lockdown," Spine says, looking up from the map. "I've tried to spread out the non-Stokers through the groups." I find my name listed in the same group as Spine, Atlas, and Dewey under the heading "Navy Pier." "The groups are meeting now to determine their team strategy. We have the smallest of the teams, since ours is the most challenging target. The four of us will be working with Huck and Flap. Stacks will join us for the end of the run if he has time after his primary assignment. We'll work in partners, each starting at a different point, then fanning in to the pier."

When Atlas and I nod, she continues, "Dewey and I figure we'll have forty-five minutes at most to hand out the tickets before returning here or to a safe house."

"There are some that claimed time was on the side of truth, but when the Marshals are dispatched, time will certainly not be our friend." Dewey turns to me. "The time we gain through the shifting-focus part of this plan will be essential."

"Stacks will leave for that task in thirty-three minutes," Spines says, checking the clock on the wall. "He'll drive to the stadium, plant his evidence, and once he's clear he'll call in the tip."

If it works, the Marshals will believe there is a large group of people handing out pages with the word "verify" roaming the area in and around the White Sox's baseball stadium—on the other side of the city from where we'll all be. The government will have to send a lot of their resources to cover that much space. It should make it harder for them to respond quickly to what we are doing on the

North Side and increase the window Rose will have to search for information about her brother's whereabouts.

I hope.

Atlas hands me a bottle of water and a plate with a slice of pizza. The idea of food makes my stomach churn. Between the planning and fleeing the Lyceum and Atlas . . . I haven't had time to think about the risks everyone is about to take. Now that I am and the time is approaching, I feel ill.

"Trust me," Atlas says. "You need to be at the top of your game tonight. Eat."

I take a bite and force myself to chew, even though it tastes like ash. Then I tell the team I had another idea that, if it works, will give us a warning as to when the Marshals learn of our real locations.

Rose answers on the first ring. She sounds tired, but the steely determination that I've always envied is present as she tells me she's on her way to meet her father. "He tried to convince me I should stay home with Mom, but I told him I needed to see that he was working to get Isaac home. I can tell he knows more than he's admitting."

"There's something else I need your help with," I tell her. "The minute your father starts getting calls that upset him and give you an opening to do your search, let me know."

"I can do that."

I think about what could be happening to her brother and swallow hard. "Be careful, Rose. Please."

"I know how to handle my father."

That's what I'm counting on.

"Speaking of fathers . . ." Rose pauses. "Yours called a little while ago looking for you. He said you weren't answering your phone. I told him you must have forgotten it in my room when you went to get me a latte. Meri . . . he sounded strange."

I rub my forehead as pressure builds behind my eyes. "He's just worried. I'll give him a call. Don't worry about it. Focus on your dad and on finding something that can help us locate Isaac."

Rose assures me she'll be fine and hangs up as Spine yells for the teams to assemble on the third floor to go over the final plans before we head out. I tell my team I'll meet them up there. When they exit, I take a deep breath and dial my father. He answers on the first ring.

"Honey, I was hoping you'd be home by now." His words sound strained, but strong and sober. "Rose filled me in on what's happening with her brother."

"Then you understand that I have to help her."

"Rose needs your support, but we have to talk. Why don't I come by and pick you up. We could get dinner and you can go back to Rose's after."

"I've already eaten."

He lets out a sigh. "I know you're upset about last night. If you let me explain—"

"Explain later, Dad," I shoot back as fear and frustration and disappointment burst free. "Right now there are more important things than whatever excuse you have this time. I'll be home in a few hours," I say as someone shouts my new name from down the hall. "If you really want to talk to me, you'll be sober when I get there." I hit End and close my eyes tight to ward off the growing tension. If he's sober when I get home, I'll tell him everything, because tonight is about truth, and it is time to end the lies.

Switching my phone to vibrate, I push the ache in my heart to the side and hurry to find Atlas and the others. Spine is standing on a chair in the center of a recreation-style room. Stewards are jammed on worn couches or milling about the tight space. Some tie and retie their laces. Others are huddled in groups, talking intently. The bags of books and papers that were brought from the Lyceum are piled near the door.

Spine nods when she spots me and lets out a loud whistle. Everyone quiets.

Nervous excitement crackles as I weave through the Stewards, almost all dressed in black sweatshirts, to stand next to Atlas and Dewey.

Spine rolls up her sleeves—the book and the flame tattoo on her forearm visible as she slowly turns on her chair to survey everyone in the room. Several Stewards pull up their sleeves or roll down their socks to display the same tattoo.

Finally, Spine straightens her shoulders and speaks with a voice that carries throughout the space. "Atticus should be the one to make this speech."

I find Atlas's hand and weave my fingers through his.

"The Stewards were founded because Atticus's father understood the power of words and did what he could to protect them. Atticus continued to lead that mission, but he decided that keeping the record of our country was not the way we should measure success. He believed that every day the lies presented as truth by our government went unchecked made it harder for the truth to be returned and embraced. And that truth valuable enough to protect was important enough to fight for."

Stewards around me nod and raise their fists.

Spine turns to face Atlas. "Atticus intended on waging this fight quietly. He did not ask for our help, because he did not want to put anyone else at risk. But he is not here to stand for the truth. He was turned in to the Marshals by one of our own who believed she understood the Stewards and our mission better than anyone else. So we will stand for the truth in his place and hope the truth will set not only Atticus but the entire country free."

She scans the room again. "This won't be easy."

Feet shuffle around me.

"Some of you have trained for months, others for years, to avoid the Marshals and keep the Stewards a secret. Today, we are asking you to use those skills to let the people of this city know what we have been protecting all these years. When the government realizes what we are doing—the Marshals will come."

Heads nod. A Steward not far from me with a shock of gray running through dark red hair jams her hands into her pockets and looks down at the floor.

When that truth settles, Spine continues. "When you see them, run. Return here or to one of the stations in the surrounding neighborhood. Keep your face hidden if there is any chance you'll be recognized by anyone in the area. If your real identity is compromised, Index will see to it that you are safely hidden until you can be taken out of the city."

Spine checks her watch. "At this very moment, Stacks is leaving for his decoy run. Anyone having second thoughts should speak up now."

The woman with the age-streaked red hair whispers to the person next to her and shakes her head. "I'm sorry. I want to do this. I thought I could, but I can't." She then hurries to the door with tears in her eyes.

When the woman is gone, Renu steps forward. "We can divide

up her work among the rest of the group." Her eyes are determined behind her dark glasses. "We have it covered. Right?"

A muscular gray-haired man next to her nods. "Damn right."

Spine's smile is grim. "She's right to be scared. What we do tonight is dangerous. The government is counting on us to be afraid. They think fear will keep us quiet, but we will be silent no more. Removing words changed our country to what it is today. Returning them will start the process of giving back the freedoms that have long been denied to everyone—the ones our founders believed in. While they fought with weapons to gain the freedom they sought, the most powerful shots they fired in that fight were ones made up of words. Today you will follow in that tradition."

Stokers pump their fists as Spine continues. "Be smart. I already know you are brave. For years you have guarded the embers of truth, and now it is time to stoke them into a fire that cannot be extinguished." She rolls her sleeve over her tattoo and puts up her black hood.

The air is still as she checks the time, then scans the room from one side to the other. I hold my breath.

"You have forty-five minutes to get into your positions. Keep your phones on in case we have any news to share with you. And now . . ." She takes a deep breath and nods. "I wish you all a safe and purposeful ride."

There are whoops and fist bumps, and under the excited shouts of "Let's go!" and "For Atticus!" is the sharp edge of fear.

"In a time of universal deceit, telling the truth is a revolutionary act," Dewey says, looking down at the battered hat in his hands. "Let the revolution begin."

"Who said that?" I ask as the first group of Stewards each grab at least two bags of books and papers off the pile near the door and head out. Their jaws are set. Their eyes are bright with determination. My stomach jumps and rolls.

"Funny . . ." Dewey places the hat on his head and smiles. "But no one seems to truly know. When this is over, we'll have to do our best to find out."

Finally, it's our turn.

I pick up two bags and groan under the weight. Awkwardly, I adjust them onto my shoulder next to my much lighter backpack, while the others, even Dewey, heave three or four of them onto their shoulders without flinching.

Spine turns to me. "I've put you and Atlas together. Our three teams of two will be approaching the pier from different sides. There will be a lot of people there, which makes it an excellent choice, but it is also the most dangerous. It could be easy to get trapped at the end of the pier without any method of escape. You requested this particular location, but I can assign you to another if you have any concerns. No one will think less of you."

"My mom used to take me to Navy Pier at least once a week when I was younger." We rode the carousel and the Ferris wheel and afterward we would sit with our tablets and draw. She with sure hands and a clear eye. I with the hope that someday I would be as good as her. As I grew older, there was less time for those adventures. But we still made a point of visiting as a family several times a year. The last was two weeks before she died. If my mother were here now, it's the location she would take. "It's the place I know best."

Spine nods. "I had a feeling you were going to say that. You're right," she says to Dewey. "She's a lot like Folio."

I hope so.

Spine goes over our starting locations one more time and reminds me to keep an eye on my phone in case Rose has information to share.

"I'll let you know if I hear anything," I assure her.

Index appears at the doorway and motions that the previous group has left the area and the street is clear for us.

Shifting the weight on my shoulder, I start forward, only to have Spine put out her arm to stop me. "There's one more thing," she says.

"What?" I ask.

She reaches into her pocket, pulls out a small red bag, and shakes a blue pill into her palm. "This."

My heart beats in my throat as I stare at the deadman's switch.

"Every Steward has one. It's to protect the mission of truth and give you a choice when the Marshals would take all your choices away."

She holds out her hand to me, and my mouth goes dry.

Just days ago, I had never heard the word "verify." My truth was what I heard in school and learned on screens and saw when I walked down the street every day. I believed the world was safe because I was told that it was. And maybe the world could have still been safe if I'd chosen to ignore what I know. But I can't. The truth changed my life before I ever heard it spoken. And tonight the truth will change my life again.

Slowly, I take the pill from Spine's palm and roll the blue capsule between my fingers.

"I hope I never need to use it," I say, sliding the small pill into my front pocket.

"You and me both, Merriam." Spine shifts the bags on her shoulder. "Now let's ride."

EIGHTEEN

The sky is still bright, but the sun is starting to descend toward the horizon as we weave through the people chattering while they walk. We use the Steward CTA cards to take the bus to the stop closest to our destination. Spine goes over the best exits from the pier with a lanky, older blond guy with wire-rimmed glasses named Huck while Dewey chats up a sprite-like girl with at least a dozen piercings and pink-and-black-streaked hair called Flap. Atlas stays close to me as the bus jerks forward. I watch the city streets roll by, anxiety growing with every block.

Are there enough people out tonight to make this plan work? I don't know. The city streets will be busier in a few weeks when the weather is hotter and there is a festival or concert or art display on every other street corner, but there are enough—I hope—to help us fight back. To give Rose an opening to locate Atlas's dad and Isaac. To let me finish the task my mother left for me. We just need to reach a few hundred people and get them asking the right questions. That will be the spark. Those questions will get others talking. Hundreds will become thousands within days, and then there will be nothing the government can do to stop the truth from spreading. The Marshals can't possibly have the ability to silence everyone.

Spine points to the door as the bus jerks to a halt. "This is our stop."

The six of us climb onto the curb, and Spine checks her phone. "The other three groups have all reached their positions. Stacks will start his run in five minutes. We have to move."

We reach the end of the next block, and the six of us part ways.

"Five minutes until Stacks is set to ride. As soon as you have passed out all of your tickets, get back to Index's station," Spine says. "I'll send the green light as soon as Stacks gives me the go. With any luck, we'll be able to spread the truth to a lot of people and give your friend enough time to find what we need." She nods to the others. "Have a good run." With that, she starts jogging down the street. Huck and Flap fall in behind her.

Dewey shifts his bags on his shoulder and gives me what he probably considers a smile. "Whatever happens, I know Atticus and Folio would be proud. I will see both of you soon." With a parting touch to the brim of his hat, Dewey follows Spine and the others into the final rays of daylight.

Atlas and I walk in silence to our assigned starting location—an alcove of a building a block and a half away from Navy Pier. I take out my phone and wait for the message from Spine that will tell us Stacks has drawn the Marshals to the location on the south side of the city and that it is time for us to go.

Atlas eases the zippers of his bags open halfway, and I use my sweaty, shaking fingers to do the same with mine. "Hand out the dictionaries first. Each has one of the papers Dewey created stuffed inside it," Atlas says quietly. "The less you are weighed down, the faster you'll be able to run if you need to."

Good advice, I think as Atlas takes my hand and we wait— together. Just days ago, the city seemed safe. Atlas was a stranger. I felt alone. Now the city is filled with danger, and I can't imagine navigating it tonight without Atlas by my side.

My phone buzzes.

DAD JUST GOT A CALL. HE ASKED TO KEEP HIM UPDATED.

"I think Stacks has gotten the attention of the Marshals," I say as my phone sounds again and there is only one word with this message:

GO!

My stomach trips as I shove my phone into my back pocket. Before I can step onto the sidewalk, Atlas grabs my arm. "Merriam, you're going to run if you see the Marshals, right? You're not going to try to be a hero."

"I wouldn't know how to be a hero," I say. "We have to go."

"Promise me." He cups my cheek with his hand so I can't avoid his eyes. "Promise when you see a Marshal you'll run."

"I can't help Isaac or your father if the Marshals catch me," I say. "I promise."

Relief and something I can't identify fills his eyes. He brushes my cheek with his hand. I lean into his touch as I study his face, which has become so important to me in just a matter of days. Finally, he steps away and nods. "Then let's do this."

It's strange. In movies, when a character is risking everything there are explosions or major car chases. But there are no fires or floods or things falling from the sky as Atlas and I walk out of the alcove and onto the sidewalk. There is nothing about us walking in the twilight—Atlas in red shorts and a black hooded sweatshirt and me in my jeans and battered blue baseball cap—that would strike any observer as brave. I wonder what quote Dewey would have for this moment as I pull a faded *Merriam-Webster's Collegiate Dictionary* out of my bag, walk up to a dark-haired woman in a dove-gray suit, and say, "This is for you. I hope you read it."

She looks confused as she takes the book, but she takes it.

Atlas approaches a couple pushing a toddler in a stroller and does the same. Quickly, I move down the sidewalk, pulling books out of my bag and asking people to let me put the truth in their hands. There are gasps of how expensive paper is and some shouts about how we are being selfish for not recycling. A few even wonder if this is a reality show stunt as they take the books from my hands and turn them over, as if waiting for something magic to appear—intrigued by the paper—just as I was when I saw a man arrested for having it. Each time I ask them to read the paper sticking out of the book and dig into my bag for another. Every book I hand out makes me reach faster for the next, until I have no more dictionaries to give and I am reaching for the stacks of papers Dewey created.

The lights of Navy Pier shine against the darkening sky when my pocket buzzes. I practically shove a paper into the hands of an older woman and look for Atlas as I pull out my phone.

SOMETHING BIG IS HAPPENING. DAD HAS GONE INTO THE MAYOR'S OFFICE. I'M ALONE AND LOOKING NOW.

Rose's message means we might have mere minutes before Marshals arrive. But if she's just starting her search, we can't clear out. We have to reach more people and keep her dad busy long enough for her to have a chance of finding the location of the Unity Centers.

I send the prearranged alert to the team and look around. Large clusters of people are on the other side of the street, moving toward Navy Pier. So I yell to Atlas to head for the crosswalk.

Sirens blare in the distance.

The glow of the top half of the slowly moving Navy Pier Ferris wheel shines in the sky.

The light changes before Atlas can cross. Cars zoom by, and I hurry from person to person, handing out the sheets Dewey designed with the word "VERIFY" at the top.

"Isn't using paper like this against the law?" someone yells.

"Go find a recycling center."

"Whatever that is, I don't want it."

"Please, take a look," I urge. "It's important."

More sirens. Closer than before. And I haven't handed out enough papers yet. I have to work faster.

I approach a group of people dressed in long satin dresses with rhinestones and suits and ties and fumble as I try to give them each a page as quickly as possible before moving on to the next group. Out of the corner of my eye, I spot a guy standing under the Navy Pier archway just behind me—glaring at the paper in my hand.

Someone bumps me as I hurry to a group of college-age guys who push my papers aside with sneers and laughs, and I turn to look for someone else to hand them to. The sound of an electric bass coming from the pier pulses like a strobe light in my chest.

Fountains gurgle and spray.

Another siren screams in the air, and a police car comes into view.

I spot Atlas far to my left. He waves both arms over his head. He shouts something I can't hear over the cars and the band and the people laughing and the sound of the water as it swooshes up and crashes to the pavement behind me. I take two steps toward him when he shakes his head, points to a woman twenty feet away, and mouths the word "Run!"

I don't need to look at the shoes. The way the eyes of the woman in the jean jacket and button-down shirt narrow and how she begins to move when she sees the paper in my hands tell me all I need to know. I start to my right, then see a man in a dark jacket stepping out from behind a post. With my heart pounding hard in my ears, I turn toward the lights and music and run.

"Hey!"

I bump into a guy pushing a stroller, shout an apology, but I don't stop, because I can hear other shouts that tell me the Marshals are on my heels. I jump atop the long seat of a red-and-silver bench, step on the back of it, and leap over onto the stone pavement. I don't look behind me as I bolt toward the fountain park. Despite the chilly breeze coming off the lake, there are kids squealing as they skip through the dozen or so arching sprays of water. Pulling the bag of papers to my chest, I splash across the pavement, dodge the children, and veer right to the concourse side of the pier. The splashing footsteps that pound behind me tell me I can't slow down.

Lights glow against the darkening of the night. I glance behind me as I weave around a performer made up to look like a statue. The woman Marshal is about twenty yards back and moving fast. The other one is nowhere in view. Neither is Atlas or any of the Stewards I recognize. For now, I'm on my own.

Fear pushes me to go faster. I weave around advertising screens touting restaurants and boat rides and other entertainments, and then run past people and streetlamps down the interlocked stone ground of the concourse. In the middle of the summer, the pier is packed with people. A larger crowd would be easier to get lost in. I could just wait for the Marshals to pass me by without venturing too far away from shore. But it isn't wall-to-wall people today, which makes it harder to simply fade into the background.

The sounds of guitars, horns, drums, and the bass that still rings deep in my chest grow closer the farther onto the pier I run. Scents of roasting nuts, popcorn, and fried dough are carried on the ever-chillier breeze, or maybe it just seems colder because my feet are wet and I'm scared and desperate to get away from it all.

Dropping the slightly damp page in my hands into an open bag dangling off an older woman's arm, I dash to the side of a snack booth to my right, which partially hides me from view. I take off the blue baseball cap and shake out my hair so it curtains around my shoulders. Then I pull up the bottom of my shirt and tie it into a knot above my waist. I drop the black duffel, now emptied of dictionaries, behind the stand, jam my hat into one of the other bags, and make sure they are each open enough for me to grab items out of them on the fly before slinging them over my shoulder.

As far as disguises go, it's not great. But the Marshals saw me for only a few seconds. I hope they'll focus on looking for the blue hat as I hurry toward the music.

I glance over my shoulder as I weave around a woman holding a small, crying toddler. There is a man in a dark shirt and dark shoes standing with his back to me about fifteen feet away. He turns in my direction, and the familiar sharp nose and scruffy jawline get me moving again.

The music grows louder.

The lights get brighter.

I zigzag through the growing number of meandering tourists,

some holding the familiar red-covered dictionaries in their hands. The band I have been hearing is playing on a stage to my left, and I make a beeline toward the crowd in front of it. A guy shouts, "Hey, watch it," to my right. I turn and spot the female Marshal shoving her way through the dancing and singing rock band audience. And her eyes are set on me.

I wriggle my way through a group of women with their arms slung around each other. A bunch of them swear or yell at me as I search for somewhere, anywhere, to run. One of my bags slides down my shoulder. I reach for the strap to shrug it back up when something catches on the strap and pulls.

I stumble forward, hit the ground, and ignore the pain as panic screams inside me. I turn and scoot backward. Cymbals crash over and over again. The female Marshal smiles and strides closer.

"Are you okay?" A guy steps in between the Marshal and me. I watch her reach around her back as I scramble to my feet and run.

"Screw you!" the guy shouts as I duck and weave and dodge through the crowd until I am close to the front center of the stage with the female Marshal and her scary smile advancing. From the other far side of the stage I see the hooked-nosed Marshal take a step forward and nod. The female Marshal pauses. Both watch me, waiting—like lions hunting prey—ready to pounce when I make a move. There's an entrance to the inside restaurants to my right. I just need to get there, and I might have a chance.

Lights pulse. A guitar solo wails. I look for Atlas or any of the other Stewards, but if they are on the pier, they aren't here now. But thinking of Atlas gives me an idea.

I ease the backpack off my shoulder. My attention shifting between the man standing at the end of the stage and the woman bobbing back and forth with the crowd to keep me in her sights, I reach into my bag.

The drumbeat gets faster and louder. The guitar solo gains in frenzy. I pull the papers out and launch them into the air like Atlas did when we last faced Marshals. The pages fly up in the gusting breeze. The guitar wails on a high note, and the crowd cheers. The female Marshal is knocked to the side as people surge forward, grabbing at the fluttering papers, thinking it's part of the act, and I bend low and bolt for the entrance.

The female Marshal is not far behind me as I leap over a "Wet Floor" sign, dodge a family eating ice cream, and race through the wide, tiled indoor concourse that smells of grilled meat and fudge. The Marshal is still right behind me. I reach back into my bag and throw more papers as I streak by a group of costumed people singing "Happy Birthday." There are shouts of surprise, and I toss another handful of papers over my shoulder while dashing for the exit.

Immediately, I know I've gone the wrong way. The Ferris wheel looms in the air above me, inching in its slow arc of the sky, and grows closer with every step I take. But there is no going back the way I came because the Marshal hasn't given up.

I see a man and a woman flanking a drunken friend. The friend's head lolls to the side, and I realize that the girl isn't their friend at all. Pink-streaked hair flutters, and piercings twinkle as they catch the light. The woman they are dragging is Flap.

Farther down the pier I spot Dewey's hat. He leaps around a food cart with two men in pursuit.

I want to help them, but there is nothing I can do with my own Marshal closing in. I toss more papers, dart around tourists, and

climb the wide concrete steps that lead to the next level. I am gasp-
ing for air as I reach the top. Lungs burning, I hurry toward the
carousel that plays the same happy music I remember from when I
rode the colorfully painted horses as a child.

Desperate, I circle the ride and head for the Ferris wheel, turning its large, enclosed gondolas lazily in the sky.

My legs tremble. No matter how scared I am, I won't be able
to keep running like this for much longer. Thankfully, the woman
chasing me, who is now scanning the carousel, appears to have also
slowed down.

The Ferris wheel crawls to a stop. The gondola doors slowly
slide open, and when passengers start to unload I see my chance.
I duck behind the pedestal of a statue that is near the line for the
Ferris wheel and take several deep breaths. I have to get this right
because I won't have another opportunity.

The Marshal is still searching the carousel.

Screens filled with news or advertisements for cruises and restaurants flicker.

Crouching, I watch passengers climb off and new ones load on.

When the new passengers disappear through the door, I take a
deep breath, wait for the doors to slide shut, and yell, "Hey! That girl
cut in front of me. Hey!"

The Marshal's head snaps in this direction.

"Stop the Ferris wheel!" I shout as the gondola begins to inch
forward.

The Marshal takes a step toward it. Two. Then she starts to
run.

I wait for her to pass the statue, then bolt in the opposite direction to the glass atrium building on the far side. There are gardens

and fountains in there that my mother helped me draw. I know how to get to the front of the pier and the exit from there.

I reach the open doorway just as a hand latches on to my arm. Cold metal jams into the exposed skin at my waist and I go completely still.

"I don't think so," the hooked-nosed Marshal taunts. I had been so focused on the other Marshal, I'd never looked for this one.

I think about the pill in my pocket. This moment is why the deadman's switch exists. To keep those who are still fighting for the truth—like Rose and Atlas—safe. I know what I'm supposed to do now, but I can't. Maybe Scarlett was right about me not belonging in the Stewards. Maybe I'm not brave enough because I can't make the choice to die.

"Turn around slowly and come with me. No reason to be a martyr for something you can't possibly understand."

My heart roars in my chest.

"People are going to know the truth," I say as the Marshal yanks me out of the doorway. "They're going to demand answers. You won't be able to stop them."

"You want to bet on that?" the Marshal asks.

"I'll take that bet." Spine's voice comes out of nowhere. She spins. Kicks. Her foot connects with the Marshal's arm. He stumbles, and I reach into my bag for the hard-covered book I used earlier today and slam it into the Marshal's face. The man screams. Blood spurts from his nose as he lifts his gun toward me. I raise the book again, knowing it won't stop the bullet, but suddenly the man reels backward as Atlas appears and latches on to the guy's arm. The sharp crack of the gunshot makes me go cold. It strikes the nearby pavement with a loud bang. The Marshal wrenches his arm away, spins under Atlas's punch, and rams his head into Atlas's stomach, sending the two crashing to the ground.

The Marshal recovers first, gun still in his hand. Atlas starts to push up from the ground, but before he can get to his feet or the Marshal can take aim, Spine is there. She spins away from the Marshal's jab, grabs his arm before he recovers, and jams her foot into his crotch.

"Get out of here!" Spine yells.

I help Atlas climb to his feet as the Marshal gasps. Together we run to the entrance of the atrium. We glance back in time to see the Marshal sink to his knees. Spine lands another kick, then punches his already bloody face before shoving him to the ground.

Eyes bright, Spine steps toward us. She swipes a trickle of blood off her cheek and opens her mouth to speak when three pops echo in the air.

Spine jerks. Her eyes go wide, and she takes a halting step forward.

Someone screams.

There's another pop. Spine mouths one word—"Go!" Then she drops to her knees.

I spot the female Marshal near the carousel. Her gun is extended as it swings toward us.

Terrified shrieks fill the air. Atlas moves to help Spine, but I grab his hand and pull him toward the atrium entrance.

"She's dead." The words stab deep into my heart. Spine is dead, and it's because of me. My steps slow. I insisted we fight. If I hadn't pushed, she would be in the Lyceum—safe. Flap wouldn't have been taken or killed. Dewey—

There is another crack of gunfire. The bullet clangs against the doorframe beside me, and I pull myself together and get moving. Spine gave her life to save mine. I won't let that be for nothing.

People swarm off the carousel in panic, moving between us and the Marshal.

"This way!" I yell to Atlas, who gives one last look at Spine's unmoving body before turning to follow me into the atrium. Crystal water sprays in dozens of fountains. Lights glisten off the water and make the flowers look otherworldly as people scream.

"There are Marshals in the next building. Go for the emergency exit!" Atlas yells.

"It'll set off an alarm."

"That's the least of our problems."

A Marshal appears at the other end of the atrium, and the discussion is over as we run to the emergency exit. A shrill, incessant siren echoes in the stairwell as we pound down the steps to the hallway below.

"Now what?" I pant. We've left the public part of the pier. I'm no longer sure where we are or where to run next, but we're going to have to make a decision—fast.

"There are at least a dozen Marshals swarming the pier," Atlas says as we head down the hall to who knows where. "They'll be guarding the exits, and they won't leave until they have checked every inch of this place."

So we can't simply stroll outside, and we can't stay here. "What about the boats?"

Somewhere above us a door slams open. Footsteps sound as I dump the book I'm still holding in my bag and race to keep up with Atlas. He shoves open an exit door, and we head out into the night.

I can barely catch my breath as we fall in step next to a group of five guys and three girls who appear to be only a handful of years

284

older than us. I force myself to walk as if we belong with these people, who are currently talking about whose house they are going to next. To pretend Spine didn't just die before my eyes and her killer isn't in pursuit.

In my head I am screaming that we should run, but I keep my pace unhurried and stay close to the others. Only the nearer we get to the end of the pier, the more Marshals and police officers I count. Some are picking up fluttering papers from the ground or ripping them from people's hands. Others are stopping tourists and asking questions. A Marshal pulls a man out of a group and marches him over to the side where another waits with his arms behind his back. Neither arrested man looks familiar, but both have rich brown skin and short hair. Something that isn't lost on Atlas.

He pulls me around the side of the concession stand and puts his hands firmly on my shoulders. "We have to split up."

"What?" My heart jumps. "No. We have to stay together."

"They won't look twice at you as long as you walk through the exit with this group," Atlas whispers. Nearby a speaker blasts upbeat music about the feeling of freedom.

"No." I shake my head as the group we were walking with pass over their money and retrieve change. They'll be leaving soon. "Please . . ." I look up at Atlas. "I'm not leaving you behind."

"You promised me before tonight started that you wouldn't be a hero. That when it was time to run, you would run."

"Yes, but—"

He takes my face in his hands and cuts off my protests with his lips. They are hot and strong, and I grab his arms and hold as tight as I can because I don't want to let him go. Not now that I have just found him. That we have found each other.

Atlas leans back and just like that, the kiss—our moment—is

over. The music on the pier continues to play. The Marshals are still looking for us. The people providing our unwitting cover are collecting their nachos and drinks—getting ready to move on.

"Meri," Atlas says, his eyes hot on mine, "I'm going to fight like hell to get off this pier and back to you. But to do that, I need you to trust me enough to leave me behind. I need you to do what you promised."

I pull Atlas's head down, press my lips against his one more time, and before I can change my mind, I rejoin the laughing, carefree group and walk away. One of the guys notices me and grins. I blink back tears and return the smile as each step puts more distance between Atlas and me.

"Did you go to the concert?" I ask, spotting a Marshal near the waterside edge of the pier.

The music crackles and cuts out, and a voice over the loudspeaker announces, "Due to an electrical problem, Navy Pier is now closed."

All around, people groan.

"Yeah," the guy next to me answers. "We were there in the back. How about you?"

"I was up front. It was—"

"Hey!" A uniformed officer comes running toward me. It takes a second to realize he is pointing not at me but at something off to the side—near the water. "Hey! Stop!"

Marshals race by, and I keep pace with the growing crowd heading off the pier. "Stop him!" someone shouts.

Several people crane their necks to see what's happening. I'm bumped and jostled and I am desperate to stop and look back, but I promised to keep moving forward. So I do.

A woman's scream rakes over my heart. Four pops crack like whips against the night. I feel each resonate deep in my chest. My eyes burn with tears, but I affix Atlas's face in my mind and walk away.

Police officers are scattered around the fountain. A dozen black sedans like the one Mr. Webster drives are parked out front, with men in suits milling around. Marshals in their distinctive boots stand near the curb and grab people holding the Stewards' pages from the crowd. I keep my head down and—

Someone bumps into me hard. The jolt sends the bags I'm carrying sliding off my shoulder. As they hit the ground, the top of the dictionary slides out.

"Are you okay?" a male voice asks in the chaos, and a familiar face with a fussy red goatee leans down to help. It's Victor Beschloss—one of the heads of the City Pride Program. A man who helped murder my mother. "Here, let me . . ."

I know the second his voice stops that he's spotted the book. His eyes flick to my face and go wide. "Merriel Beckley?"

He blinks away his surprise, then raises his hand, waving to someone over my shoulder as I reach for the book. "I should have realized. You're going to have to come with—"

Without hesitation, I grab the book and jam it into his throat. As he gasps and reaches for his neck, I crack the flat cover against his forehead. He staggers and hits the ground. I scoop up my bag and weave through the still-exiting crowd with one thought pounding through my mind.

He knows who I am. Not my Steward name. My real one. Which means they'll be coming for me now. And not just me. They'll be coming for my dad.

NINETEEN

I have to get home.

There were men watching my house. If they are still there, I can't go home.

My chest aches as I dash into an alcove not far from a bus station two blocks away and blink back the panic that is clawing into my throat. The public transit card belongs to the Stewards. If they are looking for me, they won't be able to track my movements. Not with that. But my phone . . . they'll be able to track that. I can only hope they aren't doing it already.

Shaking, I dial, praying my father answers and that he hasn't been drinking.

It takes three rings. "Meri? Where are you? You said—"

"Dad! You have to get out of the house."

"I'm not going anywhere. I understand you've been upset, but you have to come home—"

"Dad!" I peer around the doorway down the street and spot the bus coming toward me from one direction and two policemen from the other. "Listen. I can't come home, and you can't stay. They're coming." There's too much to explain and not enough time. "If you love me . . ." I take a deep breath. "If you loved Mom, you will go out the back door and walk down the alley to . . ." To where? The Lyceum is locked down. The Marshals will search Dad's work and every restaurant and friend's house we're known to frequent. There's only one place I can send him—to the place where all the Stewards who survived the night will be headed—Index's station. "There's a building on the North Side of the Loop." I give him the cross streets and tell him to meet me on the corner.

"Honey, this is crazy. . . ."

"I know it sounds insane, but please. I love you. And I need you to do this. I need you to go." The city bus whines to a stop at the curb.

The silence stretches. Finally, Dad says, "Okay. I'm going to the alley now. But, Meri—"

"Leave your phone at home so they'll think you're still there." I make sure the police are looking the other way and hurry toward the bus. "I'll explain everything when I see you." I hit End and let my phone drop to the ground. Then I climb up the metal step and remain standing like Atlas taught me as the bus drives away.

I take calming breaths that do nothing to ease my worry as I navigate my way back to the cross streets where I told my father we would meet. And when I see him standing near a streetlight . . . I'm tired and sore, but, once again, I run.

He smells of alcohol, but I don't care. I hug him tight, pull him toward the station, then go through the process of entering the code. "Get in, quickly," Index says, moving to let us inside.

"Who's this?" Dewey appears at the end of the hall. His pants are ripped, and there's a bruise on his cheek, but his hat is still firmly on his head. "We expected you back before now. What happened?"

"This is my dad. I had to bring him," I say, watching the door-way, hoping to see one person who doesn't appear. "I was recog-nized," I admit, and it all comes rushing out. Spine's death. Flap being carted away. Atlas and the gunshots and finally escaping from Mr. Beschloss, who saw the book and has most likely sent people to my home.

"Index will make arrangements for both of you." Dewey sighs and holds out his hand to my father. "Your wife was a fine lady. Mer-riam is a lot like her."

"Who is Merriam?" my father asks. "What are you doing with my daughter, and how is it that you knew my wife?"

"Not the questions I would ask, but I suppose we all have to start somewhere," Dewey answers. When my father blinks, Dewey shakes his head. "Why don't we go somewhere and talk. I promise I'll do my best to speak slow."

"I should—"

"You should go upstairs," Dewey instructs as Index leads my confused and annoyed father down the hall. "There are others who have returned and are waiting."

The grief that I've kept at bay until now swells. As does the guilt. "I don't know if I can face everyone. Not after Spine and Flap and who knows how many others."

"There was always going to come a time when we took a stand. We all knew going in sacrifices would be made."

"Yeah, but I was the one that picked the locations. I—"

"Just because you lit the match doesn't mean you control the flame. Think about that before you wallow in guilt." With that, Dewey wanders off to speak to my father and I steel myself and go upstairs.

Two screens flicker in the dimly lit room. Over a dozen faces turn toward me, but it all fades when I spot the one I most needed to see, limping in my direction. He has a gash on his forehead and a bloody, makeshift bandage on his arm, but he is steady and strong, and I realize his clothes are wet when he puts his arms around me and holds me close.

"I told you to trust me," Atlas whispers.

"Why are you wet?" I ask, stepping back to look at him.

"I had to take an alternate exit."

"He got shot in the process," Stacks adds from the corner of the room. "I had to pull his sorry self out of the water. Now that you're here, maybe he'll let someone patch up that arm."

I assure Stacks that he will.

I have Atlas use his phone to send a message to Rose, then together we sit on the floor, my head on his shoulder, as we wait for her to respond.

More Stewards arrive. There are some tears, but there is laughter and pride at what has been accomplished. One by one they stumble off to their sleeping quarters, but we wait. Atlas with the phone in his hand. I with my head on his shoulder, willing Rose to make contact.

Finally, his phone rings, and Atlas passes it to me so I can answer.

"Are you okay?" I ask first.

"I'm fine. Dad isn't himself. He was so distracted most of the time he barely remembered I was there."

"Did you find where Isaac and Atticus are being held?"

The long pause conveys the answer before she says, "I thought I had, but no."

I shake my head, and the air seems to go out of Atlas. Despair floods his face as he closes his eyes and leans his head back against the wall. And there is nothing I can do to help him.

Rose keeps talking. "Dad doesn't have any paper files in his office, but he forgot to shut down his computer. You were right. He knows what happened to Isaac. I found his message to the mayor. He said he understood why Isaac couldn't be released until the Marshals were positive the flag on his ID was flawed. He then requested authorization to visit the Unity Center to check the progress of the inquiry. His request was denied, and there wasn't any information about where the center is located."

Damn. "But if he's asking to visit, then Isaac has to be in the city. Right?" And if the people we met tonight start asking enough questions, they won't be able to hide it for long.

Atlas's eyes open.

"Don't give up hope," I say. "Isaac is alive, and we're going to find him." We can still find them both.

The truth is out there, I think as the sun comes up. We just have to wait for it to take hold.

TWENTY

We assemble in the morning to watch the news for signs that our efforts are taking effect. Atlas stands close to me—his eyes glued on the screen.

There is nothing in the first news report.

Stacks changes channels. Index brings doughnuts, then returns to her efforts of ferrying Stewards who missed the lockdown out of town. Halfway through the next news report my father stumbles into the room with Dewey at his side.

The anchor discusses the weather, sports, the start of the Grant Park summer concert series. Finally there is a story about a strange power surge at Navy Pier last night.

We all go still as the chirpy anchor goes on to explain, "Several breakers were damaged, which forced those enjoying the warmer weather to leave early. But never fear, city officials tell us the problem has been repaired and those looking forward to a boat ride or taking the high-flying tour of the city from the historic Navy Pier Ferris wheel today will not be disappointed."

An hour later, a more sober newsman reports details of an unauthorized block party near Wrigley Field as well as a gas leak that shut down the streets on the Magnificent Mile. All locations we were at last night. All places we spread tickets.

People who received the tickets will hear the news report and recognize it as dishonest.

"I think this might actually work," someone says.

I call Rose on Atlas's phone and learn the police are looking for me and my father. Her father's blaming the same gang that took Isaac and is insisting Rose stay with her mother instead of visiting him at work. She promises to let us know if she is able to learn anything more before she hangs up, and I have nothing else to do but watch the reports and wait.

At first my father avoids me, but eventually, I am able to corner him in the library on the top floor of Index's station. He is holding a history book in trembling hands.

"Your mother hid all of this from me," he says quietly.

"She did it to protect you. To protect us," I say. I still wish she had done things differently, but after what I have seen and done, I understand why she believed she had to keep her secrets close.

He shakes his head. "I wish I could believe that. She risked her life . . . she thought this was so important that she died for it. She trusted Atlas's father. She trusted Dewey and all the others. Me, she left in the dark. She didn't trust me. She could have told me, and she didn't. And neither did you." He flings the book across the room, and I jump as it crashes against the window and thuds to the floor. "How do I live with that, *Merriam*? How do I live knowing that you both chose these people over me?"

I flinch at the bitter tone he uses for my code name. "I didn't

294

choose them," I shout. "I had to find out the truth about Mom, and you . . ." I bite back the angry words I want to hurl. The words about how alone he's made me feel and how there was no way I could turn to him because of all the promises he's broken. "I had to know the truth."

"Well, now you do," he scoffs. "And I know the truth, too. We no longer have a home. I don't have a job. Some guy named Stacks told me he went by our house and saw people loading our things into a moving van. So the truth is that we've lost everything. And now we have no choice but to leave."

"You want to leave? But Isaac and Atticus are still missing, and there's so much more we can do to change things. Mom would want us to—"

"Your mom didn't care what I wanted." His tone is icy calm and sends a chill up my spine. "I don't have to consider what she would want now. My first and only concern is keeping you safe, and we'll be leaving as soon as Index makes the arrangements. She says lots of people who were once part of these Stewards have started over and are living good lives. We can forget all of this ever happened."

He glares at all the books haphazardly jammed onto the shelves that line the room, clenches his fists, and walks out.

Leave? Forget? Impossible. I start to chase after him, but he's too angry to listen. *I just need to give him time*, I tell myself. The truth is hard to accept. He'll realize how important this is and understand why I did what I did when people in the city begin to share the truth we gave them.

Later that evening my father stumbles into the third-floor gathering room as the rest of us are watching the evening news. His eyes are unfocused. His face is flushed, and the smile he gives me makes me want to sink to my knees. Everything has changed between us, but nothing has changed at all.

Dewey comes to stand next to me. "John McCain said 'The truth is sometimes a hard pill to swallow. It sometimes causes difficulties.'" He gestures toward my father. "He tried several times to leave the station today in order to get a drink. He wants to forget. So we gave him what he needed."

"You did that to him? You gave him a drink?" I lash out. "How could you?"

Dewey sighs. "He was willing to risk all of us—even you—to get what he required. Would you have had me do anything else?"

I don't know. I want to say that Dad would have never had another drink if Dewey hadn't given him alcohol today, but wanting something to be true doesn't mean it is.

"Your father needs time. He's not the only one."

I glance around the room. Several sets of angry eyes glower at the screens. We had all hoped that our message would be immediately felt. Now, for some, the hope they had been operating on is fading.

"Dad wants to leave the city," I say softly. "He's insisting I leave with him."

"Perhaps that is what is meant to happen," Dewey says, nodding to the newscasts. "I suppose time will tell. I'll escort your father to his room."

I watch him take my father by the arm and lead him out. When they're gone, I cross the room to sit with Atlas—feeling his eyes and everyone else's on me. They all saw my father drunk. They all now know what I have tried to hide for so long. Having them know it makes the pain even more real.

I wait for Atlas to say something, but he just takes my hand in his. As we watch the screens, I find myself clinging to the hope that we can still save his father, since I can't do anything right now for my own.

Index brings in platters of sandwiches. Some of the Stewards talk. Others stare out the window as music plays and the next anchor comes on the air.

We don't have to wait long before the redhead behind the desk says, "Anyone out in some of the most popular areas of the North Side of Chicago last night got an intriguing surprise. Paper."

I hold my breath.

"Pages and pages of papers and books were handed out to un-suspecting passersby in an unprecedented promotion for a new movie."

My stomach drops. Everyone in the room shifts.

"Real World Studios isn't sharing details about the title or cast of the upcoming film, but if they are willing to pay the tax on all that paper to get the city abuzz, chances are it will be a blockbuster." There is a shot of a recycling center with a line going out the door.

A man in a black baseball hat gives a toothy smile to the camera as he holds up a fist full of money. "They're paying double the normal rate for those red books. Whoever came up with the promotion is a genius."

The anchor comes back on the screen as several Stewards slip out of the room. "If you know of anyone lucky enough to get one of those promotional books or single-page advertising sheets, please let the city know. We don't want them to miss out on the extra-special recycling bonus. Now for the weather with Lawrence Tapper. How is the rest of the week shaping up, Lawrence?"

None of us listen to Lawrence as what was just reported sinks in.

"Just because they are calling it a promotion doesn't mean everyone will turn them in without reading the pages," Stacks says.

A bunch of Stokers nod, but doubt shadows more than one face. I can tell there are those who wished they had followed Scarlett's edict instead of taking a stand.

The next day, Dewey spouts inspirational quotes about battles and revolution to bolster us, but by the end of the week, most Stewards have either left the station or disappeared into the city to wait for the lockdown's end. There are no more reports about the movie campaign. There is only one news report reminding people not to miss out on the special recycling deals before the reporter turns to a discussion of a weekly weather update filled with rain.

I get up each day and turn on the news, even though I know what I will see. I check on my father, who has only gotten worse. Twice he stumbled out of his room railing against the people who killed my mother. The last time, he struck Stacks in the mouth and drew blood.

"He has to leave the city," Index says gently as Dewey looks on, his battered hat clutched in his hands. "I know you were hoping you could convince him to stay here in the station, but he's not prepared to deal with any of this. We have new identities for you arranged. There's a Steward living near the state border who can help you get across into the outskirts of Madison. We have a small group there that will assist you and your father while you get settled."

"There are people who know the truth here," I say. How can I leave Atlas or Rose, or the memories of my mother? "We just need to give it more time. Or try again."

Dewey closes the door on that hope. "The experiment failed. People have moved on. If you could walk on the streets you'd see them going about their lives as if nothing happened. Since you can't, you'll have to trust me."

"Atlas doesn't believe that." He has gone out every day to search for signs that the spark has been lit. So far he hasn't found any, but so many people received those pages. There have to be some who understood the words and cared. There have to be.

"Atlas is clinging to the idea that Atticus can be found." Dewey sighs. "I wish that were true. He was a dear friend. If I thought we could gather the papers we needed to try again, or that your friend knew where to find the information about his location . . ." He shakes his head. "Unfortunately, it will take months or years before we have the supplies and manpower to mount another try."

"But—"

"Margaret Thatcher has been credited as saying you may have to fight a battle more than once to win it. We will just have to wait, Merriam, until the time is right to fight again." Dewey puts his hand on my shoulder. "Your father is waging his own battle. Perhaps that is where you need to focus your attention now." When I say nothing, Dewey nods. "The last train out leaves in two days. If you are on it, as I suspect you will be, I wish you great luck in your new life. When you need me, I will be here." He presses a kiss to the top of my head, then puts his hat on and disappears out the door.

Index tells me I should get my things together. So, I go upstairs to the room filled with now empty bunk beds I once shared with a half dozen Stewards and begin to put my few belongings into my backpack. Because Dewey is right. My dad has a battle ahead, and I can't even leave this building. What good can I do? Especially without the supplies we will need to mount another attempt to make people see the truth. Maybe by the time we get the papers necessary to try again, people will be ready to see what we see when we read those words. Or maybe . . .

My heart leaps. Maybe Dewey and the Stewards are wrong and we are the ones who need to see things differently. Maybe the battle has to be fought another way.

We know the truth. We can't help but look at the world and not see what we know. But what if we tried to see it like everyone else?

Thunder rumbles, and I think back to that night on Navy Pier. Not of the hope and excitement I felt, but of how people reacted when I handed them the books and the papers. I picture their faces and hands and hear their voices in my head. Surprised. Reluctant. Uncomfortable. At times they were angry because they saw paper the way the government told them it was supposed to be seen, not the way we see it. They saw it as selfish or indulgent or anti-country. So is it any surprise that when they looked at the words on the page or the ideas inside the covers, they saw those the same way?

Most couldn't see the truth through the lens colored by lies. So they recycled the paper as they were told to do. That means we have to present it to them in a way they don't question. That somehow feels familiar.

I sit in the gathering room alone, watching the screen, searching for a way to make that happen. Uninspired, I start to turn away but stop as an advertisement for makeup comes on. The model is stunning. Confident. Happy. Just like everyone watching wants to be as she applies the sharp red color to her lips, winks, and then goes to join a handsome man. It's the type of product advertisement I've always ignored but Rose and all the other girls in school love. The kind that

Rose's mother has in her magazine. The type that makes people study the page to see how they can be that beautiful and happy, too.

And suddenly, I have an idea.

I work on a station tablet throughout the subsequent hours as everyone else akes preparations to leave the next day. Index comes in and tells me the plan for me and Dad to be smuggled out of the city is ready. Dewey is watching my father until it is time for us to leave. A few of the remaining Stewards stop by to wish me a safe ride and to tell me they will try again when the time is right.

I nod and keep drawing.

Sharp lines. Strong colors. No longer am I trying to re-create something my mother would have drawn or something that my teacher would approve of in class. This is my vision. My passion captured with each stroke. I started this fight to finish my mother's work. But while this started with my mother, it is about so much more now. It's about me. And it's time to make the choice to do it my way.

Since I can't use my old information, I create a new email account, then send my work to Rose, hoping my friend will read a message sent from an unfamiliar address. I'm careful not to say anything the government could question, and gnaw on my cheek as I wait anxiously for a reply. Almost immediately, she responds that she knows a great place to get free makeovers and warns that I should immediately take advantage of the offer or I might miss out.

If someone finds the message, they will think Rose was just passing along a fashion-industry tip. Which is exactly what they are supposed to think. I grab the blue hat out of my bag, tuck my hair under it, and head out to find Atlas, who has grown more resigned to losing his father and saying good-bye to me.

Thunder crackles outside as I tell him, "I have an idea. Come with me."

"Where are we going?" he asks as I head for the door. "The Marshals are still looking for you. It's why you have to leave the city."

"I know," I say with confidence that helps keep the fear away as I sneak out the door into the thick air. The promised rain is on the way.

Rose is waiting for us at the open back door of *Gloss*, as I knew she would be. After all, it is where she procures the makeup she always has handy. "This way," she says as we weave through a storeroom filled with samples to her mother's office. "There's a few people working late on the next issue, so I set up in my mom's space upstairs. No one will bother us there."

"Set up?" Atlas asks. "What are we doing here?"

"We're not giving up," I say as Rose leads us to her mother's expansive office filled with images of *Gloss* covers, along with a familiar image Rose loaded onto the screen—the one I sent to her. The one she tells me her mother loves. A new logo for *Gloss*.

It's a version of the Stewards' tattoo—with sharp lines looking like pages of the magazine fluttering open and flames of every color shooting out. "We're just going to change the way we fight."

Atticus and Isaac could still be out there. People continue to disappear and are shipped off to who knows where for purposes we can't yet know. But just because we lost the battle doesn't mean the fight is over. The war has just begun.

"Ready to change?" Rose asks as she pulls out a chair next to a table piled with hair products she gathered for me. Because there is only one option if I want to stay and fight.

Am I ready to become someone new?

I look at Atlas, who is calling Index to tell her we won't be taking the Stewards' final train to safety. I think of my father and all we have been through. I love him, but as much as I want to help him, I have realized the journey he's on is one he needs to take without me. I can't change him or his drinking. And I can't shape my life around trying.

Still, uncertainty swirls as I take off Stef's blue hat and run my fingers along the lining that I will take apart tomorrow. I'm not sure if we can find the location where Atticus and Isaac are being held or what happens to those who are taken away. The truth is, I'm not sure of very much at all.

There is only one thing I am certain of. The truth changed my life without my knowing it, from the minute I first heard it.

I take a seat in the chair and nod to Rose that it is time to start. *To keep fighting for the truth now,* I think, *it is only fitting that I have to change again.*

Atlas watches as Rose cuts and colors and fusses until finally she is ready to let me see her work.

People weren't willing to see the truth the last time we fought for it. *This time,* I think, as I shake out my newly short hair, colored with streaks of bright red and white, *I am going to make the truth impossible for them to ignore.*

ACKNOWLEDGMENTS

Words have power. I don't think I understood how much power until I began to write books. I realized it anew as I sat down to tell this story. Still, no matter how much power words have, it often takes more than one voice to make sure those words are heard.

As an author, I'm lucky to have incredible voices on my side to help me through the process of story conception to publication. It's because of their chorus of support and dedication that the words I write are transformed into a book.

First and foremost, this story would never have been told had it not been for the support, guidance, and friendship of Stacia Decker. It's amazing what ideas a bunch of random emails between client and agent can spark. More amazing still is the careful attention you always give to the story I am telling and to me. You were the first to dedicate yourself to making sure my words are heard, and I am and will always be forever grateful.

Next, words are never written in a vacuum. They are written

on planes, in parks and tae kwon do studios, and most of all in my house. Thank you to all my friends and family. But especially, thank you to my husband, Andy, for understanding the late nights, my need to brainstorm when I am stuck even though you have no idea what I am talking about, and for your love. Also, to my son, Max—thank you for your cheerful certainty that I can do anything and your unflinching conviction when you tell people that I'm famous. (Spoiler alert . . . I'm not famous.) And to my fantastic author assistant and amazing mom—thanks for always meeting the bus and helping with homework when I am out of town and for your unfailing belief that my words have value even when I have no idea what I am trying to say.

So many people touch a book once it's written. To editor extraordinaire Kristen Pettit—thank you for your enthusiasm and your willingness to find the heart of the story I'm trying to tell. I also owe lots of hugs to Ro Romanello and huge applause to Elizabeth Lynch! Also, thanks to Erica Sussman for her vision for HarperTeen and for letting me be a part of it. To my amazing copyeditor Sona Vogel—you are a grammar and fact-check rock star! Edel Rodriguez—I couldn't imagine a more perfect artist or cover for this book. Thank you for lending your incredible talent to my words. And to production editor Liz Byer, incredible designer Jenna Stempel-Lobell, and the entire HarperTeen and Epic Reads team: thank you for your incredible work.

Words have power only if they are heard or read. I am so grateful to each of the librarians, teachers, booksellers, and readers for taking the time to let my words into their lives. You are the reason my words are more than just a bunch of letters on a page. It is you and your imagination that bring them to life.

And finally, I would be remiss in these acknowledgments if I didn't extend my gratitude to the men and women of the fourth estate who are the living, breathing embodiment of the First Amendment. We are counting on you to keep asking questions even if they make us uncomfortable and verifying answers no matter whether they are the ones we want to hear. Words have power. We are depending on you to keep using yours.